KYLE

HOPE CITY

MARYANN JORDAN

Kyle

Hope City

Book 5

By
Maryann Jordan

ISBN ebook: 978-1-947214-64-4

ISBN: print: 978-1-947214-65-1

❀ Created with Vellum

"Jesus."

The word was whispered, and Kyle McBride shot a glance toward his partner sitting on the passenger side of his pickup truck. Alex Freeman's gaze was pinned on the scene through the windshield. For both detectives of the Hope City Police Department, this was not their first rodeo. But seeing this level of poverty never got easier.

Having exited off one of the main highways that cut through Hope City, Kyle maneuvered along several streets and ramps, finally turning onto a pothole-strewn road. The word 'road' was a gift... more like packed dirt, crumbled asphalt, and craters. Nestled under the Highway Thirty-One Bridge, the Cardboard Cottages created a city under the city. 'Cardboard Cottages' was the moniker given to a makeshift neighborhood for the homeless, mentally ill, runaways, social outcasts, and drug addicts. And those were probably its good points.

The neighborhood was constructed from an amalgamation of cardboard, tarps, plywood, and corrugated tin. At one time, graffiti had covered the concrete walls of the underpass, but now only glimpses could be seen between the homemade structures.

Occasionally, a real tent was erected between the other homemade shelters. That was a new improvement—tents. The city had been working to clean up the area and disband those living there, but they always came back. So, several churches and those working with the homeless population had donated cold-weather sleeping bags and small camping tents in an effort to provide a more hospitable environment.

Hospitable. *Fuckin' hell.* All it accomplished was to splash color on an otherwise dreary scene.

He parked his truck at the edge, near the first burn barrel he came to. Both men sat, their gazes scanning over the area. It didn't pay to act in haste in a place where suspicion was in the eyes of everyone looking back, some with an added heavy dose of malice.

The weather had turned warm, but men still congregated around the burn barrels scattered about the area. A few tents were placed around the edges where families lived. Grass was a distant memory, and several children kicked a ball along the hard-packed dirt outside the tents.

A memory flashed through his mind of warm evenings spent playing ball in his family's large backyard. Because it was connected to their neighbors' yard and the children of the two families played together constantly, they'd joked that it was hard to grow grass between their houses. In reality, their yards were lush and well-tended compared to what he was viewing now. The cheers and laughter from times gone by were not known by these children. Desolation, hunger, cold, and fear were what these kids knew best.

The children had stopped their play, and several women alighted from the tents, gathering the children close. Knowing they feared whoever was sitting in the truck, he said, "Let's go. With the morning they've had, they're going to wonder who the fuck we are."

A call had come in early. Three men were found dead near one of the burn barrels. The medical examiner had already examined the bodies and had them transported to the morgue for autopsies. Crime scene techs had searched the area for evidence and homicide detectives had already come and gone. By the time Kyle was called in, the initial cause of death was suspected to be an accidental overdose.

Recognizing two of the men standing near one of the burn barrels, he stalked over the litter-strewn dirt, his senses heightened. The bleak area was known to him as well as many of the long-time residents of Hope City. But he would be a fool to not keep his wits about him. Poverty and hunger often led to desperation. And the police were not seen as friends.

To a casual observer, he might not appear much different than the men he was approaching. His hair was longer on the top, slicked back away from his face. Tats peeked out from below the sleeves of his shirt. His jeans were worn, frayed at the bottom, although clean. His black T-shirt had seen better days but still fit tightly across his chest. His blue denim shirt helped to hide his body armor, but to the residents of the Cardboard Cottages, his casual-rough appearance did little to hide that he was with the police force. Of course, the light blue gloves he wore on his hands were a beacon, but he wasn't about to go without protection. Not here, where illness ran rampant.

The men standing around the burn barrel stayed in their place, stretching their fingers out toward the warmth of the fire. He and Alex slid in amongst them. "Hear you had some excitement this morning."

Two of the younger men he didn't recognize shot gazes between themselves. One was caked with dirt and the body odor emanating was potent. Another one looked as though he might have had a shower within the last few weeks… or maybe took a dunk in one of the ponds at the Hope City Park, something the city council complained about often. The older man sighed. "Not much exciting happens here."

"Whatever happened, it happened right here." Kyle tilted his head in a nod toward one of the large boxes. "I know that's where you lay your head. You didn't see anything that happened twenty yards away?"

"I was sleeping."

One of the younger men decided to jump into the conversation. "Yeah, we was sleepin'."

"Shut the fuck up," the first man said. Turning his gaze back to Kyle, he shrugged. "Shit happens. You know that."

"Yeah, what I want to know is how you slept through all three getting rolled."

"When I sleep, I sleep hard."

Alex snorted, and Kyle's lips twitched as he cut his eyes toward his partner. "So, you wake up this morning to three dead, naked men around the burn barrel and aren't surprised?"

"Nothin' much surprises me around here," the older man said.

With a chin lift acknowledging he knew exactly what the man meant, he stepped back from the burn barrel and began walking toward the darker areas under the bridge. Here, the early morning light didn't penetrate so brightly. The cardboard of some of the structures was deteriorating… time for some of the residents to go dumpster diving for more boxes—as well as food.

A slight breeze blew, unable to sweep away the stench of unwashed bodies and refuse. His stomach clenched, and for a few seconds, he regretted the strong coffee he had downed on the way to pick up Alex.

Hastening his steps, he glanced to the side, seeing a woman relieving herself behind her shelter. She jerked her pants up and stumbled along, her gait unsteady. As she swung her head around, he recognized the glaze in her eyes and wondered what drug of choice had helped her sleep.

A glance inside a few of the structures revealed some residents still asleep, curled up in their sleeping bags, blankets, and a few tucked in tightly with their dogs. The animals eyed him as warily as the humans.

Another burn barrel stood nearby, this one's flames burning higher. Recognizing one of the men, he nodded. "Manny."

Manny grinned, exposing his tobacco-stained teeth —what few he had left. "Dee-tective," he greeted. "I wondered if you might show up."

"Well, me and Alex just figured we'd take a little early morning stroll around the Cottages."

Manny began to chuckle, which immediately rolled into deep-chested coughing. Alex pulled an unopened bottle of water from his pocket, untwisted the lid, and handed it to Manny.

Manny's thin fingers reached out and curled around the bottle, and he drank deeply. After several long gulps and more strangled coughing, he finally sucked in a ragged breath. Lifting the bottle slightly, he nodded. "Appreciate it."

"Yeah, well, make sure you put the empty in a recycle bin when you're finished."

Manny grinned again, shaking his head. "You know it, Dee-tective. Don't want to do no pollutin' around here."

More men closed ranks, moving toward the barrel, each looking as rough as the next. A couple of the older ones had sleep creases down their faces, their gazes pinned on the fire warming the area. Several younger men wandered over, their eyes alert as they stared at Kyle and Alex.

Turning his attention back to Manny, he asked, "You got anything for me?"

Manny scrubbed his hand through his scruffy beard, his eyes darting all around before landing back on Kyle's face. "A lot of shit going around. Far's I can tell, same ol', same ol'."

"What about those three stiffs from last night?"

Lifting his shoulders, Manny shuffled from foot to foot. "Talk this morning was old dinosaur." Shaking his head, he muttered, "Dumb fuck."

He had wondered if they'd all been using heroin. "And the younger ones?"

"Didn't know 'em. Probably crank."

"Anything else you can give me?"

"'Fraid not, Dee-tective. Didn't see nothin' and don't plan on asking about it."

The others shook their head, a few with slight grins.

Casting his gaze around, Kyle asked, "Are you sure?"

One of the younger ones replied, "Nobody saw nothin'. Not a damn thing."

Manny's gaze shot behind Kyle and he took a step back. Kyle glanced over his shoulder and spotted a friendly face walking their way. Not surprised that the residents scattered like roaches when a light went on, he lifted his chin as Detective Brody King stepped closer.

He and Brody had been best friends since birth and the King family were the neighbors he was thinking of earlier when remembering his childhood home. The three men fell into step as they walked toward the fresher air and daylight now flooding the outskirts of Cardboard Cottages.

"Amazing how three people end up dead by this burn barrel, in front of all these people, and no one saw a thing."

"Safer for them not to get involved," Brody said, glancing around. "Who has the death scene?"

"Homicide detectives were here and did the initial canvas. Crime scene techs got what evidence they could, but the bodies had been rolled. No shoes, clothes, nothing of value left on them. It sucks. So many people, so little resources to help."

"Hey, people like Tara and Brianna are doing everything they can."

Kyle nodded, acknowledging their sisters' work with the homeless. Snapping off his latex gloves, he dropped them into the burn barrel as they passed by. "True, but what brought you here?"

"We've got good intel that Peña's cartel is bringing in Gray Death. Two OD's are suspected already. Was there any indication that these three were using GD?"

Kyle shook his head. "One died with a dirty needle in his arm. H is my guess. The other two men were meth heads. If they had the money, they'd buy more crank."

"One of GD's primary components is heroin, but they cut it with elephant tranqs."

"Are you serious?" Kyle blinked up at him. "I've heard about GD, but I haven't seen it on the streets. Not here at least, thank God."

Brody nodded. "Do me a favor and keep your eyes open. When the tox comes back on that H user let me know what it says?"

"Yeah. I got a good working relationship with Miller and Tripp. I'll give them a call and give them a heads up."

"Thanks, but keep it quiet for now. We don't need

anyone talking. If Peña gets wind of us working to close down his suspected pipeline, we're screwed."

"Gotcha. I'll call and make an inquiry then. Casual."

"Perfect. You have much business in the Cottages?"

Kyle noticed Brody shoving his hands into his jean pockets and didn't blame him. The stench alone would make him crave a shower, but that only made him feel sorrier for the residents. "Always. Cheap drugs cut with everything from baby powder to drain cleaner tend to eliminate the poor suckers that are hooked on the shit, but I'm tracking an anomaly out here. Prescription drugs."

Brody's brows raised to his hairline. "No kidding?" His gaze jumped between Kyle and Alex.

"Yeah."

Brody nodded slowly and Kyle knew his friend understood. Kyle's sister, Tara, had unwittingly become entangled in prescription fraud and illegal distribution in the homeless shelter where she worked. Several months ago, she'd nearly lost her life when trying to ferret out the information. Kyle had watched as someone held a gun to Tara's head before her now-husband, Carter, saved her. Carter was also a detective, and Kyle wondered how he slept at night having witnessed that scene. *I sure as fuck can't get it out of my mind.*

Brody clapped him on the shoulder. "Let me know if I can help. We can put out feelers if you have anything to go on." He started to walk away, then stopped. "Oh, and thanks for coming to the 'rents.'"

"I'll take you up on that offer and, dude, mini-you is

a great kid. Sorry I couldn't stay longer." He jerked his head to the side toward Alex and added, "We had a call out."

"No worries. I'm glad you made it over."

"Hell, I wouldn't have missed it. You were getting pretty close to Amber. That on again?" Brody had reconnected with a girl from his past and they were all shocked to find out that he had a son.

"It is."

Brody's words held a hint of regret, and he met his friend's intense gaze. "Be careful."

"Man, not you, too," Brody huffed.

Shaking his head, Kyle chuckled. "You're my best friend. Yeah, I'm going to tell you to be careful, but I'm also going to tell you to go for it because that woman and that kid are worth the effort. I tried to kick your ass into going to see her after the accident."

"Yeah, I remember. Wish like hell I'd taken your advice then."

Brows raised, Kyle shot a glance over to Alex before turning his attention back to Brody. "So... you're saying..."

Brody huffed. "Fine. You were right."

"Damn, that hurt, didn't it?" Just as he was finished ragging on Brody, a flash of color to the side caught his attention.

"It did. I'm leaving now." Brody tossed a wave to Alex and turned toward his vehicle.

Kyle glanced around, his brow furrowed. "Yeah, okay."

"What did you see?"

"Someone that doesn't belong, which makes me edgy. Let's go to the Celtic Cock this week. You owe me a drink or ten for being right."

"Deal, take care."

Focus now zeroed in on what captured his attention, he tossed a wave toward Brody and said, "Alex, circle around to the other side and see if you see that woman who just passed by over there. She's either fuckin' nuts if she thinks this is a place to cross through, or there's something in that backpack that we need to check out."

It was not hard to follow the girl as she skirted around the outside of the Cardboard Cottages. Her red sweatshirt hoodie stood out like a beacon. Dark jeans and flat leather shoes were another giveaway that she didn't belong. As he approached from behind, it was evident the small backpack slung over one shoulder was a leather purse, and his suspicions heightened at the idea of what she carried in that bag.

Another gust of wind snapped the hoodie back, allowing tendrils of long, honey-blonde hair escaping a sloppy bun to whip about her head. Her steps hastened and he glanced ahead, seeing a small car parked near the end of one of the exit ramps leading back up to the highway.

She held a cell phone in one hand, talking low and steady, and didn't appear to hear him approach as he gained ground. "Stop! Police."

She screeched as her hand jerked up when she whirled around, eyes wide, shooting pepper spray wildly into the air. Her aim sucked, but before he could duck, the wind whipped it around both of them. It wasn't a direct hit, but it was enough that he felt the sting in his eyes and burn in his throat.

"God damnit!" he yelled, rushing toward her. Their bodies collided, and as she flailed about, he wrapped his arms around her and maneuvered her to the ground. "Stay down!"

He had not taken a direct hit from the irritant, but his eyes teared and he sucked in a ragged breath. He pinned her to the ground with one hand on her back and swiped his hand over his eyes and nose, blinking to clear his vision. Hearing rapidly approaching footsteps, he looked up and saw Alex approaching, weapon drawn.

The girl continued to wiggle and sputter, and he flipped her over. A streak of dirt mixed with a trail of tears on her cheek marred her otherwise flawless complexion. Coughing, trying to catch her breath, she blinked rapidly. Finally, her eyes stayed open, and he gasped when staring into the familiar green orbs.

For a few seconds, the underbelly world of Hope City disappeared as the two stared at each other. "You?" he growled, recognition hitting him, barely aware that she had uttered the same word in equal disbelief.

2

ONE WEEK EARLIER

The Celtic Cock was already crowded by the time Kimberly Hogan arrived, pushing through the front door underneath the sign of a rooster inside a Celtic circle. While in downtown Hope City, the appeal of the bar was its location—tourists didn't find it and college students avoided it since it was a popular hangout for the Hope City police and first responders.

The owners eschewed trendy and went for real. Mismatched bar stools, high-top tables, and chairs would have been enough for the eclectic interior, but with framed photos of first responders from days gone by adorning the walls, the effect was unique. A couple of pool tables were in the back to one side and in the other corner was a small area for dancing. Not that there was room to dance on a night when the local team was playing and the wide-screen TVs held everyone's attention.

Maneuvering her way between bodies, she skirted

closer to the bar as she continued to squeeze between people until she came upon the table of friends.

"Bekki! Caitlyn!" she called out.

"Hey, girl," they both said in unison.

Hugs ensued, and she hefted her booty up onto the stool after giving her drink order to the server. "It's been a while since we've met each other here. Jeez, it's crowded! Reminds me of the days when we'd hit the bars near campus."

"Those were the good ol' days, when the more crowded a place was, the more guys there were to meet," Bekki added while shooting a glare toward the back of someone who bumped into her stool as they walked past.

Caitlyn nodded her agreement. "I love the Celtic Cock, but it always seems like I run into my brothers here. Of course, with two of them now spoken for, it makes it a little bit easier!"

Kimberly scrunched her nose as she attempted a sip of wine while being jostled from behind.

"I have to agree. It's hard to have a conversation here and, just like Caitlyn, I find myself trying to avoid my brothers," Bekki said.

Kimberly envied the other women—she had no family to run in to and wished she did. Eagerly sipping her wine after the server set it in front of her, she tapped her foot on the rail of her stool in time to the Celtic music, but the overall noise was distracting. "Everyone has to talk so loud to be heard over the music and the music has to be loud so that you can hear it over everyone's conversations. Seems counterproductive, doesn't it?"

Caitlyn laughed and said, "Try having five hundred teenagers in the cafeteria at one time. Sometimes I think cafeteria duty is going to make me deaf! Well, that and pep rallies."

"I don't see how you do it," Bekki said, shaking her head slowly. "That many teenagers in one place... good God, think about the hormones!"

"At least the two of you have jobs in your fields," Kimberly said, sighing slightly. "Spending my day writing up brochures on the benefits of one drug over another is hardly my idea of a stimulating career. Maybe if I'd majored in marketing, I'd find it more interesting."

Bekki agreed. "I was lucky to get the internship at the news studio that led into a job."

"That type of journalism fits you so well. For me, I wanted to use my journalism degree to write human-interest stories. But here I am, five years after graduation and still working in marketing."

"Can you do that on the side?" Caitlyn asked, snagging cheesy-fries from the plate they were sharing. "Maybe write some freelance pieces?"

Taking another sip of wine, her lips curved and she wiggled her eyebrows, catching the attention of both friends.

"Ooooh," squealed Caitlyn. "Are you already doing that?"

"Thanks to a helpful hint and nudge from Bekki, yes. A small-but-growing e-magazine was looking for articles, and I've written several that they've taken. They seemed to like my work and have offered me a continuing contract." Wrinkling her nose, she shook her head. "Actually, it's not a continuing *paid* contract. No salary or anything like that. But they said that anytime I write something, as long as they have room, they'll print it, and I'll get paid." Shrugging, she added, "It's not much now, but I'm hoping to parlay that into full-time or maybe use the experience to write on my own."

Caitlyn and Bekki high-fived her and their conversation was interrupted by another friend stopping by. Sandy Carmichael, a petite blonde with a sarcastic wit and a twinkle in her eye, hugged them each.

"Grab a stool and join us," Caitlyn offered.

Flashing her wide, white-toothed smile that generally brought men to their knees, Sandy shook her head. "Thanks, but I've been here for a little while and it's time for me to head out."

"Alone?" Bekki asked, eyes wide.

Sandy shot a glance to the side, her smile falling slightly. "Yeah, I have to work tomorrow. Anyway, you girls have a nice night, and we'll grab drinks together another time."

As Sandy made her way toward the door, Kimberly leaned to the side, searching for the reason for Sandy's hasty departure.

"I can tell you what she saw," Caitlyn huffed. "My brother. Rory."

A gorgeous man with short dark brown hair and bright blue eyes was shining his killer smile on a leggy brunette who was in the process of erasing any space between their bodies. Glancing back at Caitlyn, she nodded slowly. "Damn. I didn't know Sandy was hung up on anyone."

"I think she pretends she's not, but she and Rory have danced around each other for months. I tried asking her about it, but she shot me down quickly." Bekki sipped more wine and shrugged. "I wondered if they'd hooked up sometime but I don't want to make it awkward for her, so I stay quiet."

Caitlyn checked her phone and said, "I hate to run, but it's later than I thought. I've got to be at the high school tomorrow morning to chaperone an event, so I need to get home."

"I'll say good night also." Bekki slid from her stool and looked at Kimberly. "Are you staying?"

"Nah, I'll head out also. I just need to hit the ladies' room before I leave, so I'll say goodbye now."

The friends hugged, then separated, paying their tabs. As Caitlyn and Bekki weaved their way to the front door, Kimberly shifted through the crowd toward the hall at the end of the bar leading to the bathrooms.

Exiting a few minutes later, she sighed at the mass of bodies between her and the door. Seating was such a great equalizer... the height difference between her and her friends was not so noticeable. But, standing, she did not doubt that statuesque Bekki would have been able to easily see, and even Caitlyn, who was shorter than Bekki, would have had no problem. Sandy was petite, but with her long yellow-blonde hair and cheerleader smile acting as Moses' staff, the crowd would part for her.

Me? Not so much. Inwardly, she rolled her eyes as she came upon a group of men standing at the end of the bar completely blocking her exit. As she attempted to skirt around the gathering, one of the men moved slightly and trapped her with the bar on one side, his back directly in front of her, and more people pushing toward the bathrooms on the other side.

The man directly in front of her had longish hair, haphazardly brushed back as though it had only been finger combed after a shower. Easily a foot taller than her, she hesitantly placed her hand on his back, cautious about touching someone. "Excuse me. Can I get by?"

At her touch, he jolted and twisted around, but not before her fingertips felt the hard muscle underneath his shirt. Snatching her hand back, her gaze shot up to his deep blue eyes as he pierced her with his stare.

"I'm sorry, but I can't get by."

His intense gaze softened, and his lips curved into a smile. From the front, she could see that his long hair was truly just swept back from his face. Tattoos snaked down his muscular arms and peeked from the top of his shirt. He was unshaven, his facial hair caught between scruff and a beard. His nose was straight, his mouth perfectly formed, but it was his blue eyes that held her captive.

His brow lowered and she blinked, realizing he'd spoken, but her appreciation of his physical attributes had caused her to blank out. Sucking in a quick breath, she hoped the somewhat dim lights of the bar would keep her blush from flaming.

"I said that I'm the one who's sorry. I didn't realize I was blocking the way."

His voice was smooth and clear, not a hint of inebriation. An almost-empty beer bottle dangled in his grasp, but it was either early in his evening or he held his alcohol well. He shifted to the side, placing his back against another man to clear the way for her.

Offering a smile, she nodded her appreciation and began to slide by when she was jostled by someone forcing their way through the crowd coming from the restroom hall. Bumped from behind, she slammed into the man and she emitted a squeak as his hands snapped out to catch her by the arms, keeping her from going down onto the floor.

As he steadied her on her feet, she was sure the dim lights could no longer hide her blush. "Oh, I'm so sorry," she gushed. "I'm kind of a klutz."

"No apology necessary. It was that asshole's fault. Are you okay?"

He lowered his head so that he was closer to her, but all that did was bring his mouth closer to hers. Forcing her eyes away from his mouth, she nodded. "Yes, yes. It was nothing."

"Can I buy you a drink?"

It was on the tip of her tongue to refuse, but she nodded, shocking herself. Rarely impulsive, and never when alone in a bar, it was his voice that drew her in. That—and his smile. And eyes. And muscles. Blinking, she tried to force her mouth to work when her brain was once again categorizing his attributes. "Okay, um...

sure. I was getting ready to leave since my friends have left, but I've only had one glass of wine."

"Red or white, or do you have a preference?"

"White. I could try to impress you and pick a label, but I'll just take a house white."

He gazed over her head—which wasn't hard with his height—and called toward the bartender. "House white." His smile widened and he stepped closer, just enough so that she could hear him clearly without feeling too crowded. "You don't have to do a thing to impress me. Just one look at you, Green Eyes, and I'm honored you let me buy you a drink."

She laughed and shook her head. "Kind of a cheesy line, isn't it?"

"Yeah, but is it working?"

"I'll tell you after my drink."

He reached past her shoulder and picked up the wine glass from the bar. Handing it to her, he shifted his body once more, providing a protective barrier against the jostling crowd. "Then I'll just have to keep coming up with cheesy lines, hoping that one of them impresses you."

Taking a sip, she smiled toward her wine glass. His body radiated warmth, and she was surprised she didn't feel crowded. Somehow, he managed to stand close, his attention focused directly on her, and yet, she knew that if she told him to back off, he would. Taking another sip, it struck her—telling him to back off was the last thing she wanted to do.

Kyle had not been in the Celtic Cock long when he caught a glimpse of his sister, Caitlyn, and Bekki King as they were leaving. Giving quick hugs, he promised Caitlyn he'd make it to the family lunch on Sunday, knowing their mom would grumble if he didn't. Having maneuvered his way back to his friends, he'd managed to squeeze into the group next to the bar. Just finishing his first beer, he waited for a lull in their conversation to tell his friends he was ready to head home when a soft touch landed on his back.

He instantly stiffened and jerked around, his gaze dropping as it landed on a beautiful pair of green eyes. Normally one to take in the whole package all at once, he found himself mesmerized until he noticed her gaze shifting over his body. Grinning, he took the opportunity to do the same with her.

Long honey-blonde hair hung about her shoulders. Her complexion was flawless, pale with rosy cheeks. A tiny mole was just to the side of her right eye, not distracting from her looks in the least but drawing his gaze back to her beautiful green eyes. Petite, she only came to his shoulders. He was not often attracted to short girls, and yet, with her sweet curves, gentle smile, and entrancing eyes, he couldn't look away.

She had wanted to get past him, but his brain locked on how to keep her there when chance stepped in and he rescued her from a fall. He offered to buy her a drink, almost certain that she would turn him down. When she accepted, the shock that ran through her eyes indicated her acquiescence was a surprise to her as much as him. Hoping to drown out the noise, he turned his back on the crowd and leaned closer. He threw out a cheesy line, thrilled when her laughter met his ears.

As she sipped her wine, his gaze left her face only to scan the bar, but there were no empty seats he could offer her. Bringing his attention back to her, he watched her sigh and place her wine glass back on the bar.

"Thank you for the drink." Her voice was cool, surprising him at her about-face, uncertain what brought it on.

"Don't you want to finish it? I was hoping to find a seat I could offer you, but it looks like they're all taken."

She blinked and tilted her head to the side. "Oh. I thought you were looking for... well, um... I thought your attention was diverted."

Brows lifted, he shook his head. "You thought I was stringing you along but keeping an eye out for someone else?"

"Something like that," she murmured, her gaze dropping.

He pressed the glass of wine back into her hand and leaned closer. "I assure you, Green Eyes, you have my undivided attention." The man sitting closest to her moved and she was jostled from behind. Kyle's hand snapped out to give the man a push back, then realized he was leaving. As he and his date slid from their seats, Kyle shifted his body forward to keep anyone else from moving in. Inclining his head, he asked, "Can I convince you to sit with me?"

His breath halted when she smiled her reply, and he placed his hand on her back as she stepped on the bar rail to heft her delicious ass onto the stool at the end of the bar. Thrilled she had taken that seat, he sat in the one next to her, and with his back to the crowd was able to focus all his attention on her. "At the risk of offering another cheesy line, I don't remember seeing you in here before."

Her smile widened and she shook her head. "I like the Celtic Cock, but I'm not crazy about crowds. When I get with my friends, I like to be able to hear what they're saying."

"And your friends have left?"

"I already had a drink with them. I was getting ready to leave when *someone* was blocking my path."

"The gentleman in me wants to apologize again for being in your way. But the truth is, right now, I'm thrilled you're having a drink with me, however that came to be."

She laughed, her eyes bright as they held his gaze, and she slowly shook her head.

Throwing his hands up, he said, "Damn, you're calling out all of my cheesy lines. You're never gonna believe this, but they're not lines. Or at least I don't mean them to be lines." She had captured his complete attention, and he couldn't remember the last time that had happened. Years earlier, his trips to the Celtic Cock would have ended in a tumble after a very quick drink. Back then, he looked for pretty and easy. With a few years under his belt, easy was no longer particularly interesting.

She turned her attention toward him, and he felt that she was peering deep inside. Being at the end of her scrutiny was a little unnerving, but he was curious about what she saw. Before he had a chance to ask, she set her wine glass down between them and asked, "Besides tossing out lines to ladies at bars, what do you do?"

"I'm a cop." He threw out the short answer and waited, knowing what her reaction would be. Wide eyes. Maybe even a little squeal or an 'ooh'. And then, of course, the inevitable quip about his handcuffs and what she'd like him to do with them.

She nodded politely and took another sip of wine, saying nothing.

While he wasn't looking for easy, it was a little disconcerting that she seemed to not react to his job. Elaborating, he said, "In truth, I'm a detective."

Once again, she smiled and nodded. "Do you like your job?"

Rearing back slightly in surprise, he opened his mouth then snapped it shut, lowering his brows. "Like it? Yeah. I mean, I couldn't see myself doing anything else."

"Are you called by a desire to serve or by the excitement?"

"Are you analyzing me?"

He watched as the color in her cheeks deepened, and she scrunched her nose. "Sorry, I wasn't trying to. I was just curious."

"So, what do *you* do?"

Her top teeth landed on her bottom lip, drawing his attention to her perfect mouth. "I'm a writer." Scrunching her nose again, she said, "Mostly, I work in marketing, which isn't very interesting to me. But, part-time, I'm a writer, and that's what I really want to be."

He couldn't remember the last time he'd been curious about what a woman did for a living and was so jaded with the reactions to his career that she caught him off-guard. A roar from the crowd in the back drowned out the rest of her response. *Shit...* the Celtic Cock was not conducive to conversation with a game on the large screen TV in the back corner, and the shouts from the crowd had only become louder. He'd had several people bump into him and was glad that she was in the seat closest to the wall so that she was not being continually jostled.

He leaned closer. "Is there any chance you'd like to get out of here? We can take a walk by the harbor." As soon as the suggestion was out of his mouth, he winced. *Hell, I'm a detective. The last thing she should do is accept that kind of offer from a stranger. If my sisters did that, I'd lecture them till they'd scream for me to leave them alone!*

Just as he was about to amend his suggestion, she nodded. "I'd love to get out of here. It's so loud, I can't hear myself think." She slid down from the barstool, then lifted her gaze, her eyes widening slightly as she peered up at him. "Although, I suppose... uh..."

Seeing the specter of doubt move across her face, he reached into his back pocket and pulled out his badge and credentials. She glanced up at his face, her lips curving into a smile. "Okay, Detective Kyle with the cheesy lines. Let's go for a walk."

With one hand resting gently on her back, he guided her through the crowded bar. Aware of her diminutive stature, he extended his arm to keep others from bumping into her. Once outside, the cool breeze brought in the fresh harbor air, and he breathed deeply. Glancing down at her feet, he asked, "You gonna be okay to walk in those?"

"I could give you a sexy quip like *I was born in heels* but, honestly, these aren't very high. I'm not the most coordinated person, so I don't like tempting fate with anything taller than this." Shrugging, she laughed. "Even another inch of height wouldn't help much as short as I am."

Rearing back, eyes wide, he gasped in mock disbelief as his hand landed over his chest. "You're short?"

"Oh, very funny!"

They started walking toward the harbor, and she lay her hand on his arm, lightly holding on as they strolled. He'd always felt choked with clingy women, but her light touch felt strangely comforting. "I didn't want to ask in the bar so that you'd have to yell your reply, but I don't even know your name."

She tucked her hand in the crook of his arm and continued walking. "Kimberly."

3

Kimberly had no idea why she only wanted to give her first name. Maybe because it had been forever since she'd had a one night… whatever. Cutting her eyes to the side, she glanced at him surreptitiously, having no idea what the night would bring. It had been several years since she'd given in to the urge to leave a bar with someone she had just met. She'd dated a few men in the last several years since college graduation but never for more than a few months before admitting that no spark existed. And she longed for that spark. Like the bolt she felt when her fingers touched his back. Or when he turned his blue eyes onto her.

The streets were well lit, and as they approached the Inner Harbor, the streetlamps were bright and close together, illuminating their path. The dark water undulated, slapping against the concrete pylons. Lights twinkled on the boats in the harbor, creating diamond-sparkle reflections.

"I've always loved the Inner Harbor at night," she

murmured, breathing deeply, the tang of the bay filling her senses. A rustling sound nearby startled her. "Unless, of course, I see a rat." Twisting around to look up at him, she asked, "Have you seen the size of some of the rats?" She shivered and glanced back toward the dark edge of the water, now wishing she hadn't thought about the oversized, large-toothed, long-tailed rodents.

His arm reached about her shoulder, and he pulled her closer. She felt the rumble of his mirth against her side.

"Oh, yeah, I've seen the size of them. Gotta admit they give me the creeps, too."

"I suppose talking about rats isn't exactly the topic of conversation you were hoping for, is it?" He chuckled again and she decided that the deep-chested sound might have moved into her top five sounds of all time, bacon sizzling being one of them.

Now that she thought about it, he ranked higher than bacon.

"You're unusual, I'll say that." He looked down at her, his smile wide, and added, "Unusually interesting."

She wanted to ask if he had lived in Hope City for very long. Or what his favorite restaurant was. Hell, she was even interested in his zodiac sign. Her writer's curiosity had her wanting to find out everything she could, but there was no way he'd want to divulge his inner thoughts to her. Paying more attention to the man walking next to her than the sidewalk, she stumbled over the cobblestones, grateful for the grip he had on her shoulder and his fast reflexes keeping her from falling onto her face.

"Whoa, there. Are you okay?"

"Yes, I promise I'm not tipsy. I just didn't realize that the sidewalk had turned into cobblestones."

With his embrace encircling her, she stared up into his eyes. In the bar, they'd appeared as blue as a summer sky, but in the shadows of the harbor, they were as dark and intense as the man himself. *He'll be interested in one night only.* A flash of guilt hit her at the quick assessment of a man she just met, but her instincts about people were generally right. And for tonight… one night… that was fine.

Neither spoke for a moment, then, ever so slowly, he lowered his head as she lifted on her toes. He halted when his lips were a whisper away from hers. "I'd like to kiss you."

Her fingers spasmed on his biceps and she sucked in a quick breath. She hoped her voice was steady as she replied, "I'd like that too."

Closing the slight space between them, his mouth landed on hers in a hungry, consuming kiss, obliterating all other thoughts. Her arms banded around his neck as he crushed her body to his. The tip of his tongue licked over her lips before plunging into the warmth of her mouth. Her belly flip-flopped, the sensations shooting throughout her body, culminating in her core. *Oh yeah, oh, hell yeah.*

She lost track of time as they stood under a streetlamp, kissing as the world disappeared from around them. He lifted his head, and she immediately felt the cool breeze between their faces and hated the distance. She opened her eyes at the sound of his ragged breath, his arms still holding her tightly against his body. "Are you okay?"

He dropped his chin and held her gaze. One hand slid over her shoulder and cupped her face, his thumb sweeping over her cheek. "Would it scare you away for me to tell you how badly I want you tonight?"

Her lips curved slightly as warmth unfurled deep inside. "Not at all," she whispered. Tilting her head to the side, she asked, "Where?"

His gaze looked over her shoulder before dropping back to her face, the expression of agony turning into hope. "The downtown Hilton is right behind us."

Her smile widened and she nodded. "Perfect."

"Yeah, it will be."

Standing outside the door of the hotel room, he hesitated before putting his card into the lock. "Four-thirty-one."

Her eyes widened adorably as she cocked her head to one side. "What?"

"The room number. Text it to a friend."

"Oh, smart. I should've thought of that." She pulled out her phone and quickly typed a message. Looking back up, she smiled and nodded. "Done. Although, if you were a serial killer, you probably wouldn't have reminded me to do that, would you?"

Pushing the card into the lock, he heard the click and turned the handle. He wrapped his arm around her waist and pulled her tight as he ushered her inside the room. Whirling quickly, he took her lips again as he pressed her against the wall. Aware of her diminutive size, he was surprised when she grabbed his shirt and pulled him closer.

The kiss under the streetlamp had caught him off-guard. Kissing was such an intimate act, one he avoided unless he felt something for the woman. And with Kimberly? He felt something. Getting to know her better? Certainly. Lust? Absolutely.

Now, without the constraints of being in public, the kiss flamed hot. Their noses bumped as their heads moved back and forth. Their tongues tangled and tasted, danced and discovered. His cock was aching, swollen tight against his zipper as he pressed his groin against her belly.

He pulled her away from the wall, but their lips stayed connected. Twisting and turning, clothes began flying to the floor as they stumbled their way over to the bed. He should have been embarrassed at his hasty, adolescent fumbling, but the desire to get her naked and under him had short-circuited his finesse.

She didn't seem to mind, her fingers working in a flurry to disrobe him just as quickly. Falling naked onto the bed, he forced their lips apart so that he could take in her beauty. His hand skimmed over her full breasts, discovering her flinch when his fingertips touched the ticklish spot on her belly. He barely mumbled, "Beautiful," before finding her lips again as his hand slid between her legs.

Gliding his fingers through her slick folds, he hoped he wouldn't embarrass himself with more adolescent behavior by coming the instant he entered her body. Pulling upon all his discipline, he tamed his cock, determined to focus on her pleasure first.

His fingers lightly teased over her sex before slipping inside while his thumb circled her clit. She gasped as her hips jerked upward. Her hands grabbed hold of his shoulders, her fingernails digging into the thick muscles. His mouth nibbled along her jaw, sucking the pulse point at the base of her neck before moving lower and latching onto a nipple.

She groaned and pulled him closer, her fingers now moving from his back to his head, gliding through his hair, her fingernails lightly scratching his scalp. His body was wired, electricity jolting throughout. *What is it about this woman?* Admittedly, the only relief his cock had felt in a couple of months was his hand. Work had been intense, but the desire to find a willing woman for a one-night stress relief session had held little appeal—until tonight.

With Kimberly, all senses were on fire. A light floral scent filled his nostrils. Her skin was petal-soft underneath his fingertips, and her hair felt like silk. Her lips were nectar, and her green eyes held him captive. And now, with her sex surrounding his finger, he could barely contain his desire to sink his cock deep inside.

Her breasts seemed to swell as she inhaled deeply, crying out as her inner muscles clenched his finger.

"Oh," she groaned, her eyes squeezed tightly as her body quivered underneath his. Panting, her gaze found his, and her lips curved into a perfect smile.

Sliding his fingers from her depths, he slipped them

into his mouth and sucked her juices, grinning as she bit her lip and hissed. Leaning over, he kissed her again, allowing her to taste her essence on his tongue.

Glad he'd had the foresight to snag his wallet from his jeans before they hit the floor, he reached over to the side and pulled out several condoms. As he ripped open the packet and rolled it over his cock, he felt compelled to explain. "I keep 'em with me, but it's been a while." He had no idea why that confession felt necessary, but her smile and the softening of her face made it worthwhile. Shifting his hips over her, he nestled his cock against her entrance.

Her fingers clutched his shoulders again, and her tongue darted out to lick her lips. "Your honesty deserves mine. It's been a long time for me, too." She lifted her knees, opening herself to him. "But I'm ready. And I'm glad it's you."

He fought the desire to plunge to the hilt and eased inside as her body acquiesced to his size. Her tight warmth nearly unmanned him, but he was determined to bring her pleasure again first. He was sure previous partners would not consider him to be a selfish lover, but the desire to take and give everything to Kimberly filled his mind.

Keeping his weight off her chest with his forearms planted beside her allowed him to watch her face. As he thrust, dragging his cock along her inner walls before plunging again, he was mesmerized by the honesty of her ever-changing expressions.

Eyes squeezed tightly shut, then popping open, allowing him to drown in their green depths. Sweet breath puffed over his face as she gasped. She nibbled on her bottom lip, causing him to lean over and lick the abraded flesh. And his favorite expression was when her eyes were pinned on his and her smile wide.

Shifting slightly to hold his weight with one arm, his free hand skimmed along her torso, over the mound of her breast, then squeezed between their bodies, close to where they were joined. His thrusts increased and he knew he was no longer going to be able to hold back his orgasm. His forefinger found her clit and he circled it gently, her cries creating a symphony as his body tightened and he groaned out his own release.

He continued to thrust until every drop had drained from his cock and his movements became languid. Every fiber in his body tingled and then, sapped of all strength, he collapsed on top of her. Barely registering the 'umph' leaving her lips, he found the energy to roll to the side, keeping his arms banded around her. Uncertain he would be able to move if his life depended on it, he was glad that she remained quiet, warmly snuggled against his chest, still joined in the most intimate way.

It seemed ages that he lay there trying to catch his breath. Awareness slowly crept over him in tiny increments, allowing his senses to engage. The scent of her shampoo. The light sheen of perspiration. The softness of her skin. The whisper of breath against his chest.

Rational awareness finally set in, and he needed to take care of the condom. He kissed her forehead and mumbled, "Be right back. Don't move."

"I'm not sure I can," she murmured in return.

Grinning, he stalked into the bathroom and dealt

with the condom. Returning a moment later, he was thrilled she was still laying as he left her—tousled hair spread over the pillow, kiss-swollen lips curved into a smile, languorous movements of her beautiful body as she lifted her arm to invite him close, and sparkling green eyes that roved over his body. He had no idea how she'd woven a web, capturing his attention as well as ensnaring his desire, but he didn't want to escape.

Sex for the release was always one and done. Unless he was dating someone, he never brought them back to his house, and it had been a while since he had dated anyone seriously. But, staring down at Kimberly, he could easily see her in his bed at home. Pushing those thoughts from his mind, he climbed back into the bed and pulled the covers over their cooling bodies. Tucking her in tightly, he pressed his lips against her forehead.

After a moment, she leaned back and looked into his face. "I guess I should—"

"Uh-uh. I've got more condoms."

Her body shook with mirth. "Does that mean we're going to use them all?"

"Oh, hell yeah." Rolling so that she was on top, he banded his arms about her, drinking her in.

As the moon crossed over the Hope City sky, he showed her just how creative he could be in using all his condoms. Finally, in the wee hours of the morning, he fell asleep with her in his arms. And for the first time in many nights, he really slept.

When he awoke, he was alone. *Fuckin' hell.*

4

Kimberly reached inside her backpack purse, dropping her keys inside, pulling out her employee badge, and juggling her travel mug of coffee. The queue moved slowly today, and she was glad the temperatures were moderate. Too short to see over the line, she pulled out her phone and stifled a yawn as she began to read the e-book she'd planned on finishing last night before... *yeah, before.*

Hoping no one could discern her smile and blush, she kept her head down as she shuffled toward the door leading from the employee parking lot. The memory of Kyle rushed over her, jerking her awake even though she'd only had a couple of hours of sleep. If it hadn't been for the need to pee, she might still be laying in his arms. But, having woken, she hated the idea of the awkward morning after. Quite frankly, it had been so long since she'd had a morning after, she wasn't sure of the proper protocol.

What do you say? 'Do you want to have breakfast? Wow,

the sex was really life-changing? Would you like to go home with me and stay forever?' Or, maybe, the only thing expected would be a *'Thanks for the sex and hope to see you around sometime'.*

It was the embarrassing *unknown* that had her slip back into the room, dress quietly, resist the urge to grab her phone and take his picture lying in all his tattooed, sexy-mess tangle in the sheets, and leave. She had considered scribbling her phone number on the hotel notepad but decided against it. That seemed like too much implied pressure for him to call. *No, what I did was best... just leave it at a night well spent in unbridled passion, incredible sex, and more orgasms per hour than I've ever had in my life, and if we ever meet again—*

"Excuse me, the line has moved."

Jolting at the voice behind her, she looked ahead and realized that she had been standing in the same place, lost in her thoughts. Mumbling an apology, she scooted ahead, closing the distance to the next person in front of her. Several minutes later, she finally made it into the building and through security.

Kilton Pharmaceutical Company was a sprawling industrial campus. The modern brick and glass main building housed most of the administration offices, including HR, Finance, Marketing, and Sales. The company's president, Robert Kilton, had an office on the top floor, along with most of the other vice presidents.

Other buildings held the many divisions for pharmaceutical research and development, operations, production, and warehousing. When she was first employed, she and the other new hires were given a guided tour, learning the basics of the industry. But, daily, she reported to the second floor of the administration building, making her way to the large open office space she called home for eight hours every day.

Rather boring with tile floors, windows along the back, and beige walls, the space was adorned with large, framed, black and white photographs on the wall depicting scenes of Hope City in the late 1800s. A bit incongruent with the open-concept office, she nonetheless loved the old photographs.

Like many modern offices, the cubicles were gone and the space was filled with desks and chairs arranged in clusters. She had lucked out that the desk given to her was in the corner near a large window. Craving natural light, she felt energized by her view while the angle of her desk placement kept others from staring over her shoulder constantly.

"'Morning, Kimberly."

"Hey, Sophia. Janine. Hey, Mikey," she called out. Plopping her purse onto her desk, she leaned over and fired up her computer before heading to the break room. Her travel mug of coffee was empty, and she was ready for a recharge.

"Late night?"

Stifling a yawn, she nodded toward Janine. "Does it show?"

"Throw a little more concealer under your eyes and get another cup of caffeine in you. That ought to do the trick." Cocking her head to the side, Janine smiled. "Tell me it was worth it?"

"Oh, yeah. It was worth it." Walking back to her desk with the sound of Janine's laughter ringing in her ears, she lost the battle to not smile as well. She had no plans to spill the beans on her night with the handsome detective. Even though it was only a one-night wonder, it still felt special, and she didn't want to cheapen it.

Settling into her chair, she opened the digital brochure she'd been working on. While her background had not been in marketing, her job was not difficult. She helped design the Kilton Pharmaceuticals informational materials. Some were more technical, destined for physicians. Others were more educational, destined for schools and potential patients.

She enjoyed the creative aspect of the design, found the technical brochures to be mind-numbing, and particularly liked the information for school-aged children. Looking to the side, she smiled as Marcus settled at the desk closest to hers.

"What are you working on today?" he asked, turning on his computer as he sipped his coffee.

"I'm finishing the work on the STEM brochure."

"What age group?"

"This one's pretty basic. I think they're going to use it for upper elementary and middle school. When I finish this, I have another one for high school." Hope City Public Schools had asked Kilton for information for their Science, Technology, Engineering, and Mathematics program. She had been excited to work on the project, hoping to reach some of the inner-city kids who might not know what study and employment opportunities were out there for them. "I just need to get John to approve it."

"He will… he likes your shit. Mine? He always looks it over twice."

Soon, the room was humming with low voices, soft music, and the constant tapping of fingers on keyboards. By lunchtime, she'd finished the brochure and sent it to the proofreader.

"I'm heading to the cafeteria, Marcus. You going?"

"The cafeteria? You didn't pack like usual?"

"No. I… um, slept late and didn't get to fix anything."

"I've got a deadline to meet. Looks like I'll skip lunch today."

After grabbing a sandwich, chips, and a soda, she walked past the tables already occupied with several of her friends, choosing to go outside and sit on a bench. As the other voices droned on around her, her mind slipped to thoughts of Kyle. *What did he think when he awoke this morning? Was he relieved that I was gone? Or, perhaps, a little disappointed.* Second-guessing her decision to not leave her full name and number, she shook her head. *It's too late now. And anyway, if our paths ever cross again, then maybe I can call it fate.*

After eating, she knew her afternoon would be spent battling the desire to lay her head on her desk and sleep. Approaching her desk, she halted as her name was called. Turning, she saw John heading her way. John Bennett, her direct supervisor, was in his late forties, his hair still dark although grey was creeping in at his temples and beard. The deep crinkles radiating from his eyes gave proof to lots of time in the sun. Plus, he often smiled, and she wondered if the creases were not smile lines as much as from squinting outdoors.

"Hey, John. If you're looking for my STEM brochure, I sent it to the proofer before lunch."

He nodded but waved his hand dismissively. "No, no, that's fine. I needed to let you know that Sally Gleason has requested a meeting with you."

Eyes widening, her stomach lurched. Sally Gleason was the Vice President of the entire Marketing and Sales division. Kimberly had never met her but, like most of the company's upper echelon, had only seen her from a distance. "Me? She wants to talk to me?" Her mind raced to remember what she'd screwed up but came up empty. *And if I screwed up on something, John would be the one talking to me, not the VP.*

"Don't worry. It'll be fine."

"Uh… okay. When?"

"Now."

"Now?" Eyes jerking open wide again, she stared in disbelief as her hand lifted to smooth over her hair. "I need two minutes." Not giving John a chance to object, she grabbed her purse and hurried down the hall, slamming open the door of the ladies' room. Racing to the sink, she stared into the mirror. *Shit.*

Digging through her purse, she snagged her brush and ran it through her long hair before taming it with a clip into a low ponytail. She quickly swiped powder over her face before applying her rose lipstick. With a dab of lipstick on each cheek, she gently rubbed to add a bit of blush to her face. Glad she hadn't worn jeans, she twisted back and forth in the mirror to ascertain her pants weren't wrinkled. Washing her hands, she hurried back out to find John waiting on her by the elevator door.

Before her nerves had a chance to explode, she and John were greeted by Sally's assistant and ushered into the VP's fourth-floor corner office, just down the hall from the president's. The walls were painted a pale gray and one was lined with built-in bookcases. Their footsteps were softened by the burgundy carpet, and she stubbed her toe on the thick pile. Shooting John an apologetic look, she hoped no one noticed but him.

Sally's highly-polished, oversized wooden desk sat to one side, giving her a perfect view out the windows. A quick glance outside gave evidence that Sally's view was simply more Kilton Pharmaceuticals buildings but, even without a magnificent view, she could appreciate the opulent office. Her gaze shot back to the woman rising from behind her desk, her smile welcoming while her tone was efficient. Sally's dark skin was flawless, her short hair styled perfectly. Her makeup was elegant, and her power suit managed to be as beautiful as it was professional.

Kimberly, feeling completely underdressed, offered what she hoped was a confident smile.

"John, good to see you." Waving to the two chairs in front of her desk, she said, "You must be Kimberly. It's nice to meet you. I'm Sally Gleason."

"It's nice to meet you, too, Ms. Gleason."

Sitting in the chair, she perched near the edge with her ankles crossed, shooting a glance toward John. His elbows rested on the arms of the chair, his fingers lightly linked over his stomach. His body language appeared relaxed, and she hoped it was for good reason. Being called to the VP's office had her stomach still flip-flopping... much like being sent to the Mother Superior's office for passing notes in sixth grade. Swallowing deeply, she clasped her fingers together in her lap and adopted what she hoped was an interested and composed expression on her face.

"I'm sure you're curious why I've called you here, Kimberly, so I'll get right to the point. Kilton Pharmaceuticals took a severe hit in the press several months ago when one of our low-level pharmaceutical representatives was arrested and convicted for the illegal distribution of drugs. It illuminated a security breach as well as a pipeline into the illegal supply and distribution of opioids. While this *unfortunate incident* only involved two people in a company with over eight hundred employees, the press had a heyday at our expense. Our PR representatives had to work around the clock to try to mitigate the negative image that clouded the work that this company does."

With Sally's gaze pinned on her during her speech, Kimberly had no recourse but to maintain eye contact and nod at what she hoped were the appropriate times. As Sally paused, Kimberly was uncertain if she was expected to respond, breathing easier when the VP continued.

"While most of the initial negative press has died down, President Kilton has requested that we do more to push a positive image out to the public. He gave this task to me and I've come up with what I think is a viable concept."

Mind racing with Sally's rapid-fire speech, Kimberly almost missed the next statement.

"That, Kimberly, is where you come in."

She jolted at the sound of her name. Blinking, her eyes widened. Shooting a glance to the side, John remained calm, so she drew strength from that. "Yes... um... what would you need me to do?"

"Almost everyone in John's department has a marketing background—except you. Your background is journalism, and John tells me that you have a partic-ular proclivity for human-interest stories."

Sally paused again, but Kimberly had no idea what response should be given. Wishing she'd had another cup of coffee to sharpen her mind, she fell back on a simple nod, hoping that would suffice.

"The news is full of opioid addiction. No one is denying that it's a serious problem and needs attention. But, in the world of pharmaceuticals, there is much more good being produced than harm. Antibiotics, biologics, pain relievers, cancer treatments... just to name a few and, as you know, the list goes on. Yes, I know that part of your job is to work on the brochures that are distributed to doctors, hospitals, patients, and schools that tout the benefits of our world-class pharmaceuticals. But, perhaps, what's missing is the human interest here at Kilton Pharmaceuticals."

Sally had snagged Kimberly's attention, and her grip loosened as she realized she was being asked to help on a new assignment, not reprimanded for some gregarious mistake. "What type of publication are you thinking of?"

"We would like to begin distributing stories among our other publications. Stories of employees that place us in a better light. In some of our publications, it might be nothing more than a few quotes from someone but, initially, we'd like you to develop short but in-depth articles. These could be shared with newspapers, magazines, online publications as well as go out in any other Kilton press releases."

"So, you'd like me to interview employees of Kilton Pharmaceuticals?"

"Exactly. We'd like you to have the opportunity to talk with the other VPs and some department supervisors. Also, include some of our many lower-level employees. While John has to approve what gets printed, you'd be given free rein to develop the article ideas. We think this would utilize your talents but, quite frankly, assist us as well as we attempt to alter the public's perception of our company."

Her mind began to race with possibilities, and her shoulders relaxed at the idea of her new assignment. Lifting her gaze, she saw that Sally was continuing to stare intently toward her. Nodding, she quickly assured, "Ms. Gleason, I'm very interested in this. I'd like to thank you for this opportunity."

Inclining her head toward John, Sally said, "You can thank John. When I brought the concept to him, you were the first person he thought of. When he told me of your education, background, and interests, I agreed that you'd be the best person for tackling this assignment." She stood and reached her hand over the desk.

Kimberly leapt to her feet, clasping Sally's hand in her own. Stepping back, she allowed John to do the same before following him out of the office. Barely able to contain her excitement until they entered the elevator, he laughed as she squealed.

"John, thank you so much! This is exactly what I would like to be doing!"

"She was right when she said you were the first person I thought of. You're wasting away in marketing, although I'm glad to have you on my team. That'll give you a chance to showcase your talents as a writer as well as showcase our company."

"And I can choose who I want to interview?"

"I'm going to give you a day or so to draw up a list of who you'd like to talk to and how you'd like to proceed. You and I will meet and go over your initial ideas. Once approved, you'll be able to begin."

Hurrying back to her desk, she shared her new assignment with Marcus and began to brainstorm. Pulling up the company's organizational chart, she started a list. Vice presidents, of course. Supervisors. Product line workers. The list grew longer.

Her landlord and neighbor, Bob, worked in one of the warehouses and she decided she would talk to him. He was also the reason she first interviewed with Kilton Pharmaceuticals. She had just moved in, desperately looking for employment, and he mentioned that his company was always looking for fresh blood. She hadn't been able to find a job in journalism, and he convinced her to apply to their marketing department. Using him as a reference, she'd snagged the job in the marketing department after interviewing with John.

When the news broke that the pharmaceutical rep had been sleeping with someone who worked in the warehouses, therefore getting extra drugs to distribute, she had never asked Bob about the stories. As low level as she was, she cringed telling others who she worked for... it had been embarrassing to admit she worked for the same company as the woman in the news. But now? *I've got a chance to bring dignity back to Kilton Pharmaceuticals.*

A few hours later, she said her goodbyes and walked out to her car. The afternoon had reinvigorated her but, now that the day was over, she was exhausted. Driving home, her mind slid from her new assignment and back to the night before and the memories of the tall, handsome detective. *I wonder if he thought of me?*

5

Kyle spent his day pretending to work on his cases while his mind was filled with the beautiful, elusive writer from the night before. *She left. She got up and fuckin' left, and I didn't even hear her leave.*

Uncertain if he was more frustrated with himself for falling into a deep sleep or with her for slipping away, he had searched the room that morning but came up empty-handed, unable to believe that she didn't leave her full name or phone number.

After growling at Alex three times in the past half-hour about the squeak his chair wheels made on the tile floor, Alex finally threw his hands up into the air and barked, "What the hell is your problem today?"

"Sorry." Mumbling, he slumped back into his seat.

"Don't need a fuckin' apology. What I need is to know what's going on with my partner."

Hefting his shoulders, he avoided looking at Alex. "Nothing. Didn't sleep well last night."

"So, all this is from not getting enough beauty sleep? Jesus, get the man a tiara."

He remained silent but flipped Alex off. Not hearing a response, he looked over and saw him fighting a grin. "What?"

"You didn't sleep well or didn't sleep at all? The last I saw, you were slipping out of the Celtic Cock with a blonde. Haven't seen that in a while."

The retort died on his lips, knowing Alex would see right through him. He hefted his shoulders in a shrug and sighed. "She was something else. Yeah, we burned up the sheets most of the night, but she was... I don't know. Funny. Kinda quirky. Real."

"So, give her a call and ask her out. Nothing says she has to be a one and done."

He remained quiet, his lips pinched in irritation.

"Oh, fuck. You didn't get her number."

Shooting a glare toward Alex, he had no choice but to admit his partner was right. "I didn't even get a fuckin' last name."

"No shit?" Alex shook his head, his lips quirking upward again. "So, what do you know about this woman?"

"I know I'd like to see her again, but as far as how to find her, not much. I know her name is Kimberly. She's a writer. That's it. I've got no fuckin' idea about her full name, phone number, address, or place of employment. She was at the Celtic Cock with friends, but they'd already left by the time I met her, so I don't even know if we have common acquaintances."

"Well, if she's got friends she met at the Celtic Cock, then she'll be there again."

Snorting, he asked, "What do you suggest? I go to the bar every night and stay for hours hoping to see her again?"

"You're losing your touch, man. Stop by the Celtic Cock and ask Torin or Maeve if they know who she is."

"Fuck, I can't believe I didn't think of that!"

"Yeah, just call me the precinct's Cupid. Now, pull your shit together because we've got a meeting with the captain."

As Alex stood, Kyle scrubbed his hand over his face before slurping down more of his lukewarm caffeinated sludge. He much preferred the coffee from the shop down the street, not embarrassed that he liked it strong but with cream added. But, in a pinch, the bullpen brew would do.

Grabbing the files off his desk, he followed Alex into Captain Hollister's crowded office, seeing two fellow detectives already at the table. Carter Fiske was now his brother-in-law, married to his older sister, Tara. Carter was a good detective but, more importantly, he was a good husband and father to Tara's six-year-old daughter. Carter's partner, Evan Barlow, was also at the table. Offering nods to both, he slid into a seat next to Alex.

"What have you got?" Captain Hollister asked.

"Beth Washington refused to roll over on anyone higher up at Kilton Pharmaceuticals. I've said all along that I think she's covering up something much deeper. All we got was the one man that worked in the warehouse that she was sleeping with to get her extra drugs.

We know Dr. Tiller was pushing the drugs at his clinic and taking the kickback from sales, but there's more. I fuckin' know there is."

Carter's face was tight, and Kyle knew the mention of the woman who had held the gun to Tara's head made it hard for him to keep from going ballistic. Hell, he was right there with him.

Evan said, "You two weren't allowed to interview Beth but watched me. I pushed and pushed, but she wasn't giving up anything."

"I don't see her as being altruistic," Kyle bit out. "More like fuckin' scared."

"It's hard to imagine a bitch like her willing to go to jail without rolling over on anybody else," Carter added.

"That's why I say she was fuckin' scared. Somebody higher up. Somebody with power."

"We went through her phone log, emails, and social media with a fine-toothed comb. Nothing."

Scrubbing his hand over his chin, Kyle said, "Instead of looking at the who, how about looking at the why?" Seeing he had everyone's attention, he explained. "Beth Washington didn't strike me as the kind of woman who wanted to go to prison. Hell, she looked like the kind of woman who wouldn't be able to function if her fingernail polish didn't match her lipstick."

Alex grunted, and Kyle knew his partner agreed. "So, maybe, instead of hunting for a needle in a haystack of who was jerking her chain, the question would be why. What could make her so afraid that she'd be willing to risk prison?"

"A payoff? Is she protected? Is someone making sure she remains quiet?" Carter asked.

Captain Hollister lifted his eyebrow. "If she wouldn't divulge anything beforehand, what makes you think she will now?"

"I doubt she will, but I'd like to try," Kyle said.

"Have we got anything else on Kilton Pharmaceuticals?"

Kyle shot a look toward the others at the table and shook his head. "Nothing. Not yet. But there's no way Beth Washington or Dr. Tiller came up with this scheme by themselves."

Captain Hollister nodded. "Okay, Kyle and Alex, keep digging. Follow anything that even looks like opioids, legal or not, that ties back into Kilton." Turning his attention to the other cases, Kyle let Carter and Evan take over. His mind was settled firmly on finally being able to come face-to-face with the ones who put his sister in danger.

Making arrangements to visit the women's prison the next day, he tossed a wave toward Alex as he left the station, eager to get to the Celtic Cock. It was too early for the evening crowd to have gathered and, without a local game being televised, the bar would be emptier than the previous evening. Catching the eye of Torin, he headed straight to the bar.

Hefting up on a seat, he ordered a beer and waved as Maeve came in from the back. Torin and Maeve Flanagan's grandfather had opened the Celtic Cock many years ago. The popular pub was located in the downtown area near the Briar Hill precinct. Centrally located among several of the fire stations, it had become the watering hole for many first responders since its inception.

Torin was large, muscular, with his arms covered in tattoo sleeves, and it wasn't hard to imagine he started out as a bouncer for his grandfather.

Taking a pull from his beer, he tried to think of a less revealing way to ask about Kimberly. *Oh, fuck it.* "Look, man, I need to ask you something. Do you remember the girl I was sitting with last night? We were down at the other end and you served her white wine."

Leaning his thick forearms onto the bar, Torin held his gaze. "You're shittin' me, right?"

"No."

"We were packed last night."

"You always keep an eye on this place. Man, you brag that you know who's in your bar."

"Yeah, usually. But on a night like last night, the only reason we weren't shut down by the fire department for being over the legal limit of customers was because half the fire department was in here watching the fuckin' game. I couldn't tell you who was in here." He stood straight and crossed his arms over his chest, his brow lowered. "Actually, that's not true. I saw your sister and Bekki King sitting over on the side at one time. I don't think they stayed long, though. Other than that, it was the usual crowd plus a fuck ton more."

"So, you don't remember seeing her at all?"

"Shit, Kyle. I remember you yelled for a house white and seeing a blonde sitting on the stool next to you. But her back was to me, and I figured if you were buying her a drink, she was old enough to be in my bar."

Shoulders slumping, he drummed his fingers on the top of the bar and nodded. "Yeah. Thanks anyway."

Torin leaned against the back counter, his lips quirking, and Kyle groaned.

Laughing, Torin tossed the dishrag over his shoulder and stalked away. "I'll let you cry in your beer alone, man."

He stayed for another hour, greeting some of his friends that came in, his gaze continually scanning the bar, but Kimberly never showed. The niggle of doubt crept through his mind and he wondered if she was avoiding him. *Jesus, get a grip. It was just last night.* But as he walked to his truck, the question of whether she had thought of him since leaving that morning stayed with him.

For the entire two-hour drive to the women's prison holding Beth Washington, Kyle kept up a running dialog with Alex... anything to keep from thinking of the woman they were interviewing.

"How's your sister?"

"Hannah's great. She's a Police Chief in a tiny-ass town on the Eastern Shore of Virginia."

Shaking his head, Kyle asked, "How's your dad taking that?"

"Oh, you know dad. He thinks she lost her mind

when she turned down a position with the FBI to move to a no-wheres-ville place."

"What do you think?"

"Personally, I think my sister's the shit, man. She's smart, not afraid to go for her own dreams, and I'm fuckin' proud of her. I just hope dad eventually sees the same."

Kyle pulled into the lot of the prison. After parking, he stared out the windshield, his hands still clamped onto the steering wheel. The brick buildings sat behind a wide yard of green grass. It could have been mistaken for a small college campus if it weren't for the tall, barbed-wire-topped fence surrounding the entire area and the guard gate at the entrance.

Inside was the woman who'd held a gun to his sister's head. It was his choice to come to see her, but it wasn't until his gaze landed on her incarceration facility did the punch to the gut hit him.

Grateful Alex sat quietly, giving him a moment to clear his head, he finally unclenched his hands. "Let's go."

"You got this?"

"I got this."

After passing through the prison's security checkpoints, they were escorted down a long hall. An initial antiseptic smell hit, followed by the assault of stale air from an area with lots of bodies and no windows. What struck him most was the color of the cinder block walls... pale purple.

Alex caught his eye and mouthed *'Purple?'*, and he shrugged his shoulders in response. The guard escorting them down the hall must have caught the exchange and grinned.

"The color of the walls used to be yellow. Then someone read that yellow was an energetic color, and the last warden said that blues and purples were calming." The woman snorted and added, "Can't say I've seen a decrease in irritating behavior even if we do have lilac-shit walls."

Appreciating her candor, he kept his thoughts to himself but grinned, and a little tension slid from his shoulders. Reaching a series of doors, the guard threw one open. "You can use this interview room. Ms. Washington will be escorted here in just a few minutes."

Stepping inside the room, he noted the utilitarian interior. Grey metal table bolted to the floor. Grey plastic chairs. Bare walls except for a list of rules, the corners of the tacked poster curling and frayed. The walls were painted light grey... *guess they don't care if the prisoners are calm in here.* Kyle shook his head but remained quiet. As far as he was concerned, whatever the prison officials felt they needed to do to keep the prisoners in check was up to them. Settling into a seat, he placed his forearms on the top of the cool metal of the table and clenched his hands once again. It did not escape his notice that the purple had had no calming effect on him.

Beth Washington had pleaded guilty, insisting to the end that the drug scheme was nothing more than something she and Dr. Tiller cooked up between them. The last time he had seen her this close in person, she'd been standing in the hall of the homeless shelter Tara worked in, holding a gun to his sister's head. Sucking in a ragged breath, he let it out slowly, catching Alex watching him carefully. "I'm okay."

"You sure? Cause as much as she deserves it, I don't want to have to haul you outta here for kicking her ass."

Chuckling, he shook his head, then sobered quickly as the door opened. He wasn't sure what he'd expected, but the Beth Washington he observed now was greatly different from the high-heeled, tight skirt, perfectly made-up and coiffed woman of months ago. But she still appeared more put-together than most of the women he'd seen in the prison. Her blonde hair was pulled back into a ponytail but clean. Her lips had a slight pink sheen as well as her cheeks. Uncertain if makeup was allowed, she obviously had access to some. Her outfit was the most striking difference to her former life... similar to nursing scrubs, only orange.

Her gaze darted between the two men and she hesitated before moving to the chair on the other side of the table and sat. Kyle could feel her anxiety zapping about the room, but she appeared composed.

"I'm Detective Alex Freeman, and this is Detective Kyle McBride. We're with the Hope City Police Department."

Kyle kept his eyes on her, but she gave no indication she knew him. Since his sister was using her married name at that time, he doubted she made the connection between Tara and himself. Her gaze moved between the two men, but she remained quiet.

"When you worked for Kilton Pharmaceuticals, you must've known everything there was to know about the drugs they produced." Kyle knew he'd caught her off-guard when her brows lowered and she was not able to hide her surprise.

"That's hardly a secret," she replied. "I had to learn about almost all the drugs. I was the liaison between the manufacturer and the doctors."

"More like a distributor, wouldn't you say?"

"Everything I had to say, I've already said—"

"You had a condo overlooking the Inner Harbor that, according to the real estate listing, was stunning, exclusive, one-of-a-kind—"

"So what? What's your point, Detective?"

"What's it like in here?"

Her brows lowered again, his question obviously not what she was expecting. "Why do you want to know?"

"I guess I want to know if it's what you expected."

She opened her mouth and then snapped it closed, her jaw tight as she clasped her hands together on top of the table. She remained quiet for a moment, then looked up and held his gaze. "I can't imagine that I have anything to tell you that you don't already assume. No privacy. No autonomy. No friends. No freedom."

"So, why didn't you fight this? Why weren't you willing to make a deal for a lesser sentence? Why were you so willing to give up everything you worked for? Everything you risked?"

Her back stiffened and her eyes narrowed as she sneered. "You're going over a well-trod path, Detective. I've said it before, and I'll say it again. Dr. Tiller and I came up with the scheme to distribute the drugs—"

"Bullshit. That's complete bullshit and you know it."

She opened her mouth again, but Kyle jumped in. "You might as well know, we're digging. We're going to keep digging until we find out where the trail at Kilton Pharmaceuticals leads to. You can help with that or keep sitting in here doing your full time, but we're not giving up."

She held his gaze for a long moment, then shook her head slightly and huffed. "That's a foolish endeavor, Detective."

"Might be, but you could make the process faster."

"Not going to happen."

Alex jumped in. "Because you're afraid. You're so afraid of whoever's calling the shots that you're willing to sit in prison."

"But you gotta figure, somebody's got their eye on you," Kyle added. Her nose flared, and he zoned in on the minute sign of stress. "And it's not going to be a secret that we came to talk to you." He waited to see how long it would take before the importance of his words hit her. *Not fuckin' long at all.*

She sucked in a quick breath and leaned forward. "You're using me," she hissed. "One way or the other, you'll make it look like I talked."

"Still got nothin' to say?"

Leaning back, she pinched her lips tightly together. "I've got nothing to say to you."

Kyle and Alex nodded and stood at the same time. Her gaze jumped between the two men, a questioning crease now marring her brow.

"That's it? I can't believe you came all this way just to

try to mess with me." She snorted and rolled her eyes. "Maybe I should be flattered with the attention."

Leaning forward, he placed his fists on the table. He felt Alex shift slightly, but his partner had no worries. "Nah, don't be flattered. You see, this is personal. The woman you held hostage... that was my sister." Beth's quick intake of breath echoed in the small room. Grinning, Kyle stood to his full height. "One way or the other, I'm not gonna stop digging. And when I get them, whatever protection you've got here will be gone."

Opening the door, he and Alex stalked out, nodding to the guard that they were finished. Walking back down the hall, the guard jerked her head in the direction they just left. "Don't know how, but that woman seems to always have money for the extras. Prison salon does her dye jobs. Laundry always has her uniform pressed. And protection? She's not touched by the others." As they reached the security checkpoint, she shrugged. "She's quiet and not a problem, so I don't care where her money comes from. Just thought you might like to know."

Neither man spoke until they had completed the checkout procedures and were once more inside Kyle's truck. Letting out a long-held breath, he leaned back in the seat. "So, someone is taking care of her. Someone who is paying her to be quiet."

"Could be." Alex looked his way as Kyle started his SUV. "Feel better seeing her in prison?"

Snorting, he shook his head at Alex's attempt at a joke. "I know you were worried about me going ape shit on her, but that wasn't going to happen. Instead, she let something slip."

Alex chuckled. "I wasn't sure you caught that. I thought you might have been too interested in getting your digs into her."

"You know me better than that. But when she said that one way or the other we'll make it look like she talked, she was admitting that there was somebody out there that would care. And that person is who we want."

6

Sitting outside Helen Slater's office, Kimberly ran her hand over her skirt, both to smooth out the wrinkles and to wipe her palm so that she would not greet the Sales Supervisor with a wet handshake.

She had spent the past day planning her assignment with John and was giddy with excitement over the change. She had talked to Bekki the previous evening, picking her friend's brain for the right journalistic angle for her questions.

It had been on the tip of her tongue to tell Bekki about how her Celtic Cock evening progressed, but she'd hesitated. If it had just been all fun and games, she probably would have. Bekki would have been thrilled that her dry streak had ended. But, while there was no chance her heart was involved with Kyle, it didn't seem right to joke about it. *After all, the best sex of my life is no joking matter. Especially since it'll never happen again.*

"Ms. Hogan? Ms. Slater will see you now."

Lost in thought, she startled as the assistant waved

her hand toward the office door. Leaping to her feet, she smiled. "Thank you." Wearing heels, she focused her attention on not tripping on the carpet. It was not as lush as Sally Gleason's office, certainly more utilitarian. Stepping inside the office, she smiled as Helen stood from behind her desk and approached her. Shaking hands, she settled in the seat proffered.

Up close, Helen was older than Kimberly initially thought. Closer to fifty than forty, her white-blonde hair was styled in a severe, chin-length bob.

Uncertain how she should begin, she was gratified when Helen took charge. "Sally and I have discussed this assignment, and I'm quite excited to have you cast the Sales Department in a better light. I see no reason to beat around the bush, Kimberly, so I'll be frank. When Beth Washington, who had been one of my most prolific sales representatives, was arrested and admitted to stealing drugs that she delivered to a free clinic's doctor who was selling them on the black market... well, I was shocked." Shaking her head slightly, she said, "Actually, the word shock is hardly severe enough. I was angry. Angry at her theft. Angry at her motives. Angry that I had misjudged her. And, to be honest, angry that my department took the brunt of the brutal media and had the job of cleaning up after her."

Uncertain what to say to that lengthy declaration, Kimberly nodded rapidly. "I can understand those feelings, Ms. Slater. I'm sure that was a difficult time for you."

"It's still difficult! Here at work, I try to present a positive attitude, but I'm still not sure when this is going to end!" Blinking suddenly, she rushed, "Don't write that down. That's off the record." An air of anxiety flew about the room as rapidly as her words.

"Oh, Ms. Slater, um... don't worry. I'll have questions for you that you can answer, and I'll write up my information based on that. After all, this isn't an exposé."

"Of course, of course. I'm sorry." Helen lifted her hand and smoothed her fingers over her hair. "As you can see, this entire ordeal has taken its toll on me and my department."

"Yes, well, Ms. Slater, I thought to start off with, I'd let you give me an idea of what sales representatives actually do for Kilton Pharmaceuticals."

Helen's shoulders relaxed and her lips curved slightly. "In a nutshell, a pharmaceutical representative's job is to educate physicians about the different drugs in our rapidly-changing industry. As you can imagine, new drugs are coming out all the time and, like with any industry, there is competition among the various producers of these drugs. But, unlike other industries where the product is innocuous, we have a great responsibility to make sure that our products are being purchased and used correctly."

Hearing Helen's canned answer, she shook her head. "Do you not think that simply providing doctors with written information about the various drugs would be enough? Is there a need to give samples? What about the studies on the value of giving drug samples?"

Lifting a brow, Helen tilted her head to the side and

pinned Kimberly with a penetrating gaze. "I see you've done some homework."

"I know there's a great deal of debate in this industry about the value of giving drug samples. On one hand, the idea is to get the drugs into the hands of lower-income patients who might not be able to afford their medication. Unfortunately, some studies show that less than a third of the patients receiving the medication are low income."

"Wanting to make sure that Kilton Pharmaceuticals is up-to-date on the latest information that affects my department, I'm aware of these numerous studies." Helen glanced out the window and sat quietly for a moment. She slowly shook her head and sighed. "Another study showed that nearly half of all pharmaceutical representatives surveyed reported using samples themselves or giving them to their friends or relatives." She turned and pinned Kimberly with a hard stare and added, "I'd like to believe that very few of the Kilton sales reps abuse the samples given to them to distribute. But I'd be a fool to not know that some do. Pharmaceuticals in the wrong hands... I used to never think about it and now it keeps me up at night."

Helen's face fell and her shoulders slumped as though the weight of the world was pressing down. Desperate to think of something to say, Kimberly prompted, "So, giving away drugs comes down to the positive outweighing the negative?"

Helen shrugged and said, "Some doctor's offices now refuse to accept samples. If that becomes the norm, it will completely change the face of my job."

They continued talking for several more minutes, Kimberly scribbling everything down as fast as she could. She'd walked into the office assuming that she would hear nothing but glowing news about pharmaceutical representatives from Helen and that Beth was the anomaly but, instead, she now had an interview from an employee who was beleaguered, frustrated, and uncertain about her career future. *I doubt this is what Sally Gleason wants me to write about.* Curiosity piqued, she decided to learn more about what Beth had been involved in.

Kimberly stepped off the elevator onto the plush fourth floor once again, this time to interview Thomas Kilton, the President's son and Vice President of Finance and Administration. His office was similar to Sally's—plush carpet, a wall of bookcases, a highly-polished wooden desk. The difference in his corner office was the view out the windows—he could see trees.

Thomas greeted her with a wide smile and the family resemblance was strong and quite evident with his father's picture proudly displayed on the wall. Various awards for Kilton Pharmaceuticals graced the walls as well as framed photographs of the Kilton family with numerous politicians and many of the wealthy movers and shakers of Hope City.

Thomas droned on about the virtues of Kilton Pharmaceuticals, mentioning the numerous awards the company had won, name-dropping, and how they were leading the industry in the manufacture of drugs.

He was not telling her anything new considering she had typed similar information into brochures. As her mind wandered, she began focusing on what he was wearing. Dapper, well-groomed, and expensive suit. She was fascinated with the folded handkerchief that was peeking out of his coat pocket. She doubted he ever used it since the folds and creases were perfectly aligned. It was so flat she wondered if it was a real handkerchief or simply decoration. Since the color was the exact match of his shirt, she then wondered if he had different pocket-handkerchiefs to match all his shirts.

"Do you think that gives you enough information for now?"

Blinking, she glanced down at her notepad, seeing only the words Thomas Kilton at the top and a few scribbles underneath. *Shit!* Lifting her chin, she offered a brilliant smile. "Absolutely, Mr. Kilton. It's been such an honor meeting you and having a chance to find out more about our company." She must have said the right words with the right tone because his smile was as bright as hers as he stood and walked around his desk to shake her hand.

"Would you allow me to take a photograph of you?"

He preened, straightening his already-straightened tie. "Of course." He moved to stand in front of the wall of awards and she snapped a few pictures with her cell phone.

Thanking him, she held on to her smile as she

walked down the hall in case anyone was looking, grateful when the elevator doors opened. Stepping inside and finding it empty, she slumped against the back wall. So far, she was gaining nothing to put into an article that was different than what she could have found with an Internet search.

Next on her list was another one of the Kiltons. This time she was in the HR department, sitting with Thomas' sister, Sidney Kilton. She had never met Sidney, simply seeing her picture occasionally in company news. Like Thomas, there was a strong family resemblance to their father. Thinking she would be experiencing another interview full of smiles and effusive praise, she was surprised.

"I suppose you've already been in my brother's office," Sidney began, her voice curt as she waved her hand around. "I'm not sure how long I'll have to wait before I can manage a corner office on the fourth floor."

Eyes wide, Kimberly simply nodded as she plopped into the chair offered. She stared at the tall, statuesque brunette dressed in a power suit, immaculate makeup, and glasses that were probably never shoved upon her head and used as a headband. Sidney exuded no-nonsense strength, and Kimberly was caught between admiration and fear. "Um…"

Waving her hand again, Sidney said, "Oh, forget it. Sour grapes and all that." Spearing her with a hard stare, she asked, "Now, what do you want to know? Sally's told me that she's desperate to cast her department in a better light. Personally, I think we'd do better to focus our attention on development instead of giving away tons of drugs and... well, whatever."

Sidney's rapid-fire thought process and delivery caught Kimberly off-guard, and she fought to try to keep up. Not wanting to appear like a ninny, she crossed her ankles, placed her pad in her lap, and clicked the top of her pen. "My assignment is to find out as much as I can about our company, but I'm looking more for human-interest stories. Helen gave me some very good information about the sales representatives, and I have the names of a few that I'll talk to, hopefully gaining a vastly different experience than what the news was filled with several months ago—"

"No need to beat around the bush. You're referring to when Beth Washington was arrested, and Kilton Pharmaceuticals splashed all over the news."

"Um... yes." Looking back down at her pad of prepared questions, she swallowed deeply, uncertain if any of them would lead to a less-pissed-off supervisor. "Um... before this assignment, I was working on material for STEM, and particularly for girls. Does Kilton have a proportional number of STEM men and women?"

Sidney leaned back in her chair, her elbows propped on the wooden arms and her fingertips lightly touching in front of her. She stared, unknown thoughts behind her eyes, and Kimberly could feel a trickle of sweat running down her back. Finally, a slow smile curved Sidney's lips. "Interesting. I thought perhaps you were after nothing but fluff."

Her tongue darted out to lick her dry lips, and she

continued to hold Sidney's gaze. Tilting her head slightly, she asked, "Fluff?" She winced at the mouse-like squeak when she spoke.

"Yes, fluff. I'm afraid that's what I imagine of when I think of human-interest stories. *'How Kilton Pharmaceuticals saves the day with new and innovative drugs.'*" Lifting her eyebrow, she said, "So, what are you really after?"

Pressing her lips together for a moment, she held Sidney's steady gaze and said, "My assignment is to show the good that this pharmaceutical company does. The chance to chat with some employees who are as much of the success story as the people in corner offices."

Sidney's smile widened, and she nodded. "Well, well, I'm impressed." Leaning forward, directing her attention completely on Kimberly, she said "Talk to as many lower-level employees as you can, not just the department supervisors or, God forbid, the VPs. I know you've already interviewed my brother, and I'm surprised you didn't fall asleep while listening to him wax poetic about our company—"

A snort slipped out, and Kimberly pressed her lips together tightly.

"Ah, yes. I see you know what I mean. Dad is gone on a trip and, well, you know the old saying... *While the cat's away, the mice will play.* My brother loves to pretend he's already at the helm of Kilton Pharmaceuticals."

Kimberly remained quiet, observing a woman struggling in a man's field. A sister fighting for her place in the family business. Then the hard shield fell back into place and Sidney stood, the interview obviously over.

Jumping to her feet also, Kimberly thanked her for her time.

"I hardly gave you anything newsworthy," Sidney admitted. "But I'm serious about talking to employees. If you want to dig into the stories behind the company, that's where you'll get them."

Walking out of the HR offices, her mind reeled with the variety of responses her initial questions had brought but, with Sidney's words ringing in her ears, she decided to take her advice and do some digging. *But I wonder... what will I find?*

She decided to swing by her own office to let John know how her work had progressed. Most of her coworkers had already left for the day, and the lights in John's office were turned off.

"Hey, stranger."

She looked up and smiled as Marcus sat at his desk. "Hi, yourself. I was going to check in with John, but I see he's already left for the weekend."

"Yeah, he got out a little early. I was just finishing up my work so it wasn't going to be facing me on Monday morning." Her shoes clicked on the tile floor as she walked toward the back. Glancing down, he chuckled. "Not used to seeing you in heels."

"Yeah. I know John doesn't mind us being casual in our office, but interviewing the VPs and some department supervisors, I wanted to look the part."

"How's it going?"

She wrinkled her nose and sighed. "So far, I'm not learning anything that I couldn't get from a basic, first-hire tour. All of this stuff is what we put in brochures anyway, so it's just a repetition of what I already know."

"So, no dirty secrets, right?" he asked, wiggling his eyebrows.

"I'm not looking for secrets. I just want to see a more personal side of Kilton Pharmaceuticals. Something that makes the company seem less cold and clinical. I plan on interviewing more front-line employees and first up on my list will be some of the ones who work in the warehouse."

She sat at her desk and pulled up the news reports of Beth Washington and Terry Birk, the warehouse worker. Not seeing anything she hadn't already read months ago, she began clicking through links on where illegal prescription drugs end up. Article after article talked about the opioid crisis, especially for the low-income. More clicking led her to articles on using prescription opioids as additives to heroin and other illegal drugs.

"What are you looking at now?"

Jumping, she had not heard Marcus stepping behind her, now looking over her shoulder.

"Oh, you scared me." Turning back to her computer, she said, "I started trying to find out more about the thefts here, but that led me into all these articles about prescription drugs on the black market. God, I'm so naïve."

"If you're trying to show Kilton in a good light, why are you looking at that side of things?"

"Curiosity, I guess"

"Well, just remember what they say about curiosity," he threw out, shutting down his computer.

Glancing at her phone, she saw that she had missed a text from Caitlyn.

Let's meet at CC after work.

She was tired and considered declining, but the idea of a glass of wine, unwinding with her friends, and possibly seeing the mysterious Kyle again was too strong a lure to ignore. Grinning, she headed into town toward the Celtic Cock.

7

Closing the file on his desk, Kyle ran his hand over his hair and leaned back, hearing the vertebrae snap and crackle as he stretched.

"Fuck, you sound old," Alex said, standing as he grabbed his jacket off the back of his chair. Ignoring the finger that Kyle was flipping, he asked, "You up for a drink at the Cock?"

"God, yes. This has been a long-ass week with nothing but dead ends." He said nothing to Alex, but the chance that he would see Kimberly had him anxious to get to the bar. The idea that she was avoiding him slowed his steps just slightly. *There's no way she didn't feel some kind of a connection. At least I hope that's—*

"McBride. Freeman."

Their feet stuttered to a halt at the bottom of the steps at the sound of their captain's voice. Sharing a glance, Kyle knew they were in for a long night. Whatever their captain wanted, the Celtic Cock was going to have to wait.

Jogging back up the stairs, they reentered the workroom.

"Got an armed robbery. Think you're going to want in on this. Delivery van robbed at gunpoint." He shot his gaze between the two detectives and continued, "The van? It was from Kilton Pharmaceuticals. Everything was taken."

"Fuckin' hell. Just what we need is more fuckin' drugs on the street." With a chin lift toward his Captain, he and Alex headed back down the stairs. Climbing inside his truck with Alex in the passenger seat, he put the address in his GPS. *Looks like the Celtic Cock and the possibility of Kimberly is going to have to wait. A-fuckin'-gain.*

Traffic was heavy at the end of the workday, but within fifteen minutes he pulled to a stop in an alley behind a small pharmacy. The alley was narrow but cleared of debris. Dumpster to the side, boxes broken down and placed out for recycling. The back door to the pharmacy was standing open with several officers moving in and out.

Badge hooked to his belt, he climbed from his truck. An officer lifted the yellow tape that had been wound around the perimeter to keep back the curious bystanders that always appeared whenever the police gathered anywhere.

Looking up, he noted the swipe of black spray paint covering the security camera. Mumbling, "Professional," he knew Alex had spotted the camera as well. He stalked toward the plain, white panel van. He jerked his head toward the van, looking at Alex. "Nothing on the outside indicates Kilton. Somebody knew it was coming and what it carried."

He stopped and looked through the open side door. The interior was lined with metal shelving on each side, now completely empty. Stepping back, he spied blood droplets on the pavement. A man in a navy blue uniform was sitting in the back of an ambulance. Recognizing the paramedic, he walked over. Looking back at Alex, he asked, "Robbery's not here yet. You want to call for the lab boys or have them take the whole thing in?"

"Friday afternoon? Hell, I say let's call the whole van in."

"Works for me. I'll go talk to the driver."

He stalked toward the ambulance. "Rory," he greeted the paramedic who had finished bandaging a cut on the driver's forehead.

The paramedic glanced as Kyle walked up and grinned widely. "Hey, bro."

His younger brother Rory had come home from his days in the Army and immediately began volunteering for the Hope City Fire Department. It didn't take him long to decide he wanted to become a paramedic and was still in training.

"Is he going to the hospital?"

"We advised it, especially since this happened on the job. He can file Workman's Comp anyway, so he should go."

"Sir, I'm Detective Kyle McBride. Are you up for a few questions before they take you to the hospital?" Gaining the driver's nod, he collected the basics first—

name, address, phone number, and even though his shirt had the name Kilton Pharmaceuticals embroidered over the pocket, he checked to make sure Kilton was his employer.

"Right. Now, Mr. Parson, take me through exactly what happened."

The driver winced as Rory placed the last butterfly bandage on his forehead. "Me and Charlie left the warehouse after lunch, about 1 o'clock. We got behind in our deliveries, even though we only had four to make this afternoon. We have three on the southwest side of town and then this one. The problem was there was an accident over on Market Street and they detoured us onto Harrison Drive. Well, our first pharmacy was on Market. So I called the pharmacy manager and talked to him, and we decided to move him to later."

"Did you check in with your supervisor?"

"Absolutely. I wouldn't make a change in our delivery schedule without letting somebody back at Kilton know."

"So, then what'd you do?"

"We went to the next two on our route. This was the second one. We pulled up to the back and there was another delivery truck near the entrance. I just figured the pharmacy was getting another delivery of merchandise. The back door was closed, so I stayed in the van and my partner went to the door."

Swinging around, he spied Alex talking to another man standing to the side wearing the same blue uniform. "That your partner?"

"Yes, sir."

"Go on. What happened next?"

"Charlie got out and started walking to the back door, and suddenly two men jumped out of the other truck, and one headed to Charlie, and the other came straight up to the driver's side and pointed his gun right at me. Told me to get out, so I did. They pressed us up against the side and told us to stay put. One kept his gun on us and the other got inside our van and started clearing it out."

"Did you know them? Had you ever seen them before?"

He shook his head then winced again. "No, I didn't recognize 'em, but they had on masks."

Mr. Parson weaved slightly, and Rory shot a look toward Kyle. "Okay, Mr. Parson, they're going to take you to the hospital. We'll need you to come to the station and make a statement and answer more questions. If you're able tomorrow, we'll make that arrangement." Offering a chin lift toward Rory, he walked over to where Alex was interviewing the other Kilton delivery employee.

"Mr. Fisher, this is my partner, Detective Kyle McBride. This is Charlie Fisher."

"I know you were just talking to Detective Freeman, but Mr. Fisher, I'd like you to tell me what happened since I've just been speaking to Mr. Parson."

Charlie's gaze shot to the side, and he asked, "Are they taking Joe to the hospital?"

"Yes. He'll get checked out. Now take us through your day."

Charlie's version began much like his partner's. It

was their afternoon run. An accident kept them from making it to the first pharmacy so, after they called and cleared it with the pharmacy and Kilton, they went to the second one on their schedule. After that delivery, they drove to their current location. They pulled in behind the other delivery truck, assuming the pharmacy was accepting merchandise from another vendor.

"Joe told me to get out and ring the bell on the pharmacy's back door. By the time I walked around to the front, two men got out of the truck, both had guns and pointed right at me. Don't mind telling you, scared the piss outta me."

"Did Joe stay in the van?"

"Yeah, he stayed there and one of the men headed toward him. I was focused on the man closest to me. He told me to lean back against the van and by that time Joe was out and right next to me. One of them kept his gun on us and the other one went around and started emptying all the boxes that we had in our van."

"Did Joe try to be a hero? Is that why he got hit?"

Charlie's face scrunched in thought, and he shook his head. "No, it didn't happen then. After the other man got the boxes out of our van and put them in his truck, the one with us told us to get on our knees and face the other direction. I don't mind telling you, Detective, I figured I was going to get a bullet through the brain. They had masks on so I couldn't have told you what they look like, but I couldn't think of any other reason why they want us to get on our knees. Joe said something to one of them. 'Not now', or something like that. The man that had a gun on us grabbed him by the arm and hauled him around to the other side. I could hear voices but don't know what they were saying, and then I heard what must've been Joe getting hit and he cried out."

"But you didn't see it? Joe getting hit?"

"No. No, but I wasn't moving. Not an inch. Not until both men jumped into their truck and started driving away. When I was sure I wasn't gonna get shot, I raced around to the other side. Joe was on the ground with blood gushing out of his head."

"Who knows your delivery routes? Are they standard?"

"Standard?" Charlie asked, lifting a shaky hand and rubbing it over his forehead.

"The same all the time."

"Oh, uh... not like every day. Kilton delivers to pharmacies all over the city, county, and those are just the local deliveries. Hell, they deliver all over the country. Me and Joe are part of the local delivery team... just here in downtown Hope City."

"So, who knows about your routes?" Alex reiterated.

"Well, the people who make up the routes would know. We go to different places every day, but we tend to have a team that goes to some of the same pharmacies. Well, that brings to mind... the people at the pharmacies know we're coming."

"So, other than the employees at Kilton Pharmaceuticals that need to know about the delivery routes and the pharmacies you deliver to, no one else knows which road you take, what times you're delivering, or even what you're carrying, right?"

Nodding, Charlie agreed. "That's right, Detective. We're assigned different routes on different days. And, like today, we were off our schedule due to the accident."

A detective from the Robbery Division arrived, approaching Kyle, Alex, and Charlie. While Alex continued to get information from Charlie, Kyle stepped to the side.

"Todd, good to see you. You taking the van in?"

"Yeah. Sorry, I'm late to the party. Fuckin' accident happened right in front of us as we were on the way over. My partner had to stay, so I got over here as fast as I could." Jerking his head to the side, he said, "You can catch me up. I understand you've got a special interest in this."

"We'd like to follow closely on this one. The delivery van is from Kilton Pharmaceuticals and it was cleaned out. Alex and I are working on the Kilton angle, but I don't want to step on your toes. We're looking at fentanyl that's getting out and ending up in heroin on the streets."

"You thinkin' an inside job?"

"Let's just say I'm not dismissing it."

Nodding, Todd sighed. "Jesus, all we need is more of this shit gettin' out and hittin' the streets. And don't worry about stepping on toes… we're buried in cases, so if you want this one, I can talk to my captain. What have you got so far?"

"The driver was carried to the hospital. Not bad. Few stitches in his forehead and maybe a concussion. His name's Joseph Parson, goes by Joe. I talked to him first. Told him he'd need to come in and make a statement." Inclining his head in the other direction, he added "Charlie was just giving his rendition, but I haven't heard enough to know if it was completely aligned with Joe's."

"I'll take Charlie in now and get his statement. As soon as I can get Joe in, I'll give you a call. You want to sit in on it?"

"Absolutely. If there's even a chance that this was an inside job, I want to see if we can get one of these men to give us an in to Kilton."

Two hours later, initial reports finished and Charlie's questioning and statement given, Kyle and Alex walked into the Celtic Cock. If it wasn't for the desire to see if Kimberly was at the Cock, he would have just gone straight home. The pub was packed, typical for a Friday night. He grabbed a beer from Maeve, then managed to maneuver through the crowd enough to determine that she wasn't there.

By the time he finished his beer, he clapped Alex on the shoulder and said, "I'm heading home. If I find out when Joe's coming in, I'll give you a call." With goodbyes ringing out from his other friends, he left the pub. Tired. Pissed off. And alone.

8

"Good morning!"

Kimberly peeked out the window in her back door and could see her neighbor waving from over the top of the fence. His mother had lived in the two-story, two-bedroom townhouse where Kimberly now lived, never letting Bob, who lived next door, make any changes. When she'd died four years earlier, Bob looked for a renter that would allow him to refurbish the townhouse while living there for reduced rent.

Now, the workmen came during the day when Kimberly was at work and were usually gone by the time she came home. At worst, she had to go without a kitchen for a week. With two bathrooms upstairs, she was never without a shower.

Grinning, she threw open the door and called out, "Good morning, Bob!"

"I just realized I'm outta coffee and wondered if you had any."

"I'm a pod-coffee girl. Come on over!"

Leaving the door unlocked, she walked through her laundry room and into the kitchen. By the time Bob slipped through the gate of the fence dividing their small back patios and stepped into her house, she already had an extra mug pulled from the cabinet and was pouring the coffee.

"You're a lifesaver," he gushed. "I ran to the market yesterday and didn't get coffee because I thought I had some."

"I made muffins this morning so, if you'd like one, have a seat."

"Damn, Kimberly. I might have to forget my coffee more often."

After handing him a muffin, she sat in the seat across from him and they ate in companionable silence for a few minutes. Finishing, he thanked her, then carried his plate and mug over to the kitchen sink, rinsing them out.

"Oh, I almost forgot. You had a couple of pieces of mail that came through my letterbox." He reached into his jacket pocket and pulled out two envelopes, handing them to her.

"Hmm, one's a piece of junk, and the other is from Kilton, although it looks like junk, too. I swear I don't know why they have your address down for me. I've called HR twice about that."

Shrugging, Bob said, "It's not like we get a lot of mail anymore. And, certainly, the couple of pieces that come through are no problem for me to bring to you."

"Well, thanks anyway." She walked him to the back door, waving as he headed over to his house. Rinsing the rest of her breakfast dishes, she sighed thinking about the previous evening. She'd entered the Celtic Cock with nervous anticipation, both desperately hoping that Kyle would show up and fearful that he would but ignore her, giving evidence to the certainty of a one-and-done. But he never came in, and she finally left when her other friends went home.

She had spent time the previous week trying to convince herself there was nothing between her and Kyle other than an immediate, combustible lust. And yet, the desire to see him again was so strong. *Stop, just stop!* Shaking her head to clear the cobwebs of unrequited... whatever they had, she decided to spend her day giving her townhouse a thorough scrubbing before going out. *Nothing like a little hard work to keep my mind off Mr. Gorgeous.*

Kimberly walked along the sidewalk between the old brick buildings, the path so familiar she could have walked it with her eyes closed. The grass was neatly trimmed, and early-spring flowers were popping up in beds around the trees. Deep-green ivy climbed the brick on the wall surrounding the area.

Coming to the massive wooden door, she pushed it open and stepped inside the cool, dark hallway. The tile, old and worn, had seen the footsteps of many children over the years. She walked down the hall and knocked on the doorframe that led into a small office. The woman sitting at the desk looked up, recognition immediately settling on her face along with a wide smile that deepened the multitude of creases. She stood, her arms outstretched. The white dress that fell to just below her knees was covered in a black cape. Her hair, once brown, had moved beyond gray and was now white, still covered with a black veil.

Moving with haste that belied her age, the nun circled her desk. "Kimberly, my child. How lovely to see you!"

"Sister Honoria," she greeted, reveling in the feel of her mentor's arms around her, just as tight and comforting as they had been when she first came to the orphanage school twenty years ago. Sacred Heart was now a private girl's school in Hope City, but when it had been established in the 1800s, it was originally an orphanage. Slowly through the years, other orphanages were started, but Sacred Heart continued to serve a small population.

For Kimberly, it had been her home from the time her parents had been killed in a car accident when she was seven years old. Against all stereotypes of hard discipline, lean living, and scary nuns, Kimberly found the Sisters at Sacred Heart to be warm, caring, and nurturing. It wasn't the same as her parents, but she was still surrounded by love.

"I was just going to go for a little walk," Sister Honoria said. "I would enjoy your company."

She smiled, taking the older nun's arm. "I'd love to go with you." They walked slowly down the hall, and Kimberly peeked inside a few classrooms, remembering years gone by.

"There are very few of us still left, I'm afraid," Sister Honoria said. "There are only two teachers that are nuns and two of us that are administrators. The orphanage dormitories are now used for boarding students since the Diocese and the Hope City Department of Social Services came together to provide a different location for the orphanage."

"I remember this place fondly," she admitted. "I sometimes miss the calm atmosphere."

"Most of our children could not wait to graduate and go off into the world."

Chuckling, she nodded. "And probably, like me, most found that the world was often a noisy, crowded, unpredictable place." Seeing Sister Honoria's sharp gaze land on her, she hurried to add, "I'm happy, but that doesn't mean I don't sometimes long for simpler times."

Sister Honoria patted her arm. "The world sometimes seems to be less contemplative, doesn't it? Although, that just means we have to find and take the time to be alone with our thoughts and God."

They had left the school building, circling around the brick sidewalks that meandered between the trees. The large Sacred Hearts Chapel rose before them, anchoring one corner of the campus, and they sat on a bench, both staring up at the grey stone and stained-glass windows.

"What are your favorite memories of this place?" Sister Honoria asked.

Kimberly thought for a moment, her mind filtering through the past. "I remember Sister Grace threatening us with extra laps at PE if we didn't pay attention in class. We knew she was only kidding, and we'd laugh, but still, we'd get quiet. I remember singing in the choir. Practice was fine in the school building, but then, when we'd sing in the church, it was awesome to hear the acoustics."

"Oh, yes, lovely memories."

"I remember when Father James would take some of us with him when he delivered food and gifts to some of the people with need. I used to help him even when I was in college but haven't done that for a couple of years and miss it." She sighed. "I started my job, moved into a townhouse, and I suppose it was easier to walk away from those in need than it should have been."

"There is so much need in the world." Sister Honoria's gaze twinkled as she said, "Father James still goes there. He has a group that delivers some items to the homeless that are unable to get into shelters. If you ever want to help, just let us know."

"I do," she said, nodding with enthusiasm. "I feel as though I've lived very selfishly for a while. Is Father James around? I'd like to find out when his next delivery day will be."

Sister Honoria chuckled and pointed to a side door of the church. "You're in luck. He's coming out now."

She waved to him and smiled as he walked closer, recognizing her as he neared. He had come to Sacred Heart as a young priest when she was a child. Enthusiastic and fun at heart, the children had loved him. Now, the mantle of middle age had settled about his shoulders, but his smile was just as wide and his eyes twinkled just as bright.

"Kimberly, how lovely to see you."

"That's exactly what I said," Sister Honoria added. "Kimberly came for a visit and has decided she would like to help you with your next blanket and food donation."

Clapping his hands, he exclaimed, "You're just in time! I've got a group going in a couple of days. We visit the Cardboard Cottages, underneath the 31st Bridge. There is so much need and suffering. If you'd like to come, you can help us hand out what we've gathered."

"I'd love that." After making the arrangements, she waved goodbye as he continued down the path and she and Sister Honoria began the walk back toward the school. Seeing her mentor safely ensconced back into her office, Kimberly wandered the halls alone for a few minutes, allowing her memories to wash over her.

Each year was a little different, new children coming and old friends leaving. While the orphanage and school had been a happy place forming an ever-changing family, the memories stirred a wistful longing inside. As she walked back toward her car, she reached inside her bag and pulled out her wallet. Tucked inside was one of the pictures she kept close to her always. Her parents, smiling at the camera with her held in their laps.

Giving her head a little shake to dislodge the cobwebs of the past, she slid the picture back inside her bag, looked over her shoulder, and smiled at the familiar buildings that made up part of her past, then turned and jogged to her car.

Kyle drove to one of the large neighborhoods in the northern part of town. He wasn't surprised to see the number of cars parked in the driveways and on the street. As usual, when there was a King or a McBride gathering, most everyone showed up. He wondered if they'd be in the backyard already, but it appeared quiet.

Walking into his parents' house, he could hear voices coming from the kitchen. As was so often the case, his mom was bustling around, pulling plastic wrap off platters, while his dad was manning the grill outside with Sean and Carter. Tara, Harper, and Caitlyn were helping his mom in the kitchen. Erin and Rory were coming in from the garage, each carrying an ice chest filled with beer bottles.

Tara's daughter, Colleen, was standing at the sliding glass door, looking toward the Kings' backyard. Bouncing on her toes, she waved as he walked into the room and said, "I see them! They just got there!"

The Kings were gathering in the backyard, getting ready to welcome their newest members. Brody had gotten back together with his old girlfriend, Amber, and discovered they had a son. This was going to be the welcoming party for Brody to introduce Gage to his family. He knew Brody was also nervous about his family being around Amber again and promised his best friend that the McBrides would be there to make sure things went smoothly.

Throwing out greetings to his family, he stepped over to the door and placed his hands onto Colleen's shoulders, feeling the excitement vibrating through her small body. She twisted around and looked up at him. "Uncle Kyle? Do you think he'll play with me?"

He knew Gage was several years older and figured, like most boys, the idea of hanging with a little girl would not be his idea of fun. Uncertain what to say, he was rescued when Tara called out, "Sweetie, you know we talked about this. Gage will be overwhelmed meeting everybody, and he's older than you. I don't know that he'll want to play, but I'm sure he'll be nice."

Bending, he whispered, "Just think, Colleen. You'll always be our little princess." Rewarded with a grin, he looked out the door and watched as Brody, Amber, and Gage chatted with Hannah and Chauncey King. They were soon joined by Blay and Bekki, Brody's siblings.

His mom walked over, placed a kiss on Colleen's head, then wrapped her arm around Kyle. "I told Hannah we'd give them about ten minutes and then we'd head over." She turned and looked at the others and said, "Why don't we go a few at a time? We don't want to overwhelm them too much."

Just then, Chauncey waved toward their house, and Kyle's parents walked through the yard first. Sean and Harper, Carter and Tara with Colleen in tow, walked over next. Kyle watched carefully, glad when Gage smiled at Colleen. Heading over, he watched as Brody offered a chin lift as he approached.

"Amber, it's good to see you," he said, bending to kiss her cheek. Clapping Brody on the back, he smiled as Gage was called over.

Brody placed his hand on his son's shoulder and

said, "I'd like you to meet my best friend. This is Kyle. And this is my son, Gage."

Kyle greeted him warmly, but the shock surprised him. Looking at Gage was exactly like looking at a ten-year-old Brody. Smiling, he shook his head slightly. "Gage, it's great to meet you. You look just like your dad did when he was your age."

He stepped to the side and allowed Rory, Erin, and Caitlyn to be introduced also. Gage's eyes were wide, and Kyle had no doubt it was a lot to take in. For the next hour, a table full of food was brought over and everyone ate their fill. Amber's expression was wary, but Gage appeared to be completely at ease.

It did not take long for a football game to start in the backyard, and it felt like old times. Brody was keeping one eye on Gage while watching Amber sit with his mom. Kyle hoped that conversation was going well but, since no fireworks had gone off, he assumed it was.

His phone rang and he glanced down. Alex. He jogged over to the side of the yard to take the call. Officers had broken up a teenage party and found prescription drugs at the scene. Quickly saying his goodbyes, his mom walked him to the front door.

She reached up and patted his cheek. "You're not working too hard are you, Son?"

"No harder than anybody else. Stop worrying."

"I'm a mom. It's my job to worry."

Chuckling, he pulled her in for a hug. He was almost out the door before she added, "I'm hoping you'll bring somebody home soon."

Looking over his shoulder, he rolled his eyes. "Mom,

just because Brody got together with Amber doesn't mean I'm next."

"Well, Marguerite at church told me that she's got a lovely niece. I think she's a choir teacher."

Exaggerating his horror, he threw his hands up into the air. "Good God, Mom! I don't think that would be a good match!"

"Oh, you!"

Kissing her cheek again, he said, "Don't worry. I'm sure I'll find somebody when I least expect it." With a wave, he headed down the front walk to his truck.

Driving home, the memory of Kimberly filled his mind. *Yeah, I did meet somebody when I least expected it. And I fuckin' let her slip away!*

9

Kyle and Alex were escorted past security and into the warehouse of Kilton Pharmaceuticals. Stepping into the cavernous building, Kyle's brows lifted as they silently followed their escort. The warehouse was as large as any found near the Hope City docks. He was struck with the cleanliness of the entire building. The concrete floors and massive metal shelving units that filled the space, rising forty feet toward the ceiling, appeared like new. Men and women walked around, the sound of talking mixed with the beeping of the forklift alarms.

Kyle and Alex continued to follow their escort through the massive rows of shelves stacked with plastic-wrapped cardboard boxes. Passing through a doorway near the back, they came to a brightly-lit, tiled hallway with offices on either side. Their escort knocked on the door and said, "Mr. Myles, the police are here."

With a chin lift offered to their escort, he and Alex stepped into the office. A glance gave evidence that it was not small, but very utilitarian. Tile floor. Metal bookshelves and desk. No window. The man standing behind the desk was not wearing a tie but had a suit jacket on a hook with a tie draped over the coat hanger. It was hard to determine his age—his hair was already streaked with grey, but his face was not creased with lines.

Kyle showed his identification. "Detective Kyle McBride and my partner, Detective Alex Freeman. We're assisting the Robbery Division detectives and have a few questions."

"Welcome to Kilton Pharmaceuticals, detectives. I'm Porter Myles, the supervisor of our Materials Management and Warehouse. Please, sit down."

Not wasting time, Kyle launched into his questions. "Our concern is the whereabouts of the stolen contents of the van. We've interviewed the two drivers of the van involved in the theft on Friday afternoon. The lab has gone over the van, but there are no fingerprints other than the two drivers. Do your loaders wear gloves?"

"Yes. Obviously, the pharmaceuticals are packed in boxes, categorized and labeled, but we want to maintain the integrity of the product and anyone handling the boxes wears gloves." Porter lowered his brows and said, "I'm assuming that would indicate the thieves wore gloves as well?"

"That's what was reported by Charlie and Joe. I'd like to get a little information about those two. How long have they been working here? How long have they been working together? How long have they been on that particular route? And then we need to know the specifics of your routing system, including who knows the routes."

Nodding, Porter turned to his laptop and, with a few taps, began calling out, "Charlie Fisher. Forty-seven years old. He's been employed with us for almost twenty years. He worked a number of years in Plant Support Services... originally part of our janitorial staff. He eventually moved into the warehouse and has been on driving runs for us for the last six years."

He did not need to look over at Alex to know that his partner was taking meticulous notes. Kyle wrote when necessary, but his handwriting was chicken scratch and Alex was faster. "And Joe Parson?"

"He's forty-two years old and has been with us for seventeen years. He began working in the warehouse, eventually moved to forklift driver, and about five years ago became a delivery driver."

"Any problems with either of them? Any concerns?"

"Detective, I assure you if I had concerns, they would've already been addressed. Neither Charlie nor Joe has ever had a blemish on their employment records."

"Okay, let's talk about your routing system for deliveries."

"For that, you'll need to speak to Tammy. She's been doing the delivery routings for us for many years. If you'll follow me, I'll take you to her."

A moment later, they stepped into a much smaller office, greeted by an older woman who bounded toward them, shaking their hands with enthusiasm. "Detectives, it's so nice to meet you. I'm Tammy Rutgers and if you've got questions about routing, I'm the person to talk to!"

Once seated, Kyle began. "If you could just tell us—"

"Routing is so different than when I first started. I've been at Kilton since it began twenty years ago and started as a secretary. Back then, that's all they let me do. We weren't called fancy things like *administrative assistants*. No, sir! We were just secretaries. But I was tickled to be working in a big factory, so I didn't care what they called me. I worked for the man that did the routing, and we used to have a big room with maps all over the tables. That's how it was done back then. We just handled the local deliveries, and let me tell you, that took all our time!"

Leaning forward, he said, "I'm sure. Now, if you could just tell us about—"

"I used to work for a man named Sam Billings. Now, he was old and old-school. I started figuring out some ways that we might make the routing easier, but no, no! He was a nice man, but he wasn't about to have a *woman* tell him what to do. Well, one day he had a heart attack —God rest his soul—and everybody here ran around like chickens with their heads cut off! But not me. I knew what to do, and I took it over. I ran the routings for almost a month before someone finally said should we hire somebody to take over the job. I tell you, detectives, I jumped to my feet and told them that I wasn't going to train anybody that was going to come in and be over me. I'd been doing it for years and they could pay me to keep on doing it or I was walking!"

He shot a glance to the side, seeing Alex fighting the

smile that was threatening to erupt. Deciding Tammy was better off talking than just answering questions, he leaned back and nodded.

"I had things running smooth as silk, but oh, my Lordy, when the Internet came along and we ended up with Google maps, I thought I'd died and gone to heaven! Our drivers ended up with GPS systems that eventually went straight to their phones. We could plot out the quickest routes for our pharmacy and hospital deliveries. I even won employee of the year! That's my plaque right up there on the wall!"

Kyle's gaze moved from the bright-eyed face in front of him over to the wall where he was greeted with a large, framed picture of the same bright-eyed face staring at the camera while shaking hands with Robert Kilton. Shifting his gaze back to her, he smiled, murmuring, "Congratulations, Ma'am. That's quite an honor."

Hearing the slight snicker coming from beside him, he fought the urge to kick Alex the way he used to kick his brothers under the table. Clearing his throat, he said, "If you could give us an idea how Charlie and Joe's route works and who else knows about it, that would be such a great help to us."

He seemed to find the magic words that appeased Tammy's sense of assistance when she whirled her laptop around and exposed her screen.

"Oh, Detectives, I've stayed in this job long enough to see the miracles of technology! We now have a route manager program. I got to be on the task force to decide which one was best, and after looking at quite a few, this is the one we chose. Now, don't get me wrong. It's not like I don't have anything to do. But it's so much easier. I input all the deliveries that we have to make in Hope City and the surrounding areas. I put in the number of vans that we have available on any given day to make those deliveries and the timeframe in which we are working. This program does its magic and *Poof*, it creates delivery schedules for us. All I have to do is tweak them if needed and then print them out!"

Finally getting to the information he was seeking, Kyle jumped in quickly before she found another tangent to go off on. "I'm afraid we're short on time, Ms. Rutgers. We need to know how far in advance the drivers are given their routes and who has access to the routes."

Her face fell and she scrunched her nose in obvious disappointment at not continuing her tales. "Oh, I do realize you're very busy, detectives. To answer your questions, the drivers are given their routes weekly. I don't do it further out than that because there can always be changes. A pharmacy calls to change what they need. A new pharmacy is added to our client list. One of my drivers might be sick. But, first thing on Monday mornings, my drivers pick up their routes for the week and then, if I need to make changes during the week, I call them in to see me and give them an amended printout."

"So, for the deliveries made last Friday by Charlie and Joe, they would've had that information the previous Monday morning?" Obtaining her nod, he jumped in quickly, "And who at Kilton has access to the routes?"

Her brow crinkled and her ever-present smile dropped from her face. "I confess, I haven't really thought about that. Let's see, obviously me and the drivers. I know the drivers talk amongst themselves... sometimes they're convinced that someone gets an easier route than they have so they like to compare, which, quite frankly, irritates me—"

"Anyone else?"

"My direct supervisor, Mr. Trogdon, and, of course, the supervisor over the whole warehouse that you met this morning, Mr. Myles. We want to be very sure that no one gets in and messes with my system so I don't think anyone else would know what they are."

"Are the routes posted up anywhere?" Alex interjected.

"Oh, no! The drivers have to come in and see me personally to get their routes."

"And if you happen to be out..."

Her wide smile back on her face, Tammy preened. "Detectives, I haven't missed a day of work in almost twenty years. I do believe I'm up for another award!"

Kimberly met Bob at the back entrance to the warehouse. The nudge from Sidney gave her the idea to start finding out about more of the workers, and she called Bob to ask if he had anyone she could interview.

"Well, if you're looking for interesting characters that have been around for a long time, come on over."

As they walked through the cavernous building, she was fascinated at the massive, metal shelving units that held thousands of boxes of pharmaceuticals. As they weaved through the aisles, Bob would stop and introduce her to a number of the workers.

She met new hires who were excited to have the pay and benefits. She chatted with employees who had been working for many years, several sharing their stories of the changes in the pharmaceutical industry. Invited to have lunch in their workroom, she gleefully pulled out her notepad and scribbled as they continued sharing.

An older man sitting across from her said, "This warehouse is a helluva lot better than what I used to work in. I started on the docks of Hope City about thirty years ago. 'Course, that wasn't in this industry... I was working for a steel shipping company. Those warehouses were freezing in the winter and boiling hot in the summer. And dirty... have mercy, they were dirty."

"How long have you worked for Kilton?" she asked, wishing she could take his picture, wanting to capture the deep creases in his face that told of long years of hard work.

"Started at the beginning. I reckon that's been about twenty years ago. It was always a lot nicer than down on the docks, but even then, we didn't have this building. They built this about fifteen years ago. Temperature controlled. Clean. A real emphasis on safety."

"Do you feel like Kilton Pharmaceuticals has been a good company to work for?" She directed her questions to the older man but cast her gaze around the table as the men and women ate their lunches.

Almost all nodded but allowed the older man to answer. "It would be real easy to say I wouldn't be working here if it wasn't a good place, but the truth of the matter is, like most of us, I need a paycheck. But I've got no complaints. There's a lot of rules and regulations to follow considering we're handling a lot of high-powered drugs every day. We've got to make sure they're stored correctly, ready for transport the right way, and then shipped out where they're needed."

A burly man with a heavy beard leaned forward and pinned her with a hard stare. "Ms. Hogan, I know you said you work for Kilton's marketing, but we've never had anybody come down here and talk to us before. What exactly are you looking for?"

She sucked in her lips and looked at the faces staring back at her. Hoping she could find the right words to express what she was looking for, she sucked in a deep breath, then let it out slowly. "I've spent the last four years working in the marketing department, designing material that goes to doctors and hospitals, patients, even education. Most of it is very clinical, and certainly presents Kilton as a leading pharmaceutical company."

She hesitated, then plunged ahead. "A few months ago, Kilton was raked over the coals when it hit the news that some of our opioid drugs had been stolen and were being sold on the streets, encouraging addiction."

Several snorted and others rolled their eyes.

"Yeah... ol' Terry was gettin' some on the side from that sales rep—"

A hand slapped down on the table causing Kimberly and the others to jump. Blinking, she jerked her wide-eyed gaze to one of the older men.

"I work long and hard to make the money I take home to my family. I got grandkids that I teach to leave drugs alone and that shithead made a lot on the side by screwing more than that piece of skirt. Don't give him any credit for anything other than being a snake in the grass!"

The table grew quiet and the man let out a ragged breath. He lifted his gaze and, after a long moment, finally said, "Sorry, Ms. Hogan."

"No, it's fine. And that's partially why I want to show a different side of our company. The real people who work here who care a great deal about not only their job but the company."

Her response seemed to have the desired effect of nods and smiles as many of the workers around the table murmured their appreciation. She continued to write down their musings, especially the ones who had been around for years. When lunch finished, she shook their hands, thanked them profusely, and made her way back to Bob's office. Stepping inside, she said, "You know, I've never been in here."

"Hey, you work up in the big house with all the fancy people."

"Hmph. I've worked in the main building for three years, and until last week I've never been to the third or fourth floor. They've got carpet up there!"

He laughed, his eyes twinkling. "Were you nervous talking to the bigwigs?"

"Oh, my God, yes! I talked to several of the vice presidents and department supervisors. My goodness, their assistants were dressed better than I do!"

"You make good on this assignment, you might move up the corporate ladder. Who knows, one of them may want you to be their assistant."

Shaking her head, she grinned at his teasing. "No, thank you. But I figure this is good experience for continuing to write articles for the magazine. Who knows, one day I might get paid full-time to write what I want."

Just then, an older woman popped her head into Bob's office. "Oh, excuse me. I didn't know you had a visitor."

"Tammy, this is perfect timing," Bob said, standing and walking toward her. "I'd like you to meet a friend of mine who works for Kilton and is doing some articles about the people who work in our company. You'd be a perfect person for her to talk to."

Tammy was a bundle of energy, and before Kimberly knew what was happening, she was being dragged into the other woman's office and ushered to a chair.

"This is a red-letter day for me! I just got finished talking to some detectives and this afternoon I get interviewed about my job."

Having just sat down, Kimberly grabbed her pen and notebook quickly as she looked at Tammy. "Detectives?"

Bobbing her head up and down, bouncing her grey curls, Tammy said, "Yes, you just missed them. We had some excitement last Friday when one of our delivery vans got held up by men with guns and all the drugs were stolen!"

Her eyes jerked open wide. "I hadn't heard that."

"Well, that's always a threat when you're transporting pharmaceuticals. Nefarious criminals are always wanting the drugs!"

She fought a lip quirk at Tammy's description. *Nefarious criminals.* "Yes, I'm sure that's a problem." Thinking back to the research she'd started on pharmaceuticals on the black market, she murmured, "I wonder what happened to the stolen drugs. And what they were."

Tammy's brow lifted and she leaned closer, lowering her voice. "Well, I'll tell you what was stolen. It was a van full of all sorts of drugs, but it also included opioids going to a clinic. Oh, yes... that'll bring someone a pretty-penny when it's sold!"

Unable to hide her shock, she slumped back in her chair. *More bad news for Kilton!*

Glancing around the office, her gaze landed on a framed picture of Tammy shaking hands with the president of Kilton Pharmaceuticals and a certificate proclaiming her to be Employee of the Year. Hoping to get something she could print, she prodded, "Tell me about that award."

Tammy grinned widely and leaned back in her chair, her former air of concern having fled. "I've been at Kilton since it began twenty years ago and started out as a secretary. Back then, that's all they let me do. We weren't called fancy things like *administrative assistants.* No, sir! We were just secretaries. But I was tickled to be working in a big factory, so I didn't care what they called me..."

Parking in the alley behind her townhouse, Kimberly rolled her now-empty trashcan through the gate and settled it near the back door. Her day had been full, but she felt a buoyancy long missing from endless hours sitting at a computer retyping sales information into brochures. An idea had formed since she met with Tammy and she could not wait to talk to the editor of the e-magazine to see if he would be interested. The idea of doing a series of articles on interesting, everyday people in Hope City filled her mind. And the bouncy, excitable Employee of the Year would be first on her list.

After dumping her purse on the counter, she continued through her narrow kitchen to the stairs, jogging up to her bedroom. Deciding on a quick shower before dinner, she was soon back downstairs, barefoot, and dressed in comfortable clothes. Staring into the refrigerator for a few minutes, she finally decided on the leftover takeout from the day before. Once reheated, she sat at her small table and ate while reviewing the notes she had taken from the day's interviews. That afternoon, she had gained more insight into the inner workings of the company through the average employees.

Rinsing off her dishes, she grabbed her laptop and notebook and moved into the living room, piling onto the sofa. She typed up her notes, careful to pull tidbits from the recesses of her mind. After that, she developed the idea for her series and sent it to her editor.

By now, the sun was beginning to set, one of her favorite times of the day. Pouring a glass of wine, she walked upstairs and through the second bedroom to the deck.

Hope City was filled with thousands of rowhouses, most built in the late 1800s. Because of the harbor, the city had been filled with shipbuilders, carpenters, sailors, harbor workers, manufacturers, and craftsmen, all needing housing. By the mid-1900s many of the properties became derelict, and Hope City was desperate for revitalization. Many of them had been restored, snapped up at a low price, gutted and refurbished, and were now the envy of many families and young professionals.

And many, like hers, had had a rooftop deck added, something the original builders would have never considered. *Thank God, Bob did!*

Stepping through the door, she carried her glass of wine and tablet over to her comfortable lounger. She did not see Bob, but a few of her other neighbors were out on their decks, tossing a wave her way. Granted, the view was not spectacular by anyone's standards. She overlooked the other rowhouses and alley behind her building. But the sky stretched above, the setting sun painted muted colors over the blue palette, and the breeze from the harbor in the distance brought a freshness to the air. Sipping wine, she continued with more of her research.

Her phone rang and she grinned, seeing the e-magazine editor. "Chuck, did you get my email?"

"Yes, that's why I'm calling. Gotta tell you, Kimberly, I'm excited about your Faces of Hope City concept."

"Great! I interviewed a woman today who's perfect! She's worked at Kilton since the beginning and was a hoot to talk to."

"Can't wait to read what you've got. But, listen, you also mentioned more than just employees. I agree you should spread out into all walks of life. Even those that might be a little difficult to connect with."

"I'm going to the Cardboard Cottages tomorrow with a church group... I might find some to interview there."

"Absolutely. Listen, I'm not saying write an exposé, because that's not your expertise anyway. You don't have to be an investigative journalist to do some digging. Give me the faces of those affected by the illegal use of drugs. I know Kilton only wants good news, but readers would love to hear the human-interest angle of all kinds of people. At least think about it, okay?"

He sent a link to a news article, and she clicked on the link after ending the call. Quickly scanning the information, she recognized the article as one she had read earlier. It described the opioid crisis, including the illegal use of adding fentanyl to drugs such as heroin to make them more potent and more addictive.

Heading downstairs, she moved into the living room and settled on the sofa with her laptop. The article also delved into how stolen legal fentanyl was used to further addiction, creating a multi-million-dollar illicit industry. She wondered if that was what was happening to the stolen Kilton drugs. Staring at the computer screen, she continued clicking through articles. Homelessness was mentioned when many who spent all their money on their addiction often lost everything, including their homes.

Leaning back in her chair with her foot propped beside her and her chin resting on her knee, she sighed heavily. She had no idea what she would do, but a slither of curiosity snaked through her as her mind raced with possibilities.

Kimberly stared out the windshield of her small car, uncertainty slamming into her. She had helped Father James and others from the church pack up blankets and food, but now her curiosity in seeing the actual faces called to her. Need mixed with suspicion. Gratitude that made her feel humble.

The church group had taken a different exit ramp and delivered items on the other side of the highway bridge, staying at a distance, having some of the male residents come forward to take the offerings. Disappointed that they had not gotten closer, one of the helpers mentioned having seen women and children on the other side the previous week.

After saying goodbye to Father James, she drove back to the highway and made her way to a different exit ramp near the harbor. She curved around until she could view the Cardboard Cottages from the other side. Near the outer perimeter were a few tents, and she could see children playing ball on the hard-packed dirt.

No parks. No grass. No trees. Her heart squeezed at the idea of their life spent in what looked like a third world camp just on the fringes of a modern metropolis. A large metal barrel was nearby, flames barely visible from the top. The early spring morning had a chill to the air, and a few women stood around the barrel, their fingers extended for warmth as they talked and kept an eye on the children.

As her gaze roved further under the bridges, there were very few lights to illuminate the area. But what she could see appeared to be a conglomeration of metal sheets, plywood, and cardboard making up the housing.

She sat for several minutes, trying to both determine the best course of action and regain her nerves which had fled at the first sight of the area. She had dressed for comfort and warmth but wondered about her red sweatshirt hoodie. *Is it better for safety to stand out in a bright color, or am I just bringing undue attention to myself?*

Seeing a few women outside the tents, she decided to approach them. She had no illusions that they would welcome her with open arms, but perhaps a woman talking to another woman would be safer, especially with children around. She had chosen a small backpack as her purse and carried several packs of fruit gummies, wondering if the women would allow her to give them to the children. *Or would that be seen as frivolous?* Her fingers wrapped around a small canister of pepper spray. Hoping she wouldn't need it, she decided that it would be best in her jeans pocket, ready to grab if needed.

Wishing she had done more research on the homeless in the area, she sucked in a deep breath and let it out slowly. Nerves still shooting through her, she thought of Bekki's fire for investigative journalism. While investigative journalism was not Kimberly's forte, her curiosity was still piqued from her editor's call.

Throwing open the door, she slung her backpack over one shoulder and glanced down, glad that she was wearing jeans and flat shoes. Crunching over the gravel, she walked toward the burn barrel. The children did not stop playing, and she wondered if they were used to outsiders coming by. Plastering a smile on her face, she approached the women at the barrel, not missing their hard stares.

Two of them slowly stepped back, caution in their every move as they made their way over to the children playing. Two others stood firm, their gazes almost daring her to approach. Fighting the desire to run back to the safety of her car, she stopped several feet away. "I'm sure you're wondering why I'm here. I'm not really sure myself," she blurted. She winced, her words sounding stupid to her own ears, and she could only imagine what she sounded like to them.

"You some church lady who wants to come down here and think our souls need saving?" one of the women asked.

The woman was much younger than Kimberly had first imagined. Her face was thin, and while her blonde hair was not very clean, it was pulled back in a neat ponytail. Glancing to the side, she saw a little blonde-haired girl and wondered if it was hers.

Shaking her head, she said, "No. I was writing some articles when... um... well, I thought this area might... um..."

"Yeah, it sounds like you don't know why you're here," the other woman said. She was of indeterminate age, the creases emanating from her eyes and around her mouth possibly from harsh living conditions more than age.

"What kind of articles?" the blonde woman asked.

Uncertainty was no longer snaking through her but was blasting her with an icy wind. Stepping back, she shook her head slightly and said, "I'm sorry. I shouldn't have bothered you—"

"Hell, girl. If you don't get a stiffer backbone, you ain't never gonna get your story," the older woman said.

Her feet stumbled to a halt, and she recognized the tiny olive branch the woman was holding. "You're right, I won't. I'm just not sure how to ask the right questions without sounding offensive."

"Well, Margo and me ain't gonna bite, so why don't you go ahead and ask? If we don't want to answer something... we won't."

"I'm Kimberly."

"I'm Aleeta, and as I said, this here is Margo."

Looking over her shoulder at the little blonde girl, she turned back and asked, "Is she yours, Margo?"

Margo smiled, and Kimberly's breath caught in her throat at the transformation. Margo's obvious pride in her daughter gave her face a glow as she nodded.

"I'm afraid I didn't come with much, but I have some packets of fruit gummies. Would it be okay if I gave them to the kids?" Gaining their acquiescence, she pulled out the packets and held them in her hands, grinning as the children ran over. They halted several feet away, and she glanced back toward Aleeta and Margo.

"You can have 'em," Aleeta called out. "You know what to say."

The children took the packs of candy, each thanking Kimberly before they ran off with their treasures. The children were so happy with so little, and she swallowed deeply past the lump in her throat.

Turning back to the women, she let out a long breath and plunged forward. "I work for Kilton Pharmaceutical Company. I was writing a series of articles about the good that the company does. But I also know that even good drugs that get in the hands of people who abuse them or sell them lead to addiction." She observed Margo and Aleeta's faces carefully but discerned no change in expression. She looked past them into the depths underneath the bridge where the cardboard homes were shrouded in darkness and said, "I'm not brave enough to walk in there, so I'm not really sure why I'm here. I guess I thought I might find someone safe who'd talk to me."

Looking over her shoulder, Aleeta snorted. "Hell, honey. You wouldn't have to be brave to walk in there, just dumber n' dirt. Me and Margo live out here where it's safer. And we keep an eye on our kids. Just 'cause we're homeless don't mean we're stupid."

The tension in her shoulders relaxed slightly, and her lips curved. "I definitely don't think you're stupid."

Aleeta's lips quirked upward for the first time and,

117

just like with Margo, it transformed her face. Cocking her head to the side, she said, "We might not be able to tell you much, but ask your questions. Who knows? You might learn something anyway."

By now, the two other women had made their way back to the barrel, and Kimberly chatted with all four. Her initial questions fell to the side as she spent time just finding out about their lives. Their hard luck stories were as varied as the women themselves, but their determination to work to better their children's situation warmed her heart.

When she finally got around to asking about drugs, Margo shook her head.

"I've never been around drugs, and I don't want my kids near it. I know what goes on around here, but I stay away from it. It scares me."

Aleeta's face had grown hard again. She stared off into the distance before swinging her gaze back around to Kimberly. "My old man was a user. Sucked up every dime we had. Hell, by the time I left his ass, his habit had lost our home and my job. Last I saw of him he was lying on the street after we got evicted with the damn needle stuck in his arm."

Kimberly tried to hide her shock but had no doubt her opened-mouth, wide-eyed face gave her away. "I'm so sorry!"

Aleeta snorted. "I got away. Got a job, but it doesn't pay much. Least here, I've got no rent."

She sucked in her lips for a few seconds, her mind racing over the information she had been given. "What about fentanyl? Do you ever hear about that?"

"Heard my man talk about fenty. Don't know if that's what you're talking about. I guess I stuck my head in the sand, thinking that if I didn't know anything about what he was doing it wouldn't affect me. That didn't work."

Kimberly reached over and placed her hand on Aleeta's arm. "You were focused on yourself and your kids and did what you had to do."

Aleeta looked down at her arm, and Kimberly jerked her hand back. Afraid that she had offended her, she breathed a sigh of relief at the slow smile that crossed Aleeta's face.

"It's got a lot of names," one of the other women said. She shrugged when Kimberly looked toward her and added, "Everybody was a user where I came from. That shit can be added to H and make you feel invincible."

The morning's discussions weighed heavily on her. "Thank you so much for talking to me." Glancing back to the children who were now sitting on the dirt, she watched them play with makeshift toys. A strong breeze was blowing, and she was glad they had jackets but wondered what else they might need. She turned back to the women still standing at the burn barrel. "I'd like to bring something for your children. What would be the best thing?" Seeing Aleeta shake her head, she could feel Aleeta's pride settling like a cloak around her shoulders. "Please, I'd like to help. I know it wouldn't be much, but it would be for the kids."

"Fruit."

Looking over at Margo, she blinked, surprised at the

answer. Nodding quickly, she agreed. "I can do that. I can bring fruit when I come back."

Aleeta offered a swift nod. "Fruit would be good. You want to talk more, we'll be around."

Stepping back, she waved goodbye and began walking past some of the tents. She no longer felt afraid with the sun high in the sky but slipped her pepper spray into one hand while beginning to record her thoughts into her phone.

The breeze still had a nip to it, and her hoodie fell back from her face. Instead of walking directly to her car, she skirted the perimeter, not getting too close to the other tents but giving her a chance to talk through her impressions while they were still clear in her mind.

Her car was just up ahead, and she picked up her pace as she continued recording into her phone. Deeply focused on her task, she didn't hear footsteps behind her until a voice roared, "Stop. Police!"

Startled, she whirled toward the sound, instinctively lifting her hand and pressing the button. The pepper spray was immediately swept back toward her with the breeze, and she gasped as she tried to duck, blinking and sputtering in a desperate attempt to breathe.

Unable to see, her body collided with a hard wall that encircled her as she fell toward the ground. Desperate to get away, she flailed and kicked, unable to see her assailant.

"Stay down!"

Facedown in the dirt, the words he'd said earlier came back to her mind. *Police!* It felt as though there was a weight on her, but she had enough room to lift her hand and swiped at her streaming eyes and nose. She heard rapidly approaching footsteps, but her vision was blurry, and she was unable to see who was coming.

Still wiggling, she felt the weight leave just in time to be flipped over. Still wiping at her cheeks, she continued to blink while looking into deep blue eyes that were focused on her face.

For a few seconds, the underbelly world of Hope City disappeared as they stared at each other. "You?" she gasped, staring into Kyle's face, barely aware that he had growled the same word in equal disbelief.

Before she could suck in another breath, Kyle bounded to his feet, reached down to grab her arms, and hauled her upward. She landed on her feet with a jolt, jerked her arm from his grasp, and swiped at her face again.

"What the fuck are you doing here?"

Startled at the ferocity of his voice, she opened her mouth to explain, but he continued.

"And pepper spray? You sprayed fuckin' pepper spray into the wind? What the fuck were you thinking?"

"I take it you know her?"

Whipping her head around, she spied another man standing close, a badge clipped to his belt, his weapon being re-holstered. Swiping at her cheeks again, she turned back to Kyle. "I'm here for work—"

"Work? You said you worked in marketing. Try again, sweetheart. I'm not buying that."

He snatched her bag from the ground. "Do you have any needles or other sharp objects in here?"

"What?"

"Needles? Sharp objects?" he growled.

"No! I had fruit gummies."

He jerked open her bag and looked inside, his brow furrowed as he twisted his neck and speared her with a confused expression.

Her vision was clearing as she took the bag from him and reached inside to grab a tissue. Wiping her eyes and nose, she leveled her gaze back on him. "I don't have to tell you what I'm doing. Now if you'll excuse me, I was just heading to my car." She barely took a step when his hand latched onto her upper arm, firmly but not painfully.

"Oh, hell no, Kimberly. You're coming with me."

"You're arresting me?" she squeaked, her throat still raw.

"I should, but no. I'm taking you home."

He held out his hand and wiggled his fingers. She stared down for a few seconds then lifted her gaze to his face. Impatience and anger were clearly written on his expression, but she had no idea what he wanted. "What?"

"Keys."

"Keys?"

He wiggled his fingers again. "As in *give me your keys*," he said enunciating each word.

Glaring, she said, "I don't need to give you my keys. I'm leaving, and I'm driving."

"Only part of that is right," he growled in return. "You are leaving, but I'm driving so give me your keys."

Glancing toward the other man who was now openly smirking, she said, "This is police brutality." As soon as the words left her mouth, she was stunned that Kyle's expression could become even scarier.

He looked toward the other man and said, "I'm taking her home." Tossing a set of keys to him, he added, "Take my truck back to the station, and I'll call you in a little bit."

The other man caught the keys easily in his hand and grinned. "You sure you got this?"

Kyle looked from the other man back to her. "Oh yeah, I've got this."

She continued to watch in stunned silence as the other man tossed a two-fingered salute and walked toward an old pickup truck. With Kyle's hand still on her arm, he began walking. She wanted to pull back, but there was a small crowd growing at the edge of the Cardboard Cottages, and she didn't want to be left there. Stumbling to keep up, they made it to her car. He whirled her around and pressed her back against the passenger door, sliding her bag off her shoulder. After he reached inside, the jingle of her keys could be heard, and he pulled them out. Opening the door, he ordered, "Get in."

Determined he would receive his verbal thrashing once they were in the car and away from the area, she climbed in and slammed the door. *I can't believe I slept with such a jerk! I can't believe I've been thinking of him all week!*

Kyle started her car, determined to stay focused even though his hands were shaking from the adrenaline coursing through his body. A slew of emotions had hit him, one right after the other. Suspicion morphed into surprise when she shot pepper spray on a breezy day in close range, making most of it hit her and some toward him. He was hit with a shock when the watery green eyes stared up at him, unable to believe it was Kimberly.

Then anger overtook him at her recklessness. *Jesus, they'd just had three dead bodies there this morning. If she'd stumbled onto them... Jesus.*

As pissed as he was, the next thing that slammed into him was lust when he pressed his body close to hers to get her keys. Glancing toward the side at the hard set of her jaw, he figured he'd keep that tidbit to himself. He pulled onto the main road and asked, "Where do you live?"

She remained silent.

"I'm going to keep driving around in circles using up

all your gas, so you might as well tell me where you live."

"Colbert. Turn left up here."

Recognizing the street name, he was not surprised to observe blocks and blocks of rowhouses, similar to the area of town where he lived. After a few minutes, she pointed to hers, and he parallel parked in front. She leaped out of her car and slammed the door, stalking up her front steps. He climbed out of the driver's side slowly, grinning as he waited for her to realize he still had her keys.

At the top stoop, she whirled around, held out her hand, and wiggled her fingers, mimicking his earlier actions. Instead of dropping the keys onto her palm, he reached around and unlocked her door, pushing it open.

She stepped inside and quirked her brow. "You could have just had your friend follow us here so he could take you directly away."

He placed his hand on her stomach, pushed her back gently, and stepped into her house. Sighing, he closed the door behind them. "I could have, but I'm not leaving right now. Not until I get some answers about why you were at a scene that just this morning had three dead bodies."

She sucked in a quick breath, her eyes widening before immediately narrowing again. "Were you this much of a jerk the night I met you?"

"No, but I think we both had other things on our minds that night."

She growled and whirled quickly, her ponytail whipping about, barely missing his face. Stalking through her living room, she headed toward the back.

Every rowhouse he'd been in, including his own, had the same basic layout. The front door opened straight into the living room. Stairs leading to the second floor were close by. Toward the back was the kitchen and many had no dining room. An alley or small patio was through the back door of the kitchen. His townhouse was larger, but whoever had refurbished hers had done an exceptional job. Exposed brick. Wood floors. Softly painted walls.

Her keys were still in his hand, and he followed her into the kitchen, placing them onto the counter next to where she'd tossed her bag. Her refrigerator door was open, and she had bent to pull something out. His gaze landed on her perfect ass, and he shifted, needing to adjust his cock, glad her back was to him.

She stood suddenly and turned around, hands on her hips. "Are you still here?"

"Apparently."

"I want you to leave. There's absolutely no reason for you to be here any longer. Even though I thought of you for the past week, I'm no longer interested in seeing you again."

"You thought of me?"

"That's all you focused on? I just told you that I want you to leave and am no longer interested in you."

"But in the middle of that, you said you thought of me for a week."

Throwing her hands up to the side, she blurted, "I'm hungry. I haven't had lunch. My face is a mess, and my eyes still burn. I have dirt on my clothes. I want to take a shower and eat something. And while I'm doing all that, I want to process the fact that the women I talked to this morning can't take a shower and don't have lunch to eat!"

He stared at her face, and she was right. She looked a mess. And beautiful. And right now, ending her speech in the way she had, he watched as her chin quivered. Saying nothing, he stepped closer and opened his arms. Uncertain if she might throw a right hook toward his chin, he was grateful when her face crumpled, and she stepped into his embrace. He wrapped his arms around her, pulling her tightly to his chest as her hand snaked to his back and she clutched his shirt.

He felt her body shudder, then heard soft sobs. He slowly rubbed her back, murmuring words of comfort near her ear.

She cried for several minutes, but he wasn't worried. Growing up with three sisters and the two King girls next door, he was well aware that sometimes it took a while for them to get it all out. It might be a sexist observation, but he found that usually men decided to punch something when they were upset. If he was honest, of the two reactions, he thought the women had the healthier one.

Her breathing evened, and she leaned back. Her eyes were red-rimmed, her face was splotchy, and there was a long streak of dirt on her right cheek. And, once again, he thought she was beautiful.

He wanted to know everything. What she was doing at the Cardboard Cottages this morning. Who she talked to. Who she worked for. But right now, he just wanted to offer comfort. And, if he was honest, he loved the feel of her in his arms. "Pizza or Chinese?" Her brow furrowed and, strangely enough, he thought it made her look more adorable. "There's a lot we need to talk about, babe, but first things first. You go take a shower, and I'll call for lunch. You've got a couple of magnets on your refrigerator for takeout, so would you rather have pizza or Chinese?"

He braced for her argument, but she simply continued to hold his gaze for a moment and then her shoulders slumped.

"Chinese. I think everything in life seems a little bit better with Chinese food."

He leaned forward and placed a kiss on her forehead, mumbling, "Words to live by, darlin'." When she didn't move, he gave her a slight nudge. She held his gaze for a few seconds longer, then nodded. He watched as she walked toward the stairs and heard her footsteps as she ascended to the second floor. Waiting just long enough to hear the water running, he pulled out his phone and dialed the restaurant.

With the sound of water still running from upstairs, his gaze snagged on the small backpack lying on the kitchen counter. Not hesitating, he opened it and peered inside. Pulling out her wallet, he checked her ID. Kimberly Hogan. Twenty-seven years old. The pockets that held credit cards were empty. Seeing several stacked on the kitchen counter, he was glad she had the foresight to not head to the Cottages with a full wallet of cards and money.

Reaching into the bag again, he pulled out a note-book. Before he had a chance to open it, his gaze snagged on an ID lanyard. Flipping it over, he jolted at the sight of a Kilton Pharmaceuticals employee ID badge. *Jesus, she works at Kilton! So what the fuck was she doing at the Cottages?* He flipped open the notebook, seeing handwritten notes over several pages. Remembering when he followed her at the Cottages she was speaking into her phone, he wondered who she had been talking to. Punching a few buttons, he discovered her last call was last night. Staring at the app icon, he saw Dictation was front and center.

Before he had a chance to pursue his search further, the water from the shower stopped running. Placing everything back into the bag, he made sure to arrange it on the counter the way it had been.

The restaurant must have been close because the knock on the door came a few minutes later, just as she walked back down the stairs. He accepted the food and paid for the delivery. Turning around, he faced her fully, taking her in. Fresh from the shower, she looked more seventeen than twenty-seven, but the way his cock twitched at the sight he was fuckin' thrilled she was an adult.

Her honey-blonde hair was dark, still wet and hanging down her back. Dressed in comfortable yoga pants that cupped her hips and showcased her legs and a slouchy T-shirt that hung off one shoulder, exposing the strap of a black sports bra underneath. Her face had been scrubbed clean, and her green eyes were still slightly swollen from the pepper spray and having cried earlier.

Her gaze settled on the bags in his hands, and she asked, "How much food did you order?"

"Enough for us to have our fill and plenty for leftovers. Remember, everything in life seems a little better with Chinese food."

Her snort erupted before a full-blown smile transformed her from beautiful to gorgeous. Her fresh-faced appeal slammed into him, but it was the sound of her laughter that jolted straight to his heart. His breath was shallow as though afraid any noise from him would interrupt her moment of happiness.

Deciding that all questions could wait, he walked forward with the bags in one hand, and with his other hand linked fingers with her, leading her into the kitchen. They worked in silence for a few minutes while she grabbed two plates from the cabinets and he pulled the containers from the bags. He had no idea what she might like, so he'd bought a variety. Sweet-and-sour chicken. Beef with snow peas. Egg rolls and crab rangoons. Sesame shrimp. Pork fried rice.

She stood next to him and stared down at the amount of food. "They gave us four fortune cookies."

He grinned, continuing to set out the food. "That gives us extra chances for getting a good fortune."

"I should warn you that I tend to get the worst fortunes in the history of the world."

Time stood still as their gazes locked on to each other. "Then get used to your fortune changing."

Her eyes widened, and he bent to kiss her forehead. "Let's eat, babe."

Sitting at her two-chair table after filling their plates, they began to eat. She used chopsticks, deftly maneuvering the food to her mouth with ease. Remembering she'd called herself a klutz, he smiled.

"What?" She halted mid-bite, the chopsticks still holding on to the piece of shrimp as her head tilted to the side. "What are you smiling at?"

"Sorry, but I was remembering you tripping on the cobblestones." He inclined his head toward the chopsticks. "You're perfectly coordinated with those."

She chuckled and shook her head. "My coordination seems to be off when I try to walk in high heels. Or play sports. Or dance." Shrugging, she added, "For some reason, chopsticks are easy for me. Perhaps, it's because I'm anxious for the food to get from my plate to my mouth."

He chuckled, and they continued eating in companionable silence. At the end, he picked up the four fortunes cookies and held them out. "Your choice."

She narrowed her eyes as she gazed at them, seeming to ponder the selection with the utmost consideration. Finally, she lifted one from his palm and he chose one after her. Opening them at the same time, her brows snapped down once she had unwrapped the fortune.

"Seriously?" she groused. Turning it around so he could read it, she quoted, "The early bird gets the worm, but the second mouse gets the cheese."

A bark of laughter erupted, and he flipped his

around, not able to hide his smirk. "Success lies in the hands of those who want it."

"Oh, my God. You're also a fortune guru."

"Come on, there are two more. Pick another."

Her pout was as sexy as the earlier sparks from her eyes and once again she stared carefully at the two remaining cookies. Choosing one with great deliberation, they unwrapped them together.

"You go first," she said.

Nodding, he read his then shrugged and turned it around. "Pretty innocuous one, I'd say. 'You'll get good news.'"

She nibbled on her lip as she read hers, then her eyebrows lifted, and a smile spread across her face. "When you live the life you love, then you'll love life." Looking up at him, she beamed. "I think that's the best one I've ever gotten!"

"Told you, your fortune is about to change."

She quickly sucked in her breath, holding his gaze as a slow smile spread across her face. After rinsing off their plates, he walked over to the table and linked fingers with her again. Silently leading her into the living room, he sat down on the sofa, tugging her gently to his side. "Why don't we start with the basics? The things we didn't get to the night we met."

"The basics?"

"Yeah, like I'm Kyle McBride."

"McBride. Detective Kyle McBride." She dropped her chin and shook her head slowly. "I never paid attention to your last name when you showed me your badge. You must be Caitlyn's brother."

"You know my sister?"

"We went to college together. Me, Caitlyn, and Bekki King."

That tidbit gave him pause but only for a few seconds. He remembered she'd been at the Celtic Cock with friends but had no idea that one of those friends was his sister.

"I'm Kimberly Hogan."

He held her gaze, wanting to know more. "You already know I'm a detective, but you told me you worked in marketing. Who do you work for?"

"Everything I told you is true," she said. "My marketing job is with Kilton Pharmaceuticals. I spend my days working in an office where I design marketing materials. Everything from brochures and packets that go to doctors, patients, education, blah, blah, blah."

His head jerked back as he lifted a brow. "Blah?"

"It's not that my job is boring, because I really like the people in the office. And I have to concentrate on what I'm writing because, when dealing with drugs, errors could have horrible consequences." Sighing, she shrugged again. "I think I like the brochures for education the best. They're more interesting."

Unable to believe that she worked for the company he was investigating, he continued his questions. "Okay, what about your writing?"

She shifted on the sofa and turned slightly to face him, one knee bent and her foot tucked under her other leg. "It's an e-magazine called Hope City Happenings. They publish twice weekly and are growing in subscriptions. I've been freelancing for them for over a year and, so far, the editor's been really nice and told me he'd like more from me. Everything at Kilton has been crazy lately, but I'm discovering a way to combine what I'm doing for them and what I'm doing for the magazine, as long as there's no conflict of interest."

"Okay..."

"Since you're a detective, you've probably heard that Kilton Pharma got a lot of bad press several months ago when one of the sales reps was caught stealing and part of some kind of drug ring. There was gossip galore at work, but other than what I heard on the news, I don't know what happened."

Maintaining his interested-albeit-poker face, Kyle nodded for her to continue while hiding the gut clench that always happened when he thought of Tara being caught in that nightmare.

"Anyway, because of my journalism background, I was asked by the head of marketing to do a series of interviews that could be put in promotional material. You know, the innovative research going on. The life-saving drugs. Helping the community. The people behind the company. All of that. So, what I've been doing for the past week is talking to a bunch of people at work."

Smiling his encouragement, he still hid his inner thoughts. *Holy shit, she's got an inside viewpoint, but there's no way I can fuckin' use her. But maybe...*

She shifted on the sofa again, this time waving her hands with more excitement. "As I started meeting some of the employees and listening to their interesting stories, I thought about showcasing some in an article series called Faces of Hope City. I pitched the idea to my editor, and he loved it. Of course, for anyone at Kilton, I'd have to get their permission separately from what I'm doing at work."

So far, everything she'd told him made sense—her job and freelance, her interest in journalism and people. *But what the fuck was she doing at the Cardboard Cottages?* Her eyes were bright once again and her cheeks rosy. Part of him wanted to keep her just like this. Hell, part of him wanted to take her upstairs and claim her once more, only this time not let her walk away. But as much as he hated to take away her joy, he had no choice. *I've got to know what the fuck she was doing.*

"Do you want something to drink? Beer, soda, iced tea?"

"Wouldn't mind a beer, but I'm still on duty. My partner is probably wondering what the hell is keeping me."

She sucked in her lips and her chin dropped, her focus on her hands now clasped in her lap. *Caitlyn's brother. I can't believe I slept with Caitlyn's brother.* Waiting to see if mortification would hit, she gave a rueful snort. *Caitlyn would probably offer a high-five and 'hell yeah'.* Pushing that thought from her mind, she lifted her gaze and asked, "You're going to ask me about this morning, aren't you?"

Glad she brought it up, he nodded. "Yeah, Kimberly. I need to know how you got from interviewing some Kilton employees to placing yourself in danger by wandering around the homeless community under the bridge by yourself with nothing but a fuckin' can of pepper spray and didn't have the good sense to *not* spray it when the wind was blowing."

Her mouth fell open and her eyes widened. "Wow, you can really go from sweet to a jerk, can't you?"

"Pointing out a mistake that you made is not me being a jerk."

Her mouth clamped into a tight line, and he inwardly cursed. Sighing heavily, he said, "Let me start again. Kimberly, I'm a detective. You know that. It's my job to be aware of the dangerous places in Hope City, and you were in a bad situation. It's also my job to investigate crimes, and if something had happened to you, and I was right there and had to investigate, it would totally gut me. On top of that, I think we're establishing that I'd like to see where you and I go in this relationship." Her gaze jumped back to his face, and he nodded. "So, yeah, I'm going to be interested. And I need some answers."

She tilted her head to the side, nibbling her bottom lip. "You want to see where we go in this relationship?"

"You told me earlier that you've been thinking about me for a week. Well, here's a heads up. I have too. I woke up that morning after the best night of my life and couldn't believe that you were gone. I didn't know your last name, phone number, or where you worked."

A rosy blush moved across her cheeks and she shrugged. "I'm not used to doing what we did. I don't go to hotels with strange men and, to be honest, I had no idea what the protocol was." Air quotes accompanied the word *protocol*.

He dropped his chin and shook his head. "Fuck, even finger quotes from you are cute." Holding her gaze again, he prompted, "Protocol?"

Her blush deepened and she huffed. "Yeah. Like what's expected when you wake up with someone. Have breakfast? Take a shower? Or is one person supposed to get the hell out of the room so that the other person doesn't have to deal with them? Honestly, Kyle, I had no idea. But I figured I was one night of fun for you, and I left because I thought that would be easier on both of us."

Her honesty was refreshing, something he rarely got when he met a woman in a bar. *Not that that had happened recently.* He reached over and smoothed his fingers through her almost-dry hair, tucking a strand behind her ear. "That's nice to hear. Just so you know, my younger days of picking up women in bars are long gone. I was sorry that you weren't around the next morning. So, getting back to my original statement, yeah, I'm interested."

She nodded slowly, holding his gaze. After a moment, she said, "This morning."

"Yeah, babe. I want you to tell me about this morning."

Her nose scrunched, and she huffed. "Well, it started with Father James and the blankets and then came the call and email from my editor with an article that mentioned the Cardboard Cottages, and I know Kilton had a delivery van full of opioids robbed."

His chest deflated as the air fled his lungs, her words shocking him. *What the ever-loving fuck?*

Kimberly stared at Kyle's open-mouth gasp, appearing as though he had been socked in the gut. "Um… are you okay?"

Blinking as though coming out of a foggy sleep, he growled, "No, I'm not okay. Father James? Blankets? Email? Robbery? Jesus, Kimberly, what the hell are you talking about?"

"Me? Don't start being a jerk again."

He twisted so that he was facing out in the room, his elbows pressed into his knees as his hands held his face. Even when angry, Kyle held a calmness about him, but now it was gone. Electricity seemed to snap about the room, but she couldn't define what he was experiencing. Uncertain what to say, she remained quiet.

He finally sucked in a deep breath and let it out slowly. Lifting his head away from his palms, he twisted and speared her with his gaze. "Maybe you better start at the beginning."

She nodded, uncertain where the beginning actually was. "To be honest, the bigwigs I was interviewing were pretty boring, and I just got their canned speeches of how wonderful their departments are. Then I interviewed Sidney Kilton, who is the supervisor for HR. She told me I should get away from the supervisors and talk to some of the people who do the real work in the company."

She hesitated, waiting to see how Kyle was taking her story so far. He appeared calm, offered a small nod, so she continued.

"Well, my landlord works there, and he introduced me to a lot of warehouse workers. I had lunch in their workroom, and it was really interesting. Some of them have been there for a long time and had stories about the way things used to be. Some of them came from other companies or warehouses and had thoughts on how Kilton works as opposed to other places."

Her gaze left his as she glanced out into the room, collecting her thoughts. "I know it might not sound like much, but I was interested in meeting these people and talking to them. All I could think of was what I wanted to do. Showcase the average worker doing their job." Remembering Tammy, she barked out a laugh. "I also got to meet a lady that's been working there since the company opened, and she was a hoot. I learned all about how the delivery routes were designed and she told me about the robbery."

A flash of something undefinable flew through Kyle's eyes, but it was gone as quickly as it came. He didn't say anything, so she continued. "I guess that's where I got the idea that it might be cool to not only do human-interest stories for Kilton marketing but for the readership at Hope City Happenings as well."

He nodded slowly, his gaze still pinned on her. "Okay, I get that. So, tell me who Father James is and what the blankets have to do with the call from your editor."

"No, no. The blankets don't have anything to do with my editor. The blankets have to do with Father James."

Once again, she was sure she could hear him slowly counting under his breath. "Kyle, I don't think you're paying attention."

"At the risk of being called a jerk again, Kimberly,

I'm going to have to say that you're not making a lot of sense."

She sighed heavily and began again. "When I was younger, I used to help our parish priest collect bags of things that he would give to those less fortunate. I stopped by the other day and met with him and found out that he still has a group that does that, and they deliver blankets and food to some of the people at the Cardboard Cottages. I also received a call from my editor who encouraged me to add more people to my Faces of Hope City. He sent articles about illegal opioid use and homelessness, and I started thinking that the Cottages might give me some people to talk to. You know... the real faces, not just those at Kilton but from all walks of life."

"The real faces...?" Kyle leaned back and twisted his body so that he was now facing her directly. His brow furrowed and, if possible, the intensity of his gaze sharpened. "You're not an investigative reporter—"

Nodding emphatically, she agreed. "I know, but it seemed interesting."

"Interesting?"

"The article link he sent described the opioid crisis and how a drug called fentanyl is added to other drugs making it a lot more potent and addictive—"

"Jesus, Kimberly. And that's how you wound up at the Cardboard Cottages this morning? Alone, unprotected, vulnerable."

She pinched her lips together once again, knowing no matter what she said he was not going to be happy with her decisions.

"Just like with getting your street name, babe, I'll sit here till you decide to tell me, so you might as well go ahead and get it over with."

"Jerk," she mumbled under her breath.

"Heard that before, still ignoring it. You can think what you want about me, but I want to know how you ended up there this morning."

She lifted her hand and rubbed her forehead, trying to ease the dull ache that had settled behind her eyes. "The article also mentioned how stolen fentanyl was a multi-million-dollar industry, and the woman I talked to at Kilton had mentioned that there was a delivery van that had been robbed last week. It got me thinking that this was another time where Kilton Pharmaceuticals was involved with stolen drugs. The article mentioned the homeless population is particularly susceptible to drug addiction. Cardboard Cottages was listed as one of the problem areas."

Having explained her actions, she sat quietly, wondering what he was thinking.

Continuing to hold her gaze, he urged, "Okay, go on."

She blinked in surprise. "Um... that's all."

"That's not all."

"Yeah, it is. You wanted to know why I was there, and I told you."

"What were you doing? What were you hoping to find out? Why did you go by yourself? Why did you only have a canister of pepper spray—"

Throwing her hands up in front of her, she said, "Okay, okay! I get it! I'd never been to any place that has drugs, although I've seen pictures of the Cardboard Cottages. And no, I didn't go waltzing in like Little Red Riding Hood without a care in the world. Believe me, I thought long and hard before going."

"So, what was your plan when you got there?"

"I met the group from the church and only the men were allowed to give out the food and blankets. I didn't get a chance to talk to anyone. I decided to drive to the other side and see if I could find some women to talk to. I was only getting out of my car if I saw someone I thought I might be able to approach safely. Once I got there, I quickly ascertained that the area deeper underneath the overpasses was not where I wanted to go. But I saw some kids playing on the outer perimeter and a few women standing near a fire keeping an eye on them. I thought it would be safe to talk to them."

He stood quickly and walked across the room, hands planted on his hips while he studied his boots. Suddenly turning, he asked, "What did you want to talk to them about?"

"At first, I just thought I'd see if anyone could tell me about drugs in the area. I thought I was safe since their kids were right there."

"Jesus, Kimberly. If those women had been strung out on something, they would have slit your throat right in front of their kids and not thought anything about it!"

Stomach clenching at the thought, she stiffened her spine and glared back. "Well, they didn't, did they?"

He scrubbed his hand over his face, and she could have sworn she heard him counting under his breath again. Deciding discretion was in her favor, she remained quiet.

Finally speaking, he said, "Okay, you decided to talk to them. What did you learn?"

Jumping to her feet, she began pacing. "This is where my plan completely changed, Kyle. I offered them fruit gummies for their kids, and they accepted, even making sure their kids said thank you. Then we just talked for a little bit. I didn't ask about the drugs, not at first. I let them tell me about their situations. I realized how naïve I was to not know why some people live there. Their stories broke my heart."

She rubbed her forehead again, ready for the conversation to end. When she opened her eyes, he had moved silently and was now standing directly in front of her. She battled the desire to lean into his strength. Sighing, she continued, "Yes, toward the end I asked about fentanyl. One of the ladies knew nothing about it, saying she stayed away from drugs. Another one said her ex-husband used to use it. But they admitted they lived in the tents on the outskirts so that they were safer and weren't involved in anything illegal. I believe them. They were clean, clear-eyed, completely sober."

He closed the scant distance between them and wrapped his arms around her once again, pulling her close. With her cheek resting against his chest, she said, "I just wanted to talk to them. And, after I did, I realized I cared more about their plight than I did trying to figure out anything to do with drugs. I was walking away, back to my car, when you saw me. That's it, Kyle. That's all there is."

13

If Kyle thought the myriad of emotions ran the gamut when he discovered the woman at Cardboard Cottages was Kimberly, it was nothing compared to what he was feeling now with her back in his arms. The detective in him wanted to know what she was finding out at her workplace while the protector in him wanted to rail against her foolish decision to walk unprotected into the lion's den. And the man who was interested in her found her a fascinating woman, one with many layers that he wanted to discover. But, for the moment, he settled on just holding her in his embrace, grateful he had found her again.

She tilted her head back and whispered, "What now?"

Staring into her beautiful green eyes and the feel of her body flush against his, he smiled. "Now, this." Bending, he took her lips in a kiss that started gentle and slow but soon filled with all the emotion and desire that had snapped around like electricity.

He battled to keep the kiss light, but she lifted on her toes and wrapped her arms around his neck, pulling him closer. Closer was a relative word because, with his cock pressed against her stomach and her breasts pressed against his chest, he couldn't imagine less space between them. All thoughts left his mind as his entire being focused on the moans coming from deep inside, uncertain if they were hers or his.

Drinking each other in, they kissed in an almost desperate attempt to become one. He'd discovered the first night they met that he enjoyed kissing her, which had been a surprise. It was nothing like anything he'd ever experienced. Far beyond the innocent fumblings of youth. Far beyond the seductive precursor to casual sex. Far beyond anything he'd felt in a previous relationship.

This kiss was pulling at his soul as much as his body.

He bent and, with one hand under her knees, scooped her into his arms and stalked back to the sofa. He maneuvered them both onto the cushions, miraculously never losing her mouth. He ran his hand down her torso, and her breasts were full against his palm and the heat from her core burned against his thigh as he nudged her legs apart.

His body cried out for him to strip off their clothing and plunge himself into her warmth. But, instead, he lifted his head away from hers, gasping in a ragged breath.

"Why did you stop?" she moaned as her fingers clutched his neck, pulling him back down.

Swallowing deeply, doubting his sanity at that moment, he replied, "Because we need to stop."

Her body stiffened as her eyes widened. "What? Why?"

"Because I want this."

"I think you've muddled my mind with kisses because that doesn't make sense."

A smile slipped across his face, and he leaned down to kiss her lightly again. "It's true that I want your body. I want more mind-blowing, forget-the-world, nothing-exists-except-you-and-me kind of sex."

"Yes!" she groaned, pressing her hips upward against his aching cock.

"But I'm going to say no."

Now it was her turn to suck in a ragged breath and it was warm against his face when she blew it out in a huff.

"I want you, Kimberly. I want whatever's happening between us. What I don't want is to fuck it up."

"Can't I talk you into just fucking and not fuck it up?"

Laughter erupted from deep within and he shook his head. "Jesus, girl, you're killing me."

"I don't want to kill you, I just want you to f—"

"I want to do this right. So, I'm going to call my partner to come to get me. While I'm waiting on him, we're going to plan a date for tomorrow night. I'd make it tonight, but you're exhausted and need to rest. I'm also going to get your promise that you won't do anything else on your own."

"We're going to go on a date?"

Barking out another laugh, he said, "That's what you pulled out of everything I said?"

"Yeah. Everything else we can deal with, but I want to know again that you want to go on a date with me."

He stared into her eyes for a moment, the green reminding him of a pair of jade earrings that his mother got for Christmas one year. Kimberly's eyes were that exact color. Before he gave into temptation, he slid his phone from his pocket. With a few punches of his thumb, he held the phone to his ear. "I need you to come to get me. Colbert Street. 1722. Thanks."

"I take it that was your partner."

Nodding, he kissed her again. He hefted his body off the sofa and gently pulled her to stand next to him. "Okay. First up, date tomorrow night. I'll pick you up, and we'll go to dinner. Is six-thirty okay?"

Her top teeth landed on her bottom kiss-swollen lip, capturing his attention. He gave her a little squeeze, and she nodded.

"Yeah, just let me know what I should wear."

"And you promise that between now and then you'll do no more investigating, no more checking into things, no more dangerous trips, nothing."

She nodded again and said, "I promise. Tomorrow I'll be back at Kilton and have some people in the research department that I'm going to talk to. Honestly, that'll be boring."

"Good."

He wrapped his arm around her, and they walked to the front door. Kissing her deeply, he looked out the window and saw an SUV stop on the road right in front of her townhouse. "That's Alex."

Kissing her lightly, he said, "We covered a lot of

territory today. But, don't forget, babe, the most important thing is the start of you and me. Together, a real
relationship."

She gifted him with a smile, one he was not going to
take for granted, and it speared him straight through his
heart. With a final kiss, he threw open the door and
jogged over to the SUV, climbing inside.

They drove in silence for a moment and then Alex
finally bit out, "Are you gonna talk or make me wonder
what the fuck got into you?"

"It was her. Mystery woman."

"Figured that out. What I want to know is what the
hell she was doing and what the hell you're gonna do
about it."

"You're not gonna believe this... she works for
fuckin' Kilton Pharmaceuticals."

Alex's head whipped around, and Kyle laughed. It
wasn't often that he could catch his partner off-guard.
He spent the rest of the ten-minute drive back to the
station explaining everything that Kimberly told him.
Her job at Kilton. The new assignment. Her decision to
take some of the human-interest stories to the magazine. And her reason for going to the Cardboard
Cottages.

Parking, Alex made no move to get out, just shook
his head slowly. "Okay, you got me. That's one crazy-ass
story."

Once inside, they headed straight to their desks, and

he opened his laptop. Alex plopped down at the desk directly across from him and said, "By the way, we need to talk to Todd Bartosi."

Glancing at his partner over the top of his screen, he cocked his head to the side. "The Kilton robbery?"

"Seems like Charlie and Joe's stories don't exactly match up."

Brows lifted, he nodded and dropped his gaze back to his screen. He pulled up the information on the e-magazine, but everything he could see looked legit.

"Bartosi sent over what they had, and I've got it up on the board."

Kyle leaned back, resting his hip against his desk. At the top of the board, he'd written two words. **Kilton Pharmaceuticals.** Underneath, he had a picture of Beth Washington and Dr. Tiller, with notes out to the side about the drug ring they had been involved in using stolen opioids from KP. To the side, he had placed pictures of Charlie and Joe, observing that Alex's info from Detective Bartosi about the KP van robbery was now there as well.

"We went and talked to Beth, but I'd like to see if Dr. Tiller is willing to talk more. I'll wager a few months in prison might have loosened his lips a little."

"I wonder if he's got someone protecting him as well."

"Let's make the arrangements. If we're lucky, we can get there tomorrow."

He waited while Alex made the call and then the two of them headed the few blocks away to headquarters where Bartosi and his partner were stationed. Once on the third floor, they stopped in the open workroom, poured a cup of powerhouse coffee, and found Todd sitting at his desk, staring at his evidence board as well.

His partner walked in, a statuesque brunette with a wide smile and no-nonsense manner. Sticking her hand out, she said, "McBride, Freeman. Nice to meet you. I'm Roberta Manson, known as Birdie."

Birdie was a looker, no doubt, but Kyle's mind was filled with a petite honey-blonde. One look to the side toward his partner, it was evident that Alex was more than taken with Todd's partner. Hiding a grin, he walked over to their evidence board. "Talk to me about Charlie and Joe."

"You were with us when Charlie came in while Joe was still at the hospital. That was to our advantage because they hadn't had a chance to talk between themselves. Charlie gave a detailed account of what he remembered. We questioned him, he wrote it all down, went over it numerous times, and he signed it. Birdie wanted to make sure we got Joe early, so she headed to the hospital. He didn't have a concussion and was patched up quickly. She talked him into coming with her so that we could go ahead and get his statement. They were almost identical up to a certain point and then the differences showed up."

He looked at the timeline, noting that what Charlie had told Todd was the same as what he'd told Kyle at the site. It appeared Joe's rendition followed. "Joe was driving. Accident on Market Street. They called it into Kilton, and we know they talked to Tammy Rutgers, who cleared it with her boss for them to alter their schedule. They also called the pharmacy and talked to the manager. They made their second delivery ahead of schedule and arrived at their third delivery, also ahead of schedule. They both reported that Joe stayed in the van, although Charlie said Joe told him to get out and ring the bell at the back of the pharmacy. They reported two men got out of the van, both with guns. One went to Charlie and the other one came to the driver's side pointing at Joe, telling him to get out. They lined up side-by-side with their backs to their van, one of the men held a gun to them while the other man went around to the side and began hauling boxes from the Kilton van and putting them into their delivery truck. All that's the same."

Birdie stepped around and pointed to the split in the timeline. "This is where the difference occurs. Charlie reported the man holding a weapon on them ordered them to get to their knees and face the van. He said Joe said something, but Charlie couldn't understand what he said. The man standing behind them said, 'Not now'. Charlie claims he had no idea what was going on at that time except he expected to die. He said Joe was grabbed by the arm, hefted to his feet, and taken around to the other side of the van. Charlie stayed put... on his knees, hands behind his head."

"That's exactly what he told me at the time," Kyle said. "Heard voices from the other side of the van, couldn't understand what they were saying. Then heard a sound and Joe crying out."

"Not just any voices. He specifically said he heard Joe's voice. Then footsteps running. He braced for the worst, but the truck doors slammed, the engine started up, and it pulled away. As soon as it was gone, he called out for Joe, got to his feet, and ran around, seeing Joe slumped to the ground, holding his bloody head."

Stepping slightly to the side, Kyle's gaze ran down Joe's version, which deviated when the two men were on their knees. "Joe reports not saying anything, although he admits he might've mumbled, but he doesn't remember anyone saying, 'Not now', and if they did, he couldn't imagine they were talking to him."

Alex stepped closer and pointed to the last part of Joe's interview. "He claims when he got to the other side of the van the two gunmen were arguing, not him. He remained quiet, said they were arguing over what to do with him and Charlie. One whirled around and hit him with the butt of his weapon. Joe remembers crying out and dropping to the ground."

"So, almost identical accounts except for who was talking on the other side of the van," Kyle said.

"But is that enough to go on?" Alex asked.

Birdie swung her head around and pinned her dark brown eyes on him. "I'd say yes. That one discrepancy makes all the difference."

"Charlie admits he was pissing his pants with fear. So scared he couldn't even talk. Wouldn't Joe have been the same way? Man's got a gun on you... are you gonna argue? Talk back? Ask questions?" Jerking around, Kyle looked at the others. "I watched the interview with Charlie. He didn't hesitate. He didn't seem confused. He reported without hesitation that Joe said something when they were kneeling and the man behind them said, 'Not now'. And again, without hesitation, he said he heard voices, and specifically said one of the voices was Joe's."

"What if he's lying to implicate Joe?" Birdie asked, lifting her brow.

"You interviewed him. What does your gut say?"

She pinched her lips together and shifted her gaze back to Todd. Staring at her partner for a few seconds, she then replied, "We thought about that. But our gut feeling? Joe's interview was a little more unsure, whereas Charlie's account was certain."

"What about Kilton Pharmaceuticals?" Todd asked.

"Tammy Rutgers organizes the routes and has been there since the beginning. She's not the only one who knows about the routes, and we didn't get a chance to talk to her direct supervisor, who would also have known about the change." Kyle turned and looked back at the board, shaking his head slowly. "I know it's coming from the inside. Can't prove shit yet, but I just know someone's directing the thefts of fentanyl and selling it." *Now, how the hell do I keep Kimberly out of the middle of this?*

14

"Our research involves the experimentation of the interaction of a loose, reversible binding of molecules, the chemical bond with their target sites. Receptors, macromolecules, and lipids..."

Oh, my God. Kimberly shifted in her seat, the smile she had plastered onto her face twenty minutes ago still in place, although now drooping along with her shoulders—and her mood.

The day was passing in a haze of meetings with the other vice presidents. Dr. Li Chen of Research and Development was now talking incessantly in scientific terms that she could not decipher. Dr. Abeer Patel, the VP of Quality Management, barely had time to speak to her, managing to finally give her three minutes for an interview. Much like Dr. Chen, his praise of Kilton Pharmaceuticals was effusive, but most of his comments were scientific. She wondered if perhaps they either did not know plain-speak or spoke in scientific jargon all the time. *Bet that's exciting for their wives...*

She only had one more VP to interview, Niles Cook, VP of Operations, and the idea of sitting through another mind-numbing session almost had her skip out early. One of his departments was over Warehousing, and since this was where Beth had obtained her extra drugs by sleeping with one of the men working in the warehouse, she held onto a glimmer of hope that Niles would offer a tidbit of interesting perspective.

He greeted her with a wide smile and, even though he was a VP, there was an air of ease about him that she had not found with the others. She grinned, settled into the proffered chair, less stiff than in her other interviews. "When I looked at the company's organization chart, I was surprised at how many departments come under Operations. You're in charge of everything from the manufacturing plants and production to the warehouses and support services as well as the IT for the company."

He laughed, his smile easy. "Essentially, I believe that Operations is the term for 'all departments that we don't know where else to stick them.'"

"Kind of like a Jack of all trades?" As soon as the words left her mouth, her eyes bugged. "Sorry, I just thought of the rest of that saying. I don't mean to imply that you're not a master of anything. I just meant that, well... uh..."

He waved his hand dismissively. "Don't worry about it. In many ways you're right. I am like a Jack of all trades and master of none. I only say that because, obviously, I can't be the master of how to run a manufacturing plant and know everything about IT. But that's where having good department supervisors is essential. They report to me so that I can report to the president. But, as far as the day-to-day business in each of those departments, it's the supervisor that handles everything. I'm glad you're talking to the line workers."

"Finally! I have to confess that the other VPs were less... um... informative."

"Yeah, that sounds like the stuffiness I have to put up with as well. Geez, you should hear our VP meetings. When Li Chen presents, I know it's naptime."

Unable to hold back her snort, she nodded.

Niles' smile widened. "Now, it's late in the afternoon so I can assure you that most of the dayshift people working in the warehouse will have already shut down and are planning what they want to do for the weekend. They're great people and work hard. But I also happen to know they play hard." Shrugging, he grinned. "Sounds kind of like me, so I can hardly judge them."

"I hate to bring up anything negative, but what can you tell me about the thefts from a few months ago?"

"Ah, the Beth Washington and Terry Birk news."

She nodded, glad that he did not appear to immediately close off.

"Well, the loophole that allowed that to happen has been closed off. He was responsible for sending specially packaged pharmaceuticals over to the sales department. Unchecked on my end, I might add—which got my hand slapped—and then unchecked on Sally's end, gaining her a hand slap as well. Terry would simply divide the packages so that Beth received more than her allotment and a new hire received less, not realizing the discrepancy."

As she stood to leave, she shook his hand with enthusiasm. "Mr. Cook, thank you so much for meeting with me. This was... well, what I was hoping for." Walking out, she was amazed at how easy it had been for Beth to have extra drugs to sell illegally and hoped Niles was right about the loophole being closed.

———

Kimberly sat at her desk in the marketing department, typing up her notes. Not wanting to miss anything, she included notes from the vice presidents and department supervisors but spent most of her energy on her interview with Tammy and some of the others in the warehouse.

When she made an appointment to talk to someone in Pharmaceutical Development, she specifically mentioned she was interested in the opioids that Kilton Pharma produces. She was thrilled to have received an email setting that up for the afternoon. *Easy office work in the morning, a chance to find out more about the opioids in the afternoon, and a dinner date with Kyle this evening.* She couldn't remember the last time she was this excited about her day.

"If you grin any wider, I think your face is going to split," Marcus said.

Lost in thought, she jumped at his words, her head

whipping around to see him grinning just as widely. "I'm just having a good day."

"Obviously! You want to confess what's got you so happy?"

"Once I stopped interviewing the higher-ups at Kilton, I've had more interesting interviews with regular employees. And it's made me want to write more for the e-magazine I freelance for. Marcus, it's so much more exciting to me than what I've been doing here." Glancing around to see if anyone else was listening, she added, "And I've got a date tonight."

"Damn, I can't remember the last time you went on one of those."

"Tell me about it!" Shrugging, she turned back to her laptop. "Hence, my good mood." By lunchtime, she'd finished typing her notes, sending them to her personal email so that she would be able to look at them anytime.

She grabbed her backpack and made sure her notebook and pens were inside. Pulling out a granola bar, she tossed a wave to Marcus and said, "Dr. Chen has arranged for me to visit the research and development area this afternoon."

With his goodbye following her as she left, she munched on her granola bar as she walked along the sidewalk between the various buildings of the pharmaceutical compound. The research and development building was near the production plant, and she planned on touring and talking to some of the production members soon.

Entering, she signed in with the guard and was soon met by an assistant who led her into the bowels of the building, past many glass windows overlooking the research area. Everyone was dressed in full personal protection equipment: booties on their feet, jumpsuits covering their clothing, masks, goggles, head covering, and, of course, gloves.

The assistant left her in a small conference room, telling her that Dr. Chaudra would be in to speak to her shortly. She pulled out her notebook and quickly began jotting notes of her impressions so far. The building was pristine, not a speck of dirt to be found anywhere. She described the employees in their PPE and the workstations she had seen.

The door opened and Dr. Chaudra walked in. A wide smile on her face, she stuck her hand out in greeting. "I'm Dr. Sahana Chaudra. It's nice to meet you."

Both women settled at the table, and Kimberly immediately dove into her subject. "I know you're extremely busy, and I'm thrilled you agreed to meet with me. I'm more than willing to hear anything you have to tell me about the pharmaceutical research, but I also wondered if we could speak specifically about fentanyl."

Dr. Chaudra nodded, not giving any outward expression of surprise or irritation. Instead, she inclined her head politely and said, "Of course. It was originally developed as an opioid pain medication. Opioid, of course, means it is a compound that resembles opium and its addictive properties or physiological effects. It was created for cancer pain that was not controlled by other medications. In other words, it was never meant to be prescribed for headaches or pain after surgery. It's very potent, very addictive, and has multiple side effects."

"With such power and strength, Dr. Chaudra, isn't it very risky to use, even for cancer pain?"

Nodding, she said, "Absolutely. Very risky. But, originally, it was for the pain management of someone who was at the end of their life."

Understanding dawned, and her breath rushed from her lungs. "Oh, I see. We often hear of morphine being used to help someone who's in a great deal of pain at the end of their life to pass more peacefully."

"Yes, and for some patients, morphine and other opioids are not enough."

They continued talking for several more minutes about the research and development aspect of pharmaceuticals, but a niggling question remained in Kimberly's mind. Uncertain how the topic could be perceived, she knew she had nothing to lose by asking. "Dr. Chaudra, do you sometimes find an ethical dilemma in your research? I'm thinking specifically of fentanyl. Its original use was very narrow in focus, and yet has exploded into the world of illicit drugs."

Dr. Chaudra's lips pinched ever so slightly as she nodded. "What you have to understand is in research and development we are focused on finding the chemical combinations that can be used to help. That help might be a cure or a treatment. When researching, we constantly hope to use chemistry to assist. Yes, there are those out there that will take our research and products, not use it according to our standards or even duplicate it illegally. Doctors all across the world began prescribing fentanyl as a go-to pain reliever for patients that never should have experienced it. Illegal drug manufacturers began duplicating the chemical process. And, of course, drug dealers will steal the prescription medicine and sell it on the black market."

"And adding it to heroin and other drugs?"

"From a biochemical standpoint, this makes the drug much more potent. Someone taking it will become addicted much quicker, and with no regulations on illegal drugs, it will be sold and used at will. Am I aware that people do these things? Yes. But in answer to your original question, Ms. Hogan, I'm still going to continue my pharmaceutical and biochemistry research and development to find the combinations that cure or treat patients."

The sincerity resonating from Dr. Chaudra moved through Kimberly. "Thank you so much for talking to me today. I'd love to showcase you in one of my stories. I think you're an inspiration, especially for little girls who are interested in science."

With the heavy part of the interview over, she shook Dr. Chaudra's hand and accepted the invitation to have the assistant give her a more detailed tour of the facility. She jumped at the opportunity to speak to more of the researchers and workers on the front line.

Once she was back in her office, she continued to scribble notes of what she'd seen and who she'd spoken to. With one eye on the clock, she leaped from her chair as soon as her day was over. With Marcus' laughter and well wishes ringing in her ears, she hurried out to her car.

Now, two hours later, she felt foolish standing by her front window, looking out as she waited for Kyle to drive up. *Geez, you'd think I never go out on a date!* The truth was it had been a while since she'd been on a date that she was excited about. She had rushed home, showered, dried her hair in soft waves, and applied makeup with a light hand. That had been the easy part. The hard part has been deciding what to wear.

She had sent a text to Kyle asking how to dress, and in a typical guy manner, he replied with one word —casual.

Casual? That could be a dress or jeans or anything in between. She knew he had sisters and couldn't believe that he didn't realize her question had great importance. Checking the weather app, she discovered they were in for a slightly cool evening so she decided on a dress with a little length while showcasing her figure. Over the top, she added a light denim jacket. Foregoing heels, she slipped on platform sandals that looked cute but didn't make her feel as though she was going to topple over.

She grabbed a cute cross-body purse and stood at her kitchen counter, changing the items over from the backpack bag she had taken to work.

Now, she paced in front of her small front window overlooking the street. As several SUVs and trucks came down the road, it dawned on her that she had no idea what he would be driving. Huffing, she looked down at her phone and started to send him another text.

Just then, she spied a midsize SUV expertly parallel

parking down the street from her front door. It pulled into a space that she would never have been able to maneuver into. She was so focused on the parking job, she jolted when she saw Kyle climb from the driver's seat. She threw open her front door as he was approaching and said, "I'm sorry you had to park. I was planning on just running out."

He stood at the bottom of her steps and looked up, his gaze roving from the top of her head down to her feet and back up again. She blushed under his perusal but, from the look on his face, it was evident she had chosen her outfit well.

"If you'd just run out to the street, I would've been robbed of the chance to stand here and admire you like this."

Shaking her head and rolling her eyes, she inwardly preened at his words as she locked her front door. His hand reached out and she linked fingers, walking beside him as he escorted her to his SUV. Once inside, her gaze scanned the interior. While it didn't smell like a brand-new car, it was very clean and showed no signs of wear and tear. As soon as he climbed back into the driver's seat, she asked, "Is this new?"

"It's only a few months old. I've got a pickup truck that's a clunker and use it for work. I never know where I might get called to and some of the places I go are pretty rough. I don't want to take this vehicle to a crack house."

Her eyes widened. "Yeah. I can see where you wouldn't." Unable to think of anything else to say at his mention of a crack house, she sat silent for a moment.

"You okay, babe?"

"I guess I hadn't really thought very much about where your job takes you. I know that's foolish, but I hate to think of you being in danger."

"Does my job bother you?"

With an emphatic shake of her head, she said, "No. You're a lot braver than I am, but I do hate the idea that you're in danger."

"I'm good at what I do."

With her head leaned back, she rolled it to the side to peer at him and waited.

"I don't take undue risks. I know what I'm doing when I go into a situation. And, while anything can happen at any time, I am good at what I do, Kimberly."

By now, they had pulled onto a small side street where he executed another perfect parking maneuver. "Are you like a parallel parking guru?"

Now it was his turn to twist around and stare at her. "What?"

"I know how to parallel park my little car, especially on my street. But, even then, I'm sometimes a foot away from the curb or I bump my tire onto the curb."

"Do you really want to know the truth?"

"Of course."

"I had a driver's ed teacher in high school that must've lived on one of these rowhouse streets. He was determined that every single kid he taught how to drive knew how to parallel park. I swear I think we did it for a solid week. He was a pain in the ass, but by the end of the week, I could parallel park. Been doing it ever since."

"Hmm, I think my driver's ed teacher must've skipped that lesson."

Barking out a laugh, he climbed from behind the wheel and walked around the front, assisting her down. Bending, he kissed her lightly and said, "By the way, you're beautiful tonight."

Smiling, she squeezed his fingers before looking around, not recognizing where they were. Following his lead as he held her hand, they turned the corner at the end of the block, and she spied a large red awning extending from a small storefront. *Chino's Pizza* was written in script on the awning. "Chino's?"

"Ever heard of it?"

She shook her head. "Is it good?"

"Babe, would I bring you on a date to a place that didn't have good food?"

Scrunching her nose, she laughed. "Maybe," she said with exaggeration. He pretend-growled and she said, "You gave me Chinese last night and pizza tonight. Next date, I need to fix dinner for you."

"I'll take you up on that."

He held open the door, and as soon as they stepped inside, she was immediately charmed by the interior. Red and white checkered tablecloth covered the tables, and servers wearing jeans and bright red shirts bustled around, trays of pizza pies held high over their heads as they weaved between patrons. A rotund man in a crisp white chef's jacket and red apron was behind the counter, and when he caught sight of Kyle he threw his hand up in a wave, calling out his greeting. A pretty teenager with long black hair pulled up in a ponytail hurried to them and smiled. "Hey, Kyle! I've got a table for you over here."

Kimberly glanced at him and grinned. "Oh, I'm impressed. You must have called ahead!"

"I knew it was the only way we could get seated right away."

The young server smiled at Kimberly before shifting her gaze back to Kyle. "You never bring a lady in."

"Kimberly, this is Louisa, the daughter of the best pizza maker in town. Louisa, this is my lovely date, Kimberly."

Smiling up at the bright-eyed young woman, she said, "It's nice to meet you. I'm sorry to say that I've never been here, but I'm excited to try your pizza."

"Oh, you're in for a treat because Dad's pizza is the best." Taking their drink orders, she looked toward Kyle again and asked, "Your usual?"

He looked across the table and cocked his head to the side. "Is there anything you don't want on your pizza?"

"I'm not crazy about anchovies, but everything else is good."

He grinned up at Louisa and nodded. "My usual will be perfect."

She bounced away, her ponytail swinging as she maneuvered through the tables with ease.

"I like this place already, and I haven't even had the food," she said.

"I went to school with Chino's nephew. He worked here every summer and after school, so I've been coming around for a long time. Everybody kept telling

Chino he needed to expand and open up other restaurants, but he refused. He says he only wants to have a restaurant that's as big as what he can handle. I called ahead to make sure we got a table. If this had been the weekend, there would have been a line out the door."

Louisa came back with their drinks and set a platter of fried zucchini and mozzarella sticks with homemade marinara sauce on the table. One bite and Kimberly was in love. Her granola bar had long since worn off hours ago, and she was starved. Not wanting to overstuff on appetizers, she ate slowly. Soon, Louisa came back with a large pizza with homemade crust, loads of cheese, Italian sausage, and onions.

The scent wafting from the pie was enticing, and if she had not been afraid of burning the roof of her mouth on the hot cheese, she would've jumped straight into a bite. Instead, she pulled it apart, blowing on the top to cool. Taking a big bite, her eyes immediately widened. Kyle was grinning at her from across the table as he helped himself to his own piece.

"Oh, my God! I think I've died and gone to pizza heaven!"

Chewing the huge bite he'd taken, he said, "I told you so. Best pizza in town."

When the meal was finished, she smiled as he drove toward the harbor. Remembering the last time they were there, it felt special... almost like *their* place, even though that was ridiculous since this was technically their first date and they had only been to the harbor one other time. As she stared at the handsome man sitting next to her, a twinge in her chest built at the realization of how much she truly liked him.

Beginnings were scary. Full of doubt. But he'd told her the night before that he considered this to be the start of something between them. As they parked near the harbor, they linked their fingers once again as they began their walk.

15

Kyle always enjoyed eating at Chino's, but tonight's date was by far the most entertaining. Not only was Kimberly beautiful, she was also so damn real and funny. The mirth they shared over his being the parallel parking guru had immediately taken away some of the drudge left over from his day. He knew a lot of people in law enforcement whose marriages had not been able to withstand the stress. He also knew many who made it work and, for them, their life was so much better. *Hell, my parents and the Kings are perfect examples.*

Feeling his hand jiggle, he looked down to see her staring up at him.

"Whatcha thinking about?" she asked.

"That I'm walking around the harbor with the most beautiful woman in Hope City."

Her laughter ended in a snort, which in turn caused him to start laughing as well. "I can't believe I just did that! I never used to snort when I laughed... at least, not when I was younger. Now, I do it all the time!"

"I think I've heard that's something old women do," he said, then grunted when her elbow hit his middle.

"That kind of comment will take away any chance you have of getting lucky tonight."

Leaning back in horror with his hand over his heart, he shook his head. "I'll take any punishment but that!"

They fell into an easy pace as their arms were wrapped around each other and they continued walking around the Inner Harbor.

"Oh, look! It's the Pirates!"

They turned and faced the water, watching as a tourist boat was now surrounded by smaller boats with playacting pirates shouting threats. "I wonder if my niece has ever been out to see this?" he mused aloud.

"How old is she?"

"She's seven now."

"Oh, that's the perfect age to get excited about pirates on the water."

The sun was beginning to set behind the skyscrapers toward the west, casting long shadows on the water. As they strolled along, they avoided the storefronts, keeping closer to the least-traveled path near the edge of the harbor.

He led her over to a streetlamp, stopped, and turned so that they were facing each other, bodies pressed together. She looked up at him and smiled as he bent to kiss her. Because there were still so many people around he kept the kiss light but, even so, his body tingled with her lips on his. Leaning back, they said nothing, their eyes holding an entire conversation silently.

She finally glanced around and grinned. "This is where we shared our first kiss."

"I'm glad you remembered. That's why we're here."

"I could hardly forget that kiss. Or you."

"What about what happened after that? Were you able to forget that?"

Twisting around to glance at the hotel, she laughed. "Oh, I haven't forgotten a moment of that."

Kissing her again, he mumbled against her lips, "Your place or mine?"

"Whichever is closer." Her breath was warm against his face and he shivered.

"That'll be mine. And this time, you'd better not disappear in the morning."

She grinned. "Hey, you're driving so you'll have to take me home. But you'd better not plan on kicking me out too early!"

Taking her lips in another kiss, he squeezed her and they began walking back around the harbor toward his SUV. This time, their pace was hurried.

Kyle's townhome was an end unit, so he did not have to worry about being the king of parallel parking. Pulling to the side, he turned off the engine, threw open the door, and his feet had barely hit the pavement before he jogged around to Kimberly's side. She must have been in an equal hurry because she was already out of the vehicle by the time he reached her. He grabbed her hand and they raced to the front door. He fumbled with the keys and cursed under his breath. She pressed her body against his and he groaned. "Not helping, babe."

Her laughter met his ears, and he finally managed to open the door. Dragging her inside, she had just looked around and said, "Oh, how nice—", when his lips hit hers again. He angled his head, licked her lips, and as soon as she opened her mouth, he plunged his tongue inside. This woman, this taste, was what he had been aching for since he'd seen her the previous day.

His hands moved to the lapels of her jean jacket and slid it down her shoulders, letting it puddle by the front door. Barely taking the time to make sure the door was locked, he bent and swooped her into his arms. Mumbling, "I'll give you a tour tomorrow," he stalked toward the stairs.

Her arms wound around his neck and she pulled his mouth back to hers. He started up the L-shaped stairs, then dragged his lips away. As much as he hated to end the kiss, he did not want to slam her head against the wall. Her weight was slight in his arms, and he easily made it into the master bedroom.

Setting her feet onto the floor, he glanced toward the two windows facing the street, glad he'd already pulled the blinds. He reached around the side of her and turned on the light by the bed, casting a pale glow over her face.

They stood for what felt like an eternity but could have only been a few seconds, their bodies close but not touching, their eyes pinned on each other. He leaned forward, placing a gentle kiss on the tiny beauty mark next to her eye.

Her hands slowly moved upward, resting on either side of his waist, her fingertips digging in slightly. Mimicking her actions, his hands continued higher, cupping her face.

Her lips curved slightly, and she whispered, "What are you thinking?"

"That you're the most beautiful woman I've ever seen." She started to roll her eyes, but he swept his thumbs over her cheeks and shook his head. "That's not a throwaway line, sweetheart. That's exactly what I'm thinking right now. That you're the most beautiful woman I've ever seen, and I'm the luckiest man to have you here with me."

Her grin widened and her hands slid from his waist to hers, deftly untying the belt of her wrap dress. Seeing how easily the dress flew open, his eyes widened with surprise and he considered making it a requirement that all her clothes made it that easy for her to disrobe. She allowed the material to puddle on the floor and was now standing in her green satin bra and matching panties.

His finesse left him as he stared in awe at the gift she was offering him. Her fingers moved to his shirt, starting at the top button and moving down, pulling the material from his jeans. His shirt soon joined her dress, and her fingers moved to his belt.

"Sometime you'll have to tell me all about your tattoos. I want to know each story."

Grinning, he nodded. "Love to, babe." His hands slid to her shoulders, then the fingertips of one hand drifted lower, tracing the lace at the top of her bra that covered the swell of her breasts.

She sucked in a quick breath, and her fingers fumbled on his belt. Still grinning, he took over, quickly shucking his jeans and boxers down his legs after toeing off his shoes. Jerking off his socks, he stood completely naked in front of her, loving the way her gaze drifted languidly over his body, her top teeth biting her kiss-swollen bottom lip.

"We seem to be uneven," he said as his fingers slid around her back and deftly unfastened her bra, allowing it to slide over her arms and land on the floor between them. With only her panties left on, he wrapped her in his embrace and kissed her again, maneuvering her to the bed. He covered her body with his own, then slowly kissed down her neck to the swells of her breasts where he moved between each one. The harder he suckled, the more her fingernails dragged along his scalp, the tingling shooting straight to his already-aching cock.

He kissed lower, circling her bellybutton with his tongue before shouldering her thighs apart. Grasping the satin material of her panties, he dragged them down her legs and quickly slid her sandals from her feet. Standing, he stared at her body, naked and flush, open and inviting. She lay still, giving him the perfect chance to view every inch. He had wanted to go slow but wondered if he had it in him to be so disciplined.

Kneeling between her legs, he pressed her thighs open wide, her slick folds beckoning. The scent of her arousal called to him and he dove in, licking and sucking as she cried out, wildly thrashing underneath him.

Her hands held him in place as her hips undulated as though seeking him to be closer. Inserting two fingers into her warm channel, he searched for just the right movement, soon finding it as she called his name and her body shuddered its release. Licking more, he tasted her essence, knowing it was now an addictive drug that he would always crave.

He kissed his way up her body until his mouth latched on hers again, allowing her to taste what he had just reveled in. She moaned, clutching him tighter as their tongues tangled. "I need you," she mumbled against his mouth.

He shifted to the side, stretching his body so that he could jerk open the nightstand, extracting a strand of condoms. Hating to lose her lips, he sat up, his ass resting on his heels as he ripped open the packet. Catching her raised-brow look, he assured, "I don't bring women here. Ever. These I bought today hoping you'd be in my bed." Her smile slid across her face, and the soft light from the lamp caused her green eyes to shimmer. Having rolled on the condom, he once again shifted his body over hers, placing his cock at her entrance.

With her knees spread wide and her hands clutching his ass, she repeated, her voice firm, "I need you."

Plunging in one swift movement, he barely managed to utter, "Yes, Ma'am." Her tight channel felt like velvet and he gasped as he shifted his hips and moved out before plunging in again. He started slow, but the more she clutched his ass encouraging him on, the more forceful his thrusts became.

As though they could not get enough of each other, her fingers dug in and he grunted, their animal sounds echoing against the walls. She was slick and warm, but he wanted her to come again. Knowing he was close, he slid his hand between them and lightly pinched her clit. Her fingernails dug in as she squeezed her eyes closed and pressed her head back against the mattress. Crying out through clenched teeth, he felt her body shudder underneath him as she pulsated around his cock.

Unable to hold off any longer, his expression mimicked hers as his eyes shut, his head was thrown back, and he groaned through gritted teeth as his own orgasm rocked his body. Stars—or fuckin' fireworks— exploded behind his closed eyelids and, for a few seconds, his mind left his body and he couldn't have told anyone who he was.

When the last drop left his cock, his arms gave out and he fell straight down, hearing her grunt but uncertain he could do anything about it. With a final bit of strength, he pressed down on the mattress and rolled his weight off her, keeping her wrapped in his arms so that she was half draped over him.

He lost track of time, but right then, time didn't matter. He lay with his eyes closed, his lungs trying to suck in enough oxygen to keep his heart and brain engaged. He was very aware of the warm female body pressed against his. *Never. I've never fuckin' come that hard. I'd call it a fuckin' religious experience except my mom would have to run to the priest and light a candle... then start planning a wedding.* He had no idea where that last thought came from, but instead of adding panic to his already exhausted body, he simply felt peace.

Finally, he managed to pry his eyes open, grateful that Kimberly wasn't staring at him, repulsed. Instead, her eyes were closed as well, and her cheek rested on his chest. Her breathing slowly began to match his and, finally, she shifted slightly, leaning back so that her green eyes could peer up at him.

"I was wrong earlier."

Her brow crinkled, silently asking what he meant by that statement.

He lifted his hand and slowly smoothed his finger over her forehead. "Earlier, I said you were the most beautiful woman I'd ever seen. But that was a little premature. You, here, right now, are the most beautiful woman I've ever seen."

16

Kimberly woke and stretched, her body deliciously sore in several places. She felt the hot press of Kyle's muscular form next to hers, and as she peered at him through the slight early-morning light peeking through the blinds, she grinned. The dark-haired, square-jawed man that had so thoroughly loved her body multiple times during the night was now sound asleep, his face relaxed in slumber.

She longed to reach out and smooth her hand over his brow, but the need to find the bathroom was too strong to be ignored. Slipping from the bed, she glanced down at the floor, spying the tangle of clothing. Eschewing her bra and dress, she snagged her panties and his shirt. Slipping them on, she inhaled his scent as she buttoned a few of the buttons. There were only two bedrooms on the second floor and each one had a bathroom, his being the largest. Quickly using the facilities, she snooped long enough to find an extra toothbrush, still wrapped and labeled with a dentist's logo.

She grimaced at the idea of her breath last night and brushed with vigor, hoping for more kisses this morning. A glance into the other bedroom showed it was smaller with little furniture. Double bed, dresser, and a small desk. In the hall, she glanced up the stairs leading to a third-floor bonus room. Her rowhouse did not have anything higher than the second floor but, refusing to give in to curiosity, she decided to wait and let him give her the royal tour later.

Tiptoeing back into the bedroom, she felt like a creeper but could not help staring for a moment at Kyle still sleeping. His muscular, tattooed chest was on display as the covers had dropped to his trim waist. One arm was thrown over his head, resting on his pillow, and the other hand was splayed on his stomach. She wanted to kiss each delectable inch, discovering the meanings of all his tattoos, but hesitated. They had been up late, and she wanted him to sleep as much as possible.

Her stomach growled and the idea of fixing breakfast for him called to her. Resisting the urge to crawl back into bed, she slipped down the stairs, glancing toward the living room before heading into the kitchen.

When she had been looking for a place to rent, she'd spent hours online searching the rowhouses in Hope City, discovering them to be almost identical in basic layout while uniquely refurbished.

His house was wider than hers, and taller considering there was the as-yet unexplored third floor and basement. Bob had finished her basement with a small bedroom, den, and bathroom. She wondered how Kyle's basement was finished but again decided to not explore on her own, leaving that for the tour later.

Entering the kitchen, she was delighted. Tile backsplash that complemented the tiled floor, granite countertops, new appliances. His kitchen was wide enough to allow a table that would seat four, but he didn't have a separate laundry room. Instead, the washer and dryer were behind doors in the corner of the kitchen. His windowed back door opened onto his fenced patio similar to hers. Since his unit was on the end, he had windows along the side, including one over the sink, allowing light to flood the room.

Turning to the refrigerator, she was grateful he had eggs and a package of breakfast sausage. A glance toward a basket sitting on the counter gave evidence of a full loaf of bread. Pulling the ingredients together, she decided to wait until he was awake before scrambling the eggs. Placing the sausage into a frying pan on low, the kitchen was soon filled with the scent of sizzling pork. Opening a few more cabinets she found his coffee and filters, and soon the roasted brew was tantalizing her nostrils as well.

The sound of a creaking floorboard and running water through the pipes met her ears, giving evidence that Kyle was out of bed. She had set the table for two and nervously wondered if he would mind that she'd made herself at home preparing breakfast.

A sound at the back door caught her attention and she whipped around, gasping at the sight of a woman's face pressed to the window. Screaming Kyle's name, she whirled and flew out of the kitchen toward the stairs. As she rounded the corner, she slammed into his body, his arms immediately wrapping around her.

"Someone's at your back door! Someone's peeking in!"

His lips thinned and his jaw hardened as he gently moved her to the side and stalked around the corner into the kitchen.

"Yoohoo! Kyle? Are you home?"

Her heart was still pounding, but hearing the woman call his name had her following him. He had stopped in the middle of the kitchen, planting his fists on his hips. Unable to see around his broad back, she leaned slightly to the side to see the woman's face pressed against the glass, her hands cupped around her eyes.

"Jesus, Christ!" He stalked forward and reached for the door, flipping the lock and throwing it open. "Mom! What time is it?"

"I told you I was coming by to get that bag of jumble for the church bazaar. You were supposed to leave the deadbolt off so I could—oh!"

Kimberly froze, unable to decide what was the most appropriate course of action: flee back up the stairs, stand and act like there was nothing wrong with her standing in Kyle's shirt and her panties in the kitchen, or say a quick prayer that the floor would open up and she could disappear.

The latter did not happen and, before she had a

choice between the other two, she stared as an attractive middle-aged woman stepped into the kitchen. Her silver hair was cut in a stylish bob, and she was dressed in a simple blouse and jeans. Her face was unlined except for the crinkles that emanated from her eyes, now deep from the wide smile on her face. And, staring into those blue eyes that were undoubtedly part of Kyle's DNA, Kimberly stayed rooted to the floor.

"I had no idea you had company, Kyle," his mother said. She stepped forward and extended her hand. "Since my son has forgotten his manners, I'll introduce myself. I'm Sharon McBride, Kyle's mother."

Not having a choice except to step closer and extend her own hand while praying that the length of Kyle's shirt didn't show anything untoward, she managed to croak, "It's nice to meet you. I am... uh..."

Kyle's mom lifted an eyebrow, and Kimberly knew she needed to offer her name, but suddenly the absurdity of the situation slammed into her and she stumbled over the word.

Thankfully, Kyle wrapped his arm around her and pulled her close to his body. "This is Kimberly, Mom. Now, would you like to remind me why you're here this early, scaring the shit out of my girlfriend?"

As soon as the word girlfriend left his lips, Kimberly's heart beat erratically. *Girlfriend?* They had not defined what they were and technically had only been on one date, so hearing him so casually label her as a girlfriend to his mom caused her to dig her fingers into his waist. He grunted, shot her a lowered-brow frown, then turned back to his mother. Terrified to see what expression might be on Sharon's face, Kimberly was stunned to see absolute delight.

Sharon threw her hands up in the air while looking toward the ceiling and shouted, "Hallelujah! Prayers are answered!"

"Jesus Christ," Kyle muttered again, shaking his head.

His utterance caused his mom to snap her head down and pin him with an expression that could only be described as a 'mom-look' with her lifted brow and lips turned downward. "Kyle! Don't take the Lord's name in vain—"

"Then don't shout *hallelujah* when I introduce you to my girlfriend—"

"You've never introduced me to a girlfriend at your house before—"

"Because I haven't had one in years—"

"Well, then pardon me for being excited that my son is finally growing up!"

"Jes—" Kyle stopped his utterance and growled again.

As hilarious as the mother-son exchange was, Kimberly could still feel the hot rush of embarrassment coloring her face and wondered how to escape up to the bedroom so that she could get dressed.

Sharon turned her attention to the stove. "Oh, how lovely. You were fixing breakfast. I didn't mean to intrude."

"I was just going to scramble the eggs once he got out of bed... uh..."

Silence hit the room, and she once again wished the floor would open up to swallow her whole.

Kyle's arm squeezed her shoulders and he smiled. "What Kimberly is trying so desperately to say politely is that she woke up first, was fixing the breakfast, and I just got my lazy ass out of bed."

No less mortified, she poked him in the waist again, eliciting another grunt.

"Stop poking me," he said, glaring.

"Then stop embarrassing me!" she whispered. Deciding to finally take charge of the situation, she looked up at Sharon and saw her smiling widely. "Mrs. McBride, I honestly cannot think of anything to say that's not embarrassing. I'm so sorry to meet you for the first time like this. If you'll excuse me, I'll go get dressed." Without giving Kyle or his mom a chance to say anything, she whirled and quick-walked out of sight before racing up the stairs. Throwing off his shirt, she grabbed her bra and then quickly wrapped her dress and tied it. Slipping on her sandals, she felt overdressed for breakfast but grateful to now have clothes on. She battled the desire to stay hidden in his room until his mother left but knew that would be cowardly.

Walking back down the stairs, she discovered Kyle leaning his hip against the counter, a smirk playing about his lips as he sipped a cup of coffee. When his gaze hit her, his pupils flared with lust shooting straight toward her. His lips curved into a full-blown smile, and he lifted an arm, beckoning her to him.

Walking straight to him, she accepted his hug and turned toward Sharon, offering a smile as well.

"Kimberly, dear, I want to apologize for interrupting your morning. I would never have just dropped in if I'd known you were here. But I certainly can't deny that I'm thrilled to meet you. I was just telling my son that he needs to come to dinner and bring you with him."

"Mom." Kyle's voice was low and carried a tenor of caution.

Sharon shot him a glare and said, "I'm not going to embarrass Kimberly by continuing this conversation further. I'll let you two discuss it." Now, beaming her smile upon Kimberly, she added, "I hope you'll come tomorrow." She turned and bent to pick up a box from the floor, but Kyle shifted away from Kimberly and took it from his mom. "I'll carry it to the car for you."

She watched as mother and son walked out the back door and disappeared from sight. Slumping against the kitchen counter, her mind raced with the events of the past ten minutes. Certainly not the way she expected their morning breakfast to go, and certainly not the way she expected to meet a one of his parents.

With nothing else to do, she glanced at the stove and saw that Sharon had finished the sausage. She quickly scrambled eggs, adding a bit of shredded cheese found in the refrigerator. A moment later, Kyle returned and shut the door behind him. She turned toward him and opened her mouth but discovered she had no idea what to say.

He kept walking until he stopped directly in front of her. Bending, he kissed her lightly. "Babe, I'm so sorry my mom just showed up."

"It's fine. I mean, this is your house. I just wish…" Her breath left her lungs in a rush, and she shook her head, then stared at her feet for a moment. Finally, lifting her chin, she held his gaze and groaned, "I can't believe I met your mom while standing in your shirt and my panties in your kitchen!"

"Yeah, and it was fuckin' hot. I've got to tell you that if my mom hadn't been here, I'd have bent you over the kitchen table, babe."

At those words, a rush of heat moved through her, no longer due to embarrassment. "Kyle! You can't say things like that!"

"Like what?"

"You can't talk about your mom and then talk about bending me over a table in the same sentence!"

Barking out a laugh, he pulled her close and tucked her head next to his chest. He held her tight for a minute, then mumbled low and soft. "Babe, I'm not such a man that I don't get that that scene was embarrassing for you. But honestly, it's fine. I don't spend the night with other women. My mom hasn't met a girlfriend of mine in years. I don't have women come to this house. So, the only thing you and I have to worry about today is my mom running off to the priest to reserve the church."

Now it was her turn to bark out a laugh, and she felt her chest ease. "I just didn't want to make a bad impression. Kyle, we've only had one true date."

"Are you planning on dating anyone else while you're seeing me?"

Rearing back, she shook her head. "Of course not!"

"Then, even if we've only known each other a short time, we're dating exclusively. We want to see where this goes. Sweetheart, you're beautiful. You were in my house, fixing me breakfast, and I introduced you as my girlfriend. Believe me, my mom is fine with all that."

17

Breakfast was over, dishes were rinsed, and Kyle made good on his promise to use the kitchen table for something besides eating. As he rocked into Kimberly's body, her perfect ass in his hands as she bent forward over the table, he wondered how his legs would hold them when their releases hit at the same time. Panting, he tried to suck in enough oxygen as he pulled her tight against him, his arms wrapped around her front. Slowly pulling out, he turned her so that her breasts were pressed against his chest and he took her lips in a gentle kiss.

He hated that she'd been embarrassed this morning when his mom dropped by but could not say he was sorry at all that she'd met his mother. He had only known her a few days, and yet, everything with her felt... *right*. Although, he had to admit it might be too early for dinner with the family. Thinking of her meeting all the McBrides, he now had a clear understanding of Sean's wife, Harper, and Tara's husband, Carter, when they first had to meet everyone.

After leading her upstairs, he rejoiced that he'd agreed to the extra-large shower when they put it to good use. Finally sated, he linked fingers and said, "Let me show you my view."

He led her into the hall to the stairs leading upward. At the top, they entered a bonus room, complete with a slouchy sofa, small bookcase, TV, and windows on all four walls. She was just exclaiming delight when he said, "That's not all." He then led her out the door and onto a deck that showcased a view of the harbor in the distance.

"Oh, my God! I can't believe you can see the harbor from here!"

His friends and brothers had often spent many good times up here grilling and sharing a beer, but now, seeing her standing with her arms spread wide, twirling in a circle, he couldn't imagine anything better than having her there with him.

On the way back downstairs, he showed her the second bedroom and said, "There's also a finished den in the basement."

"This place is huge!"

Pulling her close, he said, "I can't wait to make love to you in every single room." If her smile was anything to go by, she was just as excited by his suggestion as he was.

His plans for spending the rest of the day with her were shot to hell when his phone vibrated. Seeing it was Alex, he sighed. "Yeah?"

"Just got a call from the Captain. We've been approved to see Doug Tiller today at the prison."

"Today? Fuckin' today?"

"Yeah, today. What? You had something else going on?"

Staring at Kimberly, he said, "Yeah, actually I do. But it's gotta be done. You gonna drive?"

"Yeah, I'll swing by and pick you up in about thirty minutes."

Disconnecting, he watched as she stepped closer, encircling his waist with her arms. Resting his chin on the top of her head, he memorized the feel of her in his arms.

Leaning her head back, she held his gaze. "I take it you've got to go to work."

"I'm sorry as fuck, babe."

"It can't be helped, Kyle. It's what you do."

Her gentle acceptance moved through him, and he took her lips. The kiss started gentle, but with a touch of her tongue on his, he growled, pulling her tighter against him. Finally, dragging his head away from hers, he said, "Stay here. Explore the house. Eat what you want. Call for takeout—"

She stilled his words with her fingers on his lips, shaking her head. "Thanks for making me feel welcome but, honestly, Kyle, I'll be better off at my place. I have some work to do, my laptop and my e-reader are there. You need to get ready, and I can catch a cab."

He hated the idea of her not being at his place when his day was over but promised to come to hers. A few minutes later, he watched as a cab pulled in front of his house, and she climbed in. Leaning into the window, he made sure to show his badge as he handed the driver some money. "Make sure she gets home safe and you stay long enough to see that she gets inside."

"Absolutely, Sir!"

He caught her rolling her eyes from the back seat and grinned. With a tap on the top of the cab, he watched it pull away. Having just enough time to grab his jacket and secure his home, he stepped outside as Alex pulled to the curb.

Entering the men's prison was not a new experience for Kyle, but having so recently been inside the women's prison to see Beth Washington, he was struck with both similarities and differences. There was no color on these walls. They were simply painted beige. This prison was older and it showed in the wear and tear— faded floor tiles, scuffed baseboards, windows with a coat of grime on them.

With their arrangements being previously made, Doug Tiller was waiting for them in the interview room. Kyle remembered seeing him at the time of his arrest. The middle-aged, dapper physician still maintained an aura of superiority even in prison. He wondered if the doctor's money smoothed the path for him inside but, since much of his wealth had been seized by the feds, Kyle wasn't sure that offered Doug much preferential treatment.

"I'm Detective McBride, and this is Detective Freeman."

As soon as the word *McBride* left his mouth, Doug's gaze jumped to his face.

"Ah, Tara's brother. I see the family resemblance. Are you here for your pound of flesh as well?"

Shaking his head slowly, he said, "No. I allow the law and justice to take its course and, from your surroundings, I'd say that's happening. For me, I'm satisfied with knowing my sister is well, happy, and healthy."

Doug held his gaze, then shook his head. "For what it's worth, I never intended Tara to get caught up in the... situation." His face hardened as he added, "I have no idea what you think we need to talk about."

Refusing to give in to the verbal baiting, Kyle began. "The arrangement you had with Beth Washington was not just between the two of you. You helped organize the drug runners and profited, but you're just a cog in the wheel."

Doug remained quiet, his gaze never wavering.

"You pleaded guilty, so it never went to trial, but you also never gave up anyone else. Well, except those below you."

Doug continued to remain silent.

Alex took over. "You may be smart but not smart enough to organize everything. You're only a small cog, not as big as you liked to think you were."

"What is it exactly you think I'm going to say?" Doug finally bit out. "If I didn't give up anything months ago, why do you think I'm going to say anything now?"

"Because months ago you hadn't been in here." At that statement, Kyle waved his hands slightly to indicate the bars on the window and the guard standing behind him. He saw a faint flicker move through Doug's eyes and wondered if the prison was already taking its toll on him. Doug had tried to maneuver into a position of authority by volunteering in the prison's clinic. The warden didn't want him close to medications or other prisoners who might have battled addiction, so his request was denied.

Shaking his head, Doug replied, "Detectives, I've got nothing to say."

"So, you're willing to sit here in prison and let those higher up the chain get away with everything."

A slight snort was the only indication that Doug had any reaction to Kyle's question. He leveled the detectives with his gaze and said, "You're the detectives, you figure it out. If you're so sure I was in the middle of the chain, then you figure out who profited the most." Standing, he turned toward the guard. "I'm finished here."

Kyle and Alex stood also, watching as Doug stopped right before he passed through the door.

Doug looked over his shoulder and said, "There's a lot of money in *drugs*. Think about that the next time you go to pick up your aspirin at the drugstore. Advertising, pharmaceutical companies lobbying physicians and politicians... lots of money exchanges between the hands that go into that bottle you pick up when you're trying to stop your headache." Without another word, he turned back to the guard and exited.

For a moment, Kyle and Alex stood silently. Finally, Alex huffed, "What the fuck?"

Kyle nodded slowly. "I know he just told us something, but what the hell he meant, I don't know. Looks like it's back to following the money trail."

As much as she would have liked to spend the afternoon with Kyle, Kimberly could not deny that it was nice to have a chance to catch up on everything she needed to do at home. She had showered at his place but dumped her dress and underwear into the dirty clothes and hauled it to her laundry room, starting a load to wash.

Dressed in comfortable clothes, she vacuumed and dusted, neither an activity she enjoyed beyond simple tasks that everyone has to endure. Her house was smaller, but she loved Kyle's house, especially the third-floor bonus room and deck with its harbor view. Bob had finished her basement also, which would be great for a family but was rarely used by her.

Finally finished with household chores, she sat down on her sofa and pulled out the notes she'd taken from her various interviews. Opening her laptop, she typed the notes, remembrances, impressions, and even included the pictures she'd taken with her phone.

Scrolling through the photographs, it was amusing to see the different offices. Tammy's had been tiny, organized, filled with maps and files for the drivers. Bob's had been utilitarian, somewhat neat, but she had the idea that occasionally he might have to search to put his hand on something he needed. She was used to John's office but now realized it was similar to Helen's, which would make sense as they were both department supervisors, although hers was more organized. Dr. Chen's office was filled with textbooks and what appeared to be research manuals. She flipped through several more, but it was Thomas Kilton's that now caught her attention.

A large corner office with wide windows allowing in expansive sunshine, plush carpet, and heavy wooden desk, it was rivaled only by Sally Gleason's. She remembered his sister Sidney's comments on the comparison of his office with hers. She had not met the president, Robert Kilton, but if Thomas' office was anything to go by, then Robert's would be exquisite.

Thomas had allowed her to take a picture of him sitting at his desk and, not wanting the sun to be framed behind him, she managed to get his bookcase and credenza in the background. She hated to be impressed by trivial matters, but she had to admit his office was envy-inspiring.

She typed up her interview from the researcher, the information Tammy had given her on the robbery, and added the notes she had compiled from the various uses of legal and illegal uses of fentanyl.

With everything saved to her laptop, she emailed the notes to herself and decided she wanted a hard copy. Hitting print, she ran upstairs to her second bedroom where she had a small desk and collected the pages. Back downstairs, she folded them in half, put them in her notebook and slid it and her laptop into her bag.

A knock on her back door caused her to grin, thinking of this morning's meeting with Kyle's mom. She always kept her back gate locked so only Bob was able to come through the gate between their properties. She opened the door and greeted him, offering him iced tea.

"No, thanks. I just came by to drop off some mail and let you know the farmers market on Spring Avenue has opened up. It's right on the corner of Spring and Haymarket." From behind his back, he dangled a bag from his finger and grinned again. "Since I knew you wouldn't make it there this morning, I thought you might like some fresh strawberries."

Clapping her hands, she squealed. "Oh, my God, that's perfect! I can wash them and fix some right now for us."

Waving his hand, he declined. "I've already eaten my fill from what I bought this morning. Anyway, I've got plans with friends this evening, so I'll take a rain check."

Locking the door behind him after he left, she glanced at the junk mail, tossed it into the recycle bin, and carried the strawberries to the sink to rinse. Kyle had said he was coming over when he finished work today, and she decided strawberry shortcake would be perfect. She made a quick trip to the grocery store, grabbing the ingredients she needed plus a few other items. Once home again, she mixed up shortbread and put it into the oven.

A few hours later, a knock on the front door had her bounding to the window to peek out over her stoop. Her heart skipped a beat as she observed Kyle standing there, one arm extended with his hand resting on the doorframe. Certainly handsome as always, but his head was bowed, shoulders slumped as though he carried great weight. Struck with the realization that whatever he had been doing at work had probably not been a happy chore, she rushed to the door and flung it open.

He lifted his head and his blue-eyed gaze speared her. She leaned forward and grabbed his hand, pulling him in. Not waiting for a second, she plastered her body against his, wrapped her hands around the back of his head, and pulled him down for a kiss. If he was surprised by her greeting, he didn't show it, instead plunging his tongue into her mouth. Tongues tangling, noses bumping, they kissed wildly for a long moment before she finally settled back on her heels and smiled up at him.

He cocked his head to the side. "Wow, what a greeting."

"I peeked through the window and you looked so beleaguered out there. I wanted to make sure you had a proper welcome."

Grinning, he pulled her tighter against his body. "Can't think of a better one, babe." He lifted his head and sniffed, asking, "By the way, what's that fabulous smell?"

"My neighbor, Bob, brought over some fresh strawberries from the market, and I made homemade strawberry shortcake with real whipped cream!"

His eyes widened and so did his smile. "Damn, girl. I was going to carry you off to bed, but I haven't had lunch so maybe a snack first would be good."

"We want to make sure you have plenty of energy," she added with a wink before leading the way into the kitchen. As they walked the short distance, she said, "I know you were here already, but you didn't get a good look. My rowhouse is smaller than yours, but it's plenty for me." Looking over her shoulder, she laughed. "Although, I'm incredibly envious of your bonus room and deck! And the view... oh, my goodness!"

She plated the desserts, placing strawberries in the middle and on top of the shortcake, then added whipped cream piled high. As soon as he took a bite, he closed his eyes and groaned. The sound shot through her, reminding her of the sound of his coming when they were in the shower earlier that morning. Trying to force those thoughts from her mind, she asked, "Did everything go okay today?"

Shrugging, he said, "It went. Not my favorite thing to visit someone in prison, and I can't say we got anything useful so it may have been a waste of time."

A forkful of strawberries and whipped cream were on their way to her mouth, but she halted. "Prison? Oh, Kyle, I'm so sorry you have to do that."

Shaking his head, he said, "Don't worry about it."

"Yeah, but it's got to be one of the more unpleasant parts of your job."

"It's not pretty, but you know what is? Coming home to you."

Dessert finished, she walked over to the counter and grabbed the bowl of homemade whipped cream. Glancing to the side, she said, "I hope that snack built up your stamina. I'm going upstairs to bed... with the whipped cream." With that, she ran out of the kitchen and made it halfway up the stairs before he caught up to her. He swooped her into his arms, careful to keep the bowl of cream upright. She was glad... after all, she had plans for the whipped cream. And from the grin on his face, he was on board with her plans.

18

"I can't believe you talked me into this fuckin' trip."

Kimberly glanced to the side as Kyle's comment reverberated through the cab of his truck. Seeing the scowl on his face, she bit back her retort. Instead, she said, "I promised I would bring some fruit. These women have had enough promises broken to last them a lifetime. I don't want to be just one more person who does that."

Kyle's lips thinned into a straight line and then he blew out his breath in a loud huff. Reaching across the front of his old truck, he squeezed her hand "Babe, you're a good person, but I cannot be firm enough in my warning that this place is dangerous. Do not under any circumstances ever come here by yourself again."

"I know, and that's why I asked you to come with me. I understand it was foolish the last time, and I'm not going to do that again."

They pulled off the road and began the bumpy trip toward the underpass. Just like before, the dark recesses appeared scary, but near the edge, less so. The children were playing ball in the dirt again, and she said, "You can just park back here, and I'll—"

"No way, babe. I'm going to be close by."

"I don't want you to scare them—"

Her words halted as he jerked his head to the side, his glare so scorching she was surprised her eyebrows were not singed. "Okay, okay!"

"Let's get one thing straight, Kimberly. I respect you and what you're doing, but I will not go through what I went through before, seeing someone hold a gun to a loved one's head."

She had never asked him about that situation but knew they needed to have that conversation. For now, she simply nodded.

"I'm going to be nearby, and my fuckin' badge will be showing."

They parked close to the children, and she saw Margo and Aleeta come forward, suspicion in their gazes. Kyle took the bags of fruit and other items she had brought and handed them to her. Then he moved slightly away and smiled at the kids playing.

She walked straight up to the women and said, "I brought some fruit and a couple of things I thought you might could use."

"Who's he?" Margo asked, her eyes pinned on Kyle as though she were afraid he would take off with her children.

Before she could answer, Aleeta said in a hard voice, "Looks like you brought the cops."

"He's my boyfriend," she began, and Aleeta's bark of laughter stopped her words.

"You're dating a cop? Did he know you were down here by yourself last time?"

"Um... no..." She didn't want to get into the details of her personal life, so she just left the one word hanging.

Aleeta shook her head and said, "Girl, I don't know if you've got more balls or less brains. But I'm glad to see you got some protection now."

She turned toward the kids and jiggled the bags, smiling as they ran over. She handed it to the moms, waiting to make sure the mothers had the decision of what to give the kids. Both Margo and Aleeta looked inside, exclaiming over the fruit, granola bars, and boxes of crackers with peanut butter.

Holding up another bag, she said, "This has some crayons and notebooks. I thought maybe the kids would like to color or draw, especially if it's a rainy day and they have to stay inside the tents."

She handed the third bag to Margo and smiled. "I didn't know what you might need, but I brought some cleaning wipes, deodorant, moisturizer, and since we're getting into the warmer weather, I brought some sunscreen."

The uncertainty of her gift-giving fell away as the women smiled widely and called out their appreciation. While the kids sat to the side and munched on apples, Aleeta invited her to sit with the women. Glancing back toward Kyle, she observed he was keeping an eye on the kids while scanning the area.

She sat in one of the old camp chairs and for several minutes the conversation was stilted. It was hard to know what to say to someone who was living in a tent. *"How's your day? Read any good books lately? Been to the movies?"* were obviously topics that would be ridiculous to bring up. But, after a few minutes, their conversation eased as they talked about the kids, the weather, and what else they might need in the coming months.

They slowly moved on to the issues of safety and the women reported they felt safe at the Cottages as long as they were vigilant and stayed in a group. Margo talked about a man that she'd been with for a while who worked during the days and then stayed with her and the kids in the evenings. Aleeta's brother was also working, and while he was at the Cottages in the evenings, between the two of them they hoped to move into a small apartment soon.

"It'll only be one-bedroom, but he says me and the kids can have it and he'll be fine on a sofa."

They began talking about the dangers of being on the street. "I know it seems crazy to live in a tent near a bridge, but I feel safer here than I did in a park," Margo said. "There are some scary people and, yes, drugs abound. But a lot of these people are just down on their luck and want a place to get out of the weather."

Kimberly inclined her head toward the tents and asked, "Are you ever afraid that somebody's going to steal your tent or your belongings?"

"It's kind of funny, but when the church group brought these tents, a lot of the men said they wanted us women to have them."

Aleeta laughed and added, "Don't get me wrong. There are some here that would slit your throat just to steal your shoes, but most of these people will share what they have with you, even if it's not much."

Deciding she had taken up enough of their time, she promised to come back again and asked if she could write up some of their stories. They all agreed, and the kids gathered, giggling as she took their pictures. Stepping forward, she threw her arms impulsively around Aleeta before it dawned on her that the woman might not want to be touched. Aleeta stiffened for a few seconds and then relaxed, returning her hug.

Saying goodbye, she hurried over to Kyle, surprised to see a man approach. She sidled up to his side and Kyle wrapped his arm around her.

The man grinned a mostly-toothless smile as he glanced over to the children playing and then looked back to them. "Dee-tective. You bring a friend?"

"Manny," his deep voice rumbled. "This is Kimberly."

She stuck her hand out and returned his smile. "Hi, Manny. It's nice to meet you."

His smile slipped as he stared at her hand for a few seconds and then wiped his palm on his pants. He wrapped his hand around hers and she shook it firmly.

"Nice to meet you too, Ma'am. I see you brung the kids some things. That's real neighborly."

"Just a couple of things. I wanted to talk to their moms, and they'd asked for fruit." She reached into her bag and pulled out an apple. "I've got a bit left over if you'd like."

He chuckled then fell into a coughing fit. When he

regained his ability to speak, he grinned wider. "Aw, 'fraid I ain't got the chompers for an apple."

Thinking quickly, she dug around some more into her bag and came up with crackers. "How about these? And a bottle of water?"

He nodded, reaching out to take what she offered. Lifting his gaze, he stared at her for a long moment before shifting his gaze over to Kyle.

Kyle squeezed her shoulder and she understood his signal for them to leave. "Bye, Manny. Take care."

Kyle offered a chin lift toward Manny and began to turn them toward his truck.

"Dee-tective?"

Twisting, Kyle looked over his shoulder. "Yeah?"

"You ever need anything, you come to see your old friend Manny."

She held her breath, watching the thoughts move behind Kyle's eyes. He finally nodded and offered a slight smile. Pulling her back to his side, they walked to the truck. She wanted to ask what Manny meant, but Kyle was quiet. If he wanted to silently process what just happened, she'd let him. Truth be told, her mind was full of the women and kids at the Cardboard Cottages.

His mood picked up as they drew closer to her house. "I almost hate to bring it up after the morning you've just had, but how about we take a trip to my parents this evening? My family would love to meet you, but I don't want to pile too much on you today."

She rolled her head to the side and saw the concern in his eyes. Squeezing his hand, she said, "Kyle, we've only known each other a short while. I know I met your mom, but do you really think this is the right thing to do?"

He shifted slightly in his seat so that he was more fully facing her. Lifting her hand, he kissed her knuckles before placing her hand over his chest. "I know I felt something for you the first night we met. You might want to chalk that up to just lust, but there was something more. The week that we were separated, I thought of you every single day. When we found each other again, that time I knew I felt something for you. So, while we've only officially been back together for a little while, I know what's in here." He pressed her hand gently against his chest. "I don't have a crystal ball and can't see into the future, but I know I'd love to have you meet my family tonight."

She felt his heartbeat against her fingertips where he held them in place. Warmth moved through her when she thought of this man in her life. Her lips curved into a smile and she nodded.

He grinned widely and said, "All right... get ready for a McBride family dinner!"

A big family dinner was not something she was used to. Her insides quivered and she hoped his family would like her.

That evening, Kimberly was firmly ensconced in a setting completely different from the Cottages. The McBrides' massive house in the northern part of Hope

City, in an older neighborhood where each home had a unique charm, was filled with people and food. The gathering was so large, they were set up in the huge backyard where card tables and lawn chairs spilled beyond the patio.

Looking around, she couldn't imagine what it would be like when all the McBride children had significant others and possibly children of their own. *Where would they all fit?* Then she glanced toward the end of one of the tables where Sharon kept an eye over her brood, and Kimberly did not doubt that Sharon would be able to fit everyone she loved around a table.

As soon as she had walked in, Caitlyn squealed with enthusiasm, throwing her arms around Kimberly. Sharon also hugged her, greeting her as an old friend. She was soon pulled from Kyle's arms and introduced to the others. All three of his sisters were very alike in looks, almost intimidatingly so. Tall, built, with brilliant blue eyes and dark hair. Erin had just started nursing school, having come back from the military, and Tara was a social worker, married to Carter, another detective, and they had an adorable little girl, Colleen.

The oldest brother, Sean, yet another detective, was there with his wife, Harper. The youngest brother, Rory, a paramedic, threw out the charm when he met her, causing Kyle to growl and wrap his arm around her, playfully warning Rory to keep his hands to himself.

Sharon had looped her arm through Kimberly's and dragged her over to Kyle's father, Colm, who greeted her with a firm handshake, a warm smile, and a booming voice welcoming her to their home.

Kyle's large family would have been overwhelming enough, but then the neighbors began pouring out of the house next door and their numbers grew. She hadn't realized that Bekki King was part of the neighboring King family, but she was thrilled to have another friend at the meal. Sharon made sure she met Chauncey and Hannah King as well as some of their children in attendance.

Brock and Brody showed up and, from their comments, it was for the express purpose of giving Kyle a hard time. Their women, Kallie and Amber, welcomed Kimberly with knowing smiles. "We've been in your shoes," they both said, laughing in camaraderie.

Now, with dinner almost consumed, everyone was enjoying the multitude of desserts, and the conversation flowed comfortably. She overheard Tara mention something about the homeless shelter where she worked.

"I visited the Cardboard Cottages today," Kimberly said.

As soon as the words left her mouth, the massive gathering stopped talking, the silence broken only by a few birds tweeting in the trees. Kyle dropped his chin to his chest, and she wondered what she'd said to cause such a reaction from everyone.

Brody was the first to break the silence. "Are you crazy?"

Kyle jerked his head up and growled, "Brody."

Sean shook his head. "I'd say the same thing. Are you crazy?"

She opened her mouth but didn't have a chance to reply before Carter jumped in. "That's not a place you just go to. You're lucky to have gotten out unharmed."

"Jesus, you men act like she's helpless. You haven't even given her a chance to say anything," Kallie bit out, glaring around at the others.

Tara waded in. "I've been to the Cottages also, Kimberly. I try to see if we can get some of the people there into the shelter or some of our programs."

Carter's head swung around, and he looked at his wife. "You haven't been there lately. At least I hope you haven't, not without me!"

Tara narrowed her eyes as she glared at her husband but didn't have a chance to speak before the gathering erupted into a rousing debate. Overall, the participants seemed to be divided among the sexes... the men declaring it was not a place to be and the women defending Kimberly's decision to visit. Men turned toward their wives to defend their position and the women snapped back.

Mortified at the ruckus, she felt the hot sting of tears hit the back of her eyes and blinked to keep them from falling. "Kyle was with me," she said, her words not heard over the raised voices.

A shrill whistle from Kyle cut through the cacophony and the silence was immediate, all heads turning toward him. She stared in slack-jawed, wide-eyed awe as he speared the others with a fiery glare. Jaw so tight she was surprised he was able to speak, he placed one hand on her shoulder and said, "Go ahead, babe."

Suddenly unsure the words would come out, she cleared her throat. "Kyle was with me. The first time I drove down, I was with a church group and there was safety in numbers. Then I went to a different section by myself but understand I put myself at risk. I made a promise to some of the women there that I would bring some things for their children, so Kyle went with me today to take them." Not wanting any more heated words, she added, "But I also promised Kyle that I wouldn't go by myself anymore, even to visit the women."

Before anyone could say anything, Kyle spoke, his voice still hard. "It's one thing for us to have disagreements or lively debates, but to do so with someone who's met you all for the first time—"

"No, Kyle, it's fine," she whispered. She looked around at the two families, seeing the true affection between everyone. "I didn't have this growing up. This kind of… caring… enthusiasm."

Glancing toward Sean, she added, "Believe me, Kyle was not happy when I went by myself." She then shifted her gaze toward Tara. "I'd love to talk to you sometime about how I can help. I'm working on a series of articles about the different faces of Hope City and hope to showcase some of the homeless."

"Son, you're absolutely right." Colm wrapped his arm around his wife's shoulder and said, "Kimberly, you're in the presence of a lot of law enforcement. We often see the worst in people, and my Sharon tells me that I need to spend more time looking for the good. What you did today was admirable."

"Well, I think—" Hannah began.

"We agree," Chauncey interrupted, pulling his wife closer.

Sharon's glare toward Sean and Carter was only matched by Hannah's glare toward Brock and Brody.

Rory grinned his flirtatious smile and winked. "You'll get used to us, Kimberly. If you had a quiet household growing up, I'm sure this crowd seems unruly despite Mom's best efforts."

"Oh, I think this is lovely. I grew up in Sacred Heart... the orphanage."

Once more silence descended, and the only sound heard was the birds in the trees. For a few seconds, she wasn't sure they were chirping either.

"Shit," Kyle hissed as his arms spasmed, tightening around her.

"Oh, fuck," Rory breathed under his breath. His gaze jumped to hers. "Kimberly, I'm so sorry—"

Waving her hand around dismissively, she shook her head. "Oh, don't be sorry. Don't be embarrassed. It's what I knew. I remember my parents a little bit, but they were in an accident when I was very young. Sacred Heart was a nice place. I have very fond memories from there." She smiled and added, "Although, at mealtimes our conversations were not as lively, but I like this so much better."

Kyle's arm around her shoulders tugged her closer to him, and she placed one hand on his thigh and twisted so the other was on his chest, feeling his heartbeat underneath her fingertips.

"Babe, I feel like such an ass that—"

"It's all good, Kyle. I'm just sorry we haven't had a chance to talk about our pasts very much." Smiling, she added, "I love your family."

Sharon leaned back and huffed. "Well, thank goodness you love his family because right now I'm not so sure!"

Colm's actions were similar to Kyle's as he pulled Sharon close to him. Kissing her cheek, he said, "It's all good, honey."

The conversations finally settled into easy camaraderie, and when it was time to say goodbye, she hated to leave.

Harper pulled her in for a hug and whispered, "Sean and Kyle are close, and we'd love to have you two over some time."

Kallie grinned and added, "You ever need backup and Kyle's not available? You call me!"

Amber offered a hug as well and said, "Brody and Kyle are best friends. You've got to come out with us or come over for dinner."

Caitlyn and Bekki pulled her into a trio-embrace, both exclaiming they needed another girl's night at the Celtic Cock.

As Carter helped Colleen get buckled into the car, Tara grabbed Kimberly's hand. "Let's talk soon. I've got lots of ideas for your stories and also ways to help at the Cottages."

Finally, Sharon pulled her into a tight hug, and she felt emotion pouring from the older woman. Leaning back, Sharon cupped her face and said, "I'm thrilled to welcome you to our family, Kimberly. If you ever need anything, you call me."

By the time Kyle managed to extricate her from his family's goodbyes and get her into his SUV, she was exhausted.

"Babe, I am so fuckin' sorry. I would've never taken you into that mess if I'd known—"

"You couldn't have known, honey. We've never talked about it."

A moment of silence passed as they drove out of the neighborhood full of family homes. She glanced to the side, observing Kyle opening his mouth to speak several times, then snapping it shut before uttering a word. "You can ask me anything," she assured.

A sigh left his lips as he glanced toward her before looking back at the road. "You never mentioned... about your parents. Hell, I never asked."

"We're still in the getting-to-know-you phase." She shrugged, shifting so that she could see his face. "Growing up in an orphanage is not something I'm ashamed of, but it's hardly new relationship material. I wasn't keeping it from you, it just never came up."

"And your parents..."

"I was almost eight years old when my parents were killed in a car accident. My grandparents had already passed, and they had no siblings, so there were no aunts or uncles for me to go to. I was taken to Sacred Heart by a social worker with Social Services. Looking back, they probably thought it was going to be temporary, but most people looking to adopt are looking for babies. There were a lot of girls who came through Sacred

Heart that were there for temporary reasons, but there were some of us that stayed."

She watched a tic in his jaw and recognized the tension as he appeared to fight with his emotions. "It wasn't bad, no matter what you might think. It wasn't like something you see in a movie where the other girls were mean and the nuns were horrid. Quite the opposite, actually. The nuns were very sweet, and the school was excellent. The other girls were wonderful, and I had friends. Sacred Heart made sure I had grief counseling, and while there were times I cried buckets over the loss of my parents—still do, occasionally—I was loved and nurtured."

He sighed again and shook his head. "I'm just so sorry that I introduced you to my family in such an overwhelming way—"

"Kyle, stop. Don't apologize. Your family and friends are amazing. They laugh and talk and joke, and most of all, care. At first, it seemed like a lot to take all at one time, but then I realized that it's in their coming together that they exude the best about family, which is love."

He reached across the console and linked fingers with her, smiling. "Never thought about it that way."

She squeezed his fingers as she watched the Hope City skyline come into view as they neared his house. "That's the best way to think about family. Love."

19

"How do you work with this shit in your gut?" Kyle asked, grimacing after one sip of coffee while staring at Todd. He and Alex had gone back to talk to Todd and Birdie, getting a call that they had more information on the truck involved in the Kilton Pharmaceuticals thefts.

"Quit bitchin'," Todd said. "You can't tell me yours is any better."

"That's why I don't get it at the office. Got a shop down the street."

Birdie rolled her eyes. "Seriously? You're arguing about coffee?"

"Point taken." Kyle inclined his head at the file on Todd's desk and said, "What have you got for us?"

"It was a couple of blocks away, but we're pretty sure we picked up the truck leaving the scene. Tracing the tags, it's owned by Jon Ying. He runs a laundry service that has contracts with several hotels in the area. But before you get excited... he says he reported it stolen last week. We checked, and he did file a report."

"Anything suspicious about him?"

"Nope," Birdie said. "I know you want a connection, but this guy is on the up and up. He's pissed about his delivery truck being gone and is having to get another one to use. Said corporate is making him jump through hoops, hoping we'll find it for him."

Todd added, "We wanted to get this to you. It's just one of many robberies we're working on, so we can't give it our full attention. But you're more than welcome to take this information and run with it. And if there's anything you need from us, let us know."

The four sat for a few minutes, each reviewing the reports, hoping that something would stand out to them. Kyle was a firm believer that the more eyes on a situation the less something would slip through and was glad Todd and Birdie felt the same.

Looking up, he said, "Corporate?" Seeing the others stare, he added, "You said corporate was making him jump through hoops to get another truck. So, he's not just some independent business owner?"

"He didn't gain financially from the loss of the truck," Todd said. "In fact, he's out of luck until he can get another one." Dragging his hand through his hair, he shook his head. "But I didn't check to see what the fuck he was talking about when he said corporate."

Birdie began tapping on her keyboard, and the three turned their attention to her. Grumbling and cursing under her breath, she continued searching for several minutes. "It looks like he was referring to Hope City Linen and Uniform Service. I can't tell if they actually own his business or if he just has a contract with them."

"Print that off for me, if you don't mind," Kyle said, standing. "We'll take all this now and see if there's anything we can go with. A laundry service hardly ties into Kilton Pharmaceuticals, but I'm willing to go down a few rabbit holes to see if I can get something."

On their way back to their office, they detoured to talk to Jon Ying. Expecting a small dry-cleaning business, he was surprised when they pulled up to the wide, glass storefront of an old brick building. The area had seen better days, but it was bustling with activity.

Walking inside, they moved down a long counter where a young woman on one end was taking laundry and dry cleaning from walk-in customers. The noise from the large machines in the back was almost deafening, and he wondered how she could hear. As soon as she was free, Kyle stepped forward, showing his badge. "We're here to talk to Jon Ying."

Her eyes widened and she smiled. "Oh, you found my uncle's truck?"

"If you could just get him for us, please."

She hurried toward the back, and his gaze followed her as she weaved between the machinery and disappeared. A moment later, she hustled back to the counter to take the next customer, calling out, "He's just coming."

A small, dark-haired, bespectacled man came from the back, his gaze pinned on Kyle and Alex. "You are not the same police I talked to before."

Showing their badges, Kyle introduced, "That's right, sir. I'm Detective McBride and this is Detective Freeman. We'd like to ask you a few more questions, please. Is there somewhere a little quieter we can talk?"

"Quieter?" Jon seemed perplexed, and Kyle assumed the man's hearing was either gone or he simply no longer noticed the noise roaring around him.

"Yes, please."

He waved them back, and they moved around the counter, following him past the machinery. The noise grew in intensity and the scent of bleach, detergent, and indefinable chemicals combined to make his nose burn. The heat from the machines made the air stifling. Finally, they reached a small office near the back. The office was a mess of papers, files, clothing piled in a chair, forms tacked to the walls and, somehow, there managed to be just enough room for the three men to stand once the door was closed.

"Have you found my truck?"

"I'm sorry, Mr. Ying, but no. I'd like to get a little bit more information from you about what was in the report. I believe you told the other detectives that the truck was bought by the corporation, given to you to use, but you wouldn't be able to file a claim on it being stolen. Is that right?"

His head bobbing up and down, Mr. Ying confirmed. "Yes, yes. It wasn't in my name, so I don't get any money. That's why I want it found."

"Exactly what corporation were you referring to?"

"Hope City Linen and Uniform Service."

Nodding, he continued. "Now, do they own this business?"

"No, it's *my* business."

Glancing quickly in Alex's direction, he could tell his partner was confused as well. Trying again, he said, "So, Ying Laundry is your business. What does Hope City Linen own?"

"They're a big business. They do most of the fancy hotels and many restaurants in Hope City. I had room to expand here years ago, so I still run my laundry and dry cleaning out of one end but bought the huge industrial cleaners. I have a contract with Hope City Linen and Uniform Service. They provided a couple of vans so that my drivers could get around to all the locations that are assigned to us. With one truck missing, my drivers are having to work overtime to get to everywhere. I need it back."

"If the truck was actually owned by Hope City Linen, then why didn't they file the police report?"

"I called them, but they said it was my problem. If I lost the truck, then I need to find it. But I didn't lose it. The truck was stolen right from the alley behind us."

Pinching the bridge of his nose for a second, Kyle asked, "And you have no security cameras?"

Shaking his head, Mr. Ying said, "Too expensive. How am I going to make money if I have to keep buying trucks and put up cameras?"

"One last question for now. Who is your contact at Hope City Linen?"

"Contact?"

"When you call them to talk to somebody there, who do you talk to?"

"Ah, I talk to Roger Solten." Keeping his eyes on Alex's notepad, he continued, "That's R.O.G.E—"

"Thank you, sir. I've got it."

Promising to call if they found any information, they walked back through the heavy machinery and out of the building. Stepping onto the much quieter street, Kyle shook his head slightly. "Fuck, man, my ears are roaring."

"Even if there were employees around when that truck was stolen from the back, I can now see how that happened. If you're inside, you can't hear anything happening on the outside."

As they climbed into Kyle's pickup, he started the engine, then sat for a moment. "You know, it takes balls to steal a vehicle in broad daylight. Whoever did it had been in that building before. They knew that no one on the inside was going to hear them start the engine and take it. They also knew that once it made the morning run to bring linen in, it was going to sit there for several hours until it was time to start taking linen back. And they knew there was no security camera."

Alex shook his head and said, "Todd and Birdie checked out the other employees. They were all working and there's not a blemish on their records. There's nothing to tie them into the theft at all."

"Might not be somebody who works there. Could be somebody who's been there just to check it out."

"Then, with the number of people going in and out with their laundry and dry cleaning, that could be hundreds of people a week that had been in that building."

Sighing, Kyle pulled onto the street. "Let's do some digging into the Hope City Linen company. Maybe there's something up with them. Shit, anything to see if we could tie them into Kilton Pharmaceuticals."

"You know this is a fuckin' long stretch, right?"

"I know, but I've got nothing else right now but loose ends. Something's gotta start tying them together."

Kyle stopped at the coffee shop next to headquarters, getting the biggest coffee he could, dumping creamer and sugar into it. Alex refused to pay for coffee when he could get it free at the station, but Kyle was afraid that sludge would eat a hole in his gut.

Back at their desks, he pulled up his laptop and tried to find information about the Hope City Linen and Uniform Service. Once on their website, he started searching. Within ten minutes, he was ready to throw in the towel. "Who the hell knows how to dig through this business shit to figure out who owns the company?"

Alex looked up from his desk and said, "What about Harlan?"

Detective Harlan Peters was a new hire from the surrounding county. "He's a nice guy, but what makes you think he can do this?"

"Because I pay attention when info comes out about a new hire. He came from a financial fraud background. He's probably good at this shit."

Brows now raised, Kyle stood quickly and hustled down the hall to another workroom. Eyes landing on his prey, he called out, "Harlan? You got a few minutes?"

He explained to Harlan what he needed, and the young man nodded. "I can help you out with that." The two walked back into Kyle and Alex's area and he handed his laptop to Harlan, who immediately began searching.

Harlan was scribbling notes on a pad, occasionally mumbling as he worked. After almost an hour, Harlan looked up and grinned. "I think I've got it, but I don't know that it'll do you any good."

"Let's have it anyway," Kyle said.

"Okay, so I just wanted to double-check what the laundry owner told you. And that's true, Ying Laundry Service has a contract with Hope City Linen and Uniform service. Now, HC Linen is a subsidiary of Artog, Incorporated, an international shipping company."

Harlan paused and looked at Kyle with a big smile on his face. "Fascinating stuff, isn't it?"

Kyle wondered if his expression was as glazed over as it felt. One glance at Alex, and he could see his partner was in the same boat. "Gotta tell you, Harlan, it doesn't thrill me as much as it seems to excite you. But, so far, you're not giving me much."

Wiggling his eyebrows, Harlan said, "I'm not finished yet." Turning back to his notes, he said, "Artog is huge and owns a lot of different companies, but I couldn't find a tie in until I came to one that's local. Delmont. When I dug into it, it looks like it's a holding company. Doesn't really do anything except just give the owner a chance to have tax write-offs and whatever the fuck else they want to hide under it. But it's tied into Montgomery Dell."

"The congressman?"

"Ding, ding, ding... give the man a prize!" Harlan

called out. "Now, keep in mind that it's not necessarily illegal for him to have this company that doesn't do anything but own other companies. But I'd say he prefers people not to know about it since the only name associated with it is his private lawyer."

Nodding, Kyle was intrigued but still didn't feel like he had any tie into what he wanted. He sat for a moment pondering the information but, no matter how he looked at it, it seemed useless. He turned to thank Harlan but noticed the young detective was staring at their evidence board.

Harlan inclined his head toward the board and said, "You looking into Kilton Pharmaceuticals?"

Nodding, he didn't say anything else before Harlan immediately began tapping again. He looked over at Alex but received a shrug as a reply. They sat quietly for a while, letting Harlan continue to tap on the keyboard while occasionally grunting. Finally, Harlan looked up and grinned.

"Well, it seems that Hope City Linen and Uniform also has a contract with Kilton. Probably does uniforms and lab coats and things like that. And what's more… one of Congressman Dell's biggest donors is Kilton Pharmaceuticals. Last I saw on the news, he's pushing for easier FDA requirements on testing drugs."

20

Just as Kyle walked into Kimberly's house, his phone rang. Seeing it was her, he greeted, "Hey, babe. Will you be home soon?"

"Yes, I promise it's just one drink with a few people from work and then I'm coming straight home. Did you get in okay?"

"Yes, did you think the key wouldn't work?"

"I just wanted to be sure you weren't sitting outside."

She had given him a spare key the day before, wanting him to come to her house for dinner since she had work to finish. He had not reciprocated yet... but had no qualms about giving her a key to his place.

"You want me to come get you when you're ready?"

"Nope, it's good. We're actually at a little place down the street and Bob is here. Are you sure you don't want to join us?"

"Nah... it was a long day. You enjoy. I'll chill and be here when you arrive."

"Okay, see you in about an hour. Dinner is in the slow-cooker so we'll eat as soon as I get there."

"Got any more whipped cream?"

"Uh… actually, yeah. Want to use it tonight?"

He had been joking, but at her response, the blood rushed south and the image of her spread eagle on her bed, strategically placed whipped cream ready to be licked off, filled his mind. "Make it a short drink, babe."

Laughing, she disconnected, and he walked through the living room and into the kitchen. The scent of dinner cooking filled the air. Opening the refrigerator, he snagged a beer. Heading back into the living room, he noticed her laptop, notebook, and papers scattered all over the coffee table. Curious, he sat down and looked through a few.

He smiled when he saw Tammy's picture, standing in front of a big map of Hope City, and remembered his own interview with her. *Employee of the month*. He could easily see her being featured in Kimberly's Faces of Hope City articles.

As he scanned through some of the others, he noticed the picture with Thomas Kilton and his gaze zeroed in on a picture behind him. Congressman Montgomery Dell was standing with the Kilton family, his arm around Sidney. There were interviews with warehouse workers, some who knew Terry when he was sleeping with Beth. She had notes on the various uses of fentanyl and how the biochemist worked on the compounds. A niggle of guilt moved through him, but he grabbed his phone and began snapping pictures of her notes as well as the printed pages, including photographs from her laptop.

Placing everything back the way he found it, he settled back onto the sofa and began surfing the Internet on his phone to see what he could find between the congressman and the Kilton family. Time passed quickly, and he jumped when he heard Kimberly's voice outside the front door saying goodbye to Bob. Shutting his phone down, he quickly glanced at the coffee table, satisfied that it was just as she left it. Throwing open the door, he waved to Bob as he dragged her inside, kissing her in the middle of a giggle.

She immediately wrapped her arms around his neck, pulling him down and holding him close. A growl erupted from deep inside his chest. Lifting her in his arms, she wound her legs about his waist, and he swore he could feel her heat against his cock through the layers of clothing.

Still kissing her, he managed to mumble, "Will dinner keep?"

She nodded as their lips and tongues stayed connected. He turned and stalked toward her stairs. Not sure how he was able to continue kissing her while maneuvering up the staircase, he nonetheless made it to the bedroom without incident. He slid one hand to her ass, giving a little squeeze, and she dropped her legs so he could set her feet onto the floor.

This was no slow seduction but a wild tossing of clothes while their hands and mouths devoured each other. Soon they were both naked, and she stepped back, grinning. She crawled onto the bed on all fours, tossed her long hair over her shoulder as she wiggled her perfect, heart-shaped ass at him. Thankful he'd started keeping condoms within easy reach at her house, he quickly covered his aching cock. Climbing onto the bed behind her and with no finesse, he slapped her ass gently as he mounted her. Plunging in from behind, he kept one hand on her hip and the other he wound through her long hair.

He thrust hard and fast, his hand occasionally jerking lightly on her hair. The only sounds in the room were the grunts emitted from both of them. He glanced to the side where their reflections were captured in the mirror over her dresser and could see her breasts bouncing in time to his movements.

Sliding his hand from her hip, he captured her breasts, squeezing and palming the globes before rolling the nipples between his fingers. He could see her hands clutching wads of the bed covers and as she tired, she dropped her forearms to the mattress. This only served to tilt her ass up more, and he took full advantage of the position.

He let go of her hair and planted his hand next to hers on the bed, his chest now pressing against her back. His other hand curved around, finding her swollen bud, pinching just enough to send her over the edge as her orgasm raced through her. She threw her head back, bumping his chin, but the force of her inner muscles grabbing his cock made him impervious to everything but the feel of his own release.

Her limbs gave out, and she fell flat onto her stomach, his body spread out over hers. His cock was still buried deep inside and, for a few seconds, he wasn't sure he could move. Rational thought finally crept in and he knew he must be crushing her. Rolling to the side, he lay on his back sucking in great gulps of air. His hand gently rubbed her ass as he asked, "You okay, babe?"

She grunted her affirmative to his question, and he grinned. Neither moved for several long minutes until, finally, she rolled into him, arms and legs tangling.

Lifting her head, she grinned. "That was quite a homecoming. I might have to go drinking without you more often if that's what greets me when I get home."

A chuckle erupted from deep inside and, forcing his body to move, he gathered her into his arms. "What I need to do is convince you to stay with me all the time and then we don't even have to worry about homecomings." The words leaving his mouth surprised him, having not been planned. And yet, the idea of them moving in together did not frighten him.

She lifted her head and stared down at him, her top teeth pressing firmly into her bottom lip as her green eyes held his gaze. "Stay with you all the time?"

"Maybe not right away, but soon. At least think about it."

"Why?"

His arms jerked slightly, startled by her simple question. "Why? Lots of reasons. We sleep together every night, just bounce between one house and the other. I like your house, but mine is bigger, closer to work, is owned and not just rented—"

"And has an amazing deck with a view."

He laughed and nodded. "Yeah. It has an amazing deck with a view."

They sobered and remained silent for a moment, and he lifted his hand to brush her hair back from her face so that he could see her clearly. "If you had asked me a month ago if I believed in love at first sight, I would have said no. Lust at first sight? Absolutely. But what I feel for you, I've never felt before. Not with any woman. You're the first thing I think of when I wake in the morning, and I don't want to go to sleep without you in my arms every night."

Her lips curved gently, and she whispered, "This is scary."

"What's scary about it, sweetheart?"

"Because I feel the very same way. But it's also scary because I've never felt this, so I don't know what to expect."

"Then we take it one day at a time until we're both at the same place."

Kimberly barely roused from her deep sleep when Kyle kissed her early the next morning. With his lips still pressed to her forehead, he whispered, "See you tonight, babe."

She heard him go downstairs and woke just enough to feel guilty that she had not given him a better send-off. Pushing the covers back, she padded to the top of the stairs and had just started down when she heard his voice near the front door.

"Alex, I'm heading in early because I may have found a way to tie some of our loose ends together at Kilton. I went through Kimberly's notes yesterday and discovered that there's a personal tie between the Kiltons and Congressman Dell. She has pictures from inside their office and they're all pretty chummy. Yeah, yeah, I know that's not unusual for politicians and donors, but I'd like to follow the money trail a little more. I know I can't use her for inside information on Kilton, but her insight gives me the idea that we should dig into them more. This might shut the Kilton pipeline down. Okay, see you when you get there."

Her front door opened and closed, the sound of Kyle's heavy boots fading as he walked toward his truck. She remained rooted to the floor, her heart pounding. *I went through Kimberly's notes. Discovered a tie. Shut Kilton down.*

Her legs gave out and she plopped her ass onto the stairs. The sting of tears hit her eyes as her heart spasmed. She lifted her fist and pressed it against her breastbone, wondering if someone her age could have a heart attack or if it was simply breaking.

Kyle dragged his hand through his hair, pacing in front of the evidence board while Alex leaned against their desks. He had printed out the information he'd photographed from Kimberly's notes, including the organizational chart of Kilton Pharma.

"I kept thinking it might be somebody lower down. Somebody from the warehouse. Somebody who could get hold of the driver schedules easily. But with this tie into the congressman, I'm now looking at this differently. Someone with pull and money put the fear of God into Beth Washington and Doug Tiller. I thought in terms of somebody who had possible reaches into prison, but now I'm thinking it came from higher up." He stopped pacing and glanced over to Alex. "What have we got on Congressman Dell?"

Alex grabbed the folder sitting next to him on the desk and flipped it open. "Artog International Shipping. Hope City and New York are their two major eastern city ports. They have ships that span the globe, with headquarters in New York, Guangzhou, China, and are based out of St. Petersburg. Interpol lists them as having ties to Russian Mafia, but then it appears that a lot of what comes out of Interpol is controlled by Russia anyway. The FBI has certainly had their eyes on them."

"Is there anything to tie the congressman into that shipping company? Russian Mafia? And does that even have anything to do with the drugs coming out of Kilton?"

"Artog is used as a shipping company by Kilton. They not only do port shipping but air shipping as well."

"So, we can definitely tie Kilton with Artog shipping, tie them to the congressman, and tie them to the company that owns the truck that stole pharmaceuticals from Kilton?"

"Right," Alex agreed. Holding his gaze, he added, "But this is a huge mess. What do we do about it?"

"Break it down."

Both Alex and Kyle turned around at the sound of their captain behind them. Rick Hollister moved closer, stared at the board, then turned around and looked at the two detectives. "Look, you've got a lot of links to some pretty impressive players in this game. But if you start chasing every angle right now, you're going to lose sight of trying to close the pipeline of opioids from Kilton Pharmaceuticals. Focus on that. The other," he said, waving his hand toward the board, "shipping company, Russian ties, congressman… all that can wait. Now, you can use that to put some pressure on Kilton. Don't get sidetracked with what your case is all about."

With that, he offered a curt nod and headed back to his office.

Dropping his head and staring at his boots for a moment, Kyle then lifted his chin and stared at the board once again. "Captain's right. Whatever we find on the other can be turned over to the FBI. But it can be used as leverage." A slow grin spread across his face, and he said, "How about we take a little visit to Kilton?"

Walking into Thomas Kilton's office, Kyle was impressed. Even though the building itself had a modern feel, Thomas' office resembled a throwback to old money. The carpet underneath his feet gave credence to the glare from the assistant staring at his and Alex's boots, probably wondering if they were tracking mud. He glanced down to assure that he was not.

One wall was lined with wooden bookcases filled with books, manuals, and photographs in silver frames. His desk was huge, made of solid wood. His corner office windows afforded him an expansive view.

Glancing toward the shelves, Kyle observed the pictures he had seen in the photographs Kimberly had taken. Various members of the Kilton family with a multitude of politicians, Congressman Dell being one of them.

Thomas walked through the connecting door, his smile wide as he approached, dressed to impress with his dark, expensive suit, pale shirt with its matching handkerchief tucked into the pocket, and silk tie. His hair was trimmed and slicked back away from his receding hairline, and he turned his bespectacled gaze upon the detectives.

"I'm Detective McBride, and this is my partner, Detective Freeman."

"How may I be of service, detectives?"

"We're investigating the stolen drugs from the Kilton Pharmaceuticals' delivery van," Kyle began.

"Of course, of course!" Thomas enthused, waving them toward the two wooden and leather chairs opposite his desk. He settled into his own seat, assuming the position of power. With his elbows on the arms of his chair and his fingers steepled in front of him, he asked, "Is it too much to hope for that they've been found?"

"No, we haven't found them. We know, of course, that they would be unsellable if they are found."

"We would have to destroy them. We've already taken the loss financially."

"And I assume all your shipments, including foreign, national, and local are insured?" Alex asked.

"Absolutely," Thomas said. "As Vice President of Finance and Administration, that arduous task falls to me."

"While we haven't found the drugs, we have discerned that the truck used in the theft had been reported stolen from a laundry service in town."

Thomas held his gaze steadily, his eyebrows rising slightly at that information.

"What's more interesting," Kyle continued, "is that the truck was not owned by that laundry, but by a larger linen service in Hope City. We continued to follow that trail and discovered that the true owner is Artog Shipping which, interestingly enough, is the company that Kilton Pharmaceuticals uses to ship overseas."

Nodding slowly, Thomas said, "You're right, Detective, that is interesting. I'm not quite sure where this leads us since you haven't been able to recover the drugs."

"We've been looking into the possibility that whoever held up the Kilton van had inside information on the routes used by the drivers. The truck was there waiting for them even though their schedule had changed. What we find interesting is that the truck used in the holdup can also be traced to Kilton."

"So, you're thinking of an inside job? I believe that's the terminology," Thomas chuckled. "Or perhaps I'm just showing my interest in detective shows on TV."

"You're right. We're looking at the possibility that this was, indeed, an inside job."

"I see. While this is very interesting, I'm not sure why you're giving me this information. If you're considering more of an inside job operation, then you should be talking to Niles Cook, the Vice President of Kilton Operations. The warehouse and all shipping go through his departments."

"Actually, we'll be seeing him next. But there was another interesting loose end we're trying to tie up that could concern the Finance Division. The shipping line is also tied to Congressman Dell." Inclining his head toward the wall, he added, "I see the members of your family are well acquainted with the congressman. So much so that each of you individually as well as your company have made donations to his campaigns."

His voice now sharper, Thomas asked, "What are you implying?"

"As I said, we're trying to tie up all the loose ends. The possibility that this was an inside job from this pharmaceutical company. Possibly involving a truck that was owned by a company that has ties to both Kilton and the congressman. This congressman, by the way, works on legislation to ease up FDA requirements for testing of certain drugs that I know Kilton is producing. The street value of what was stolen is probably close to about $1.2 million. Big stakes, big plans. Right now, Mr. Kilton, we're simply looking at all the information to see where it leads."

"Well, I can assure you it doesn't lead here. My father built this company from the ground up, and it's been a life's pursuit and lifeblood of the Kilton family. While I would like to assure you there's no way the theft had anything to do with a Kilton employee, I obviously can't make that claim. But I can tell you that the campaign donations to any politician have always abided by campaign laws. I know that the congressman is an old golfing buddy of my dad and we're certainly not trying to buy favoritism."

"It just helps to have everything out in the open, Mr. Kilton. Thank you for your time." Kyle and Alex stood at the same time and walked out of the office, leaving Thomas still sitting at his desk.

Once outside, they drove to the other building indicated by the security guard to talk to Niles Cook. His office was in the building next to the warehouse where they had talked to Porter Myles and Tammy Rutgers. Even though he was also a vice president, his office was much more modest. He had a large window, but it over-looked the warehouse loading area. Instead of floor-to-ceiling bookcases, he had wooden filing cabinets lining part of the wall. His desk was also wooden, but not nearly as opulent as Thomas'. The tile floor did little to disguise the sound of their boots.

While in a dress shirt and tie, Niles had eschewed a suit jacket, and the sleeves of his shirt were rolled up at the bottom. He welcomed them in, waving them toward the chairs.

"Welcome, detectives. I understand you were in last week and had a chance to meet with Porter and the irrepressible as well as indispensable Tammy. What can I help you with today?"

"Thank you for meeting with us. We've just been talking with Thomas Kilton—" a snort interrupted Kyle, and Niles immediately threw up his hands. "I'm so sorry, detectives. That was incredibly rude."

Kyle hesitated, tilting his head slightly to the side, waiting to see if Niles had anything else to say. He watched as a slight blush crept over the man's face.

"If you've been to see the exalted Thomas right before coming here, I'm sure you're stunned that while we have equal positions in the company, equal is a rela-tive term, especially when it comes to office space." Shrugging, he added, "Although an office at the 'big house'—as we over here like to refer to it—really isn't my style. Anyway, please forgive my rude interruption."

Fighting a lip quirk, Kyle continued. "Upon investigating the stolen drugs, we believe that it was either an inside job or assisted by someone inside Kilton. Exactly where inside, and by who, we don't know."

Eyes wide, Niles leaned back. "I see. Well, I have to admit, that's disturbing news."

"We talked to Tammy but wondered who else is privy to the information about the routing software. We asked her but realized she might not know how far up the chain that goes."

Nodding, Niles said, "You're probably right. The drivers may share some of the routing information with the other drivers, but the programming would not be available to them. Besides Tammy, her direct boss is Bob Trogden, and the Department Supervisor, Porter Myles, also has access to that program. I requested him to become familiar with it several years ago."

Bob Trogden... Kimberly's neighbor? Keeping his face blank, he nodded. "Why is that?"

"Technology is a wonderful thing, detectives, but programs can also be finicky. For a company our size, to only have a couple of people who know a particular program that's vital to our daily company needs is not a good plan. A few years ago, Tammy thought she might have surgery and would be out a few weeks. We were scrambling to cover what her responsibilities are. So, we made sure that Bob and Porter had that particular routing program. As it turned out, she didn't need the surgery, but the result was good nonetheless."

He smiled and added, "For full disclosure, I also have access to the routing programs, but I'll be honest to say that I've never been trained on it. I'm not sure that I would even be able to understand it if I pulled it up, but I certainly have it installed on my computer."

"The other thing we're concerned about is that the truck involved in the theft had been reported stolen but is owned by a sister subsidiary company of Kilton."

Niles' brow lowered and he shook his head slowly. "I'm not sure I understand exactly what you're saying, but I don't know anything about that, detectives."

Thanking him for his time, Kyle was about to suggest to Alex that they talk to Bob Trogdon when Alex's phone rang. Answering it, he said, "We'll be right there." Looking at Kyle, he added, "The truck's been found."

Arriving at an old strip mall where half of the stores were closed, they could see the white delivery truck sitting off to the side. A patrol car with two officers stood nearby, and as they drew closer, they could see Todd and Birdie there as well. Parking, he and Alex climbed from his truck and walked over.

"Before you ask, yes, we'll have it taken in. As usual, there's a backlog at the lab, but at least we can see if there's anything," Todd said.

"I opened it up and looked inside. It's clean from what I can see," Birdie added. "My guess would be our guys were professional, they would've kept everything in boxes and used gloves."

Kyle looked around, hoping to see security cameras but was disappointed.

"Yeah, I checked with the manager of the store over there—one of the few still open—and he said there haven't been security cameras around here in years. Not since the grocery store that anchored them on the corner went out of business."

"So, they chose a place in plain view, no cameras, but so little traffic that a truck can sit here for days and no one would notice or complain." Looking toward the two officers, he asked, "Did they discover it?"

"Yeah," Todd replied. "Because it looks so new, it caught their eye and they decided to ask the guy if it was his. He's the one that told me it's just been sitting here for a few days. They ran the plates and then called it in."

"Well, once processed, I guess Mr. Ying will be glad to get his truck back," Alex said, eliciting a chuckle from the others.

22

Kyle's day had been long, and he drove to his house, concerned that Kimberly had not confirmed that she was going to meet them there. They had bounced back and forth between houses and he hoped she would be waiting for him. Going through the front door, his gaze snagged immediately on the coffee table. A key lying on top of a piece of paper was in plain sight. Snatching the paper up, he could easily see it was from her, already recognizing her handwriting.

I suppose I'm taking the chicken way out by leaving your key and this message. I heard you talking to Alex this morning and know that you read over my notes from work. If you have to investigate my employer, I can respect that. But I can't respect or condone you using me to that end. I'm giving back your key because right now it feels disingenuous to keep it. Kimberly

He read the note three times then tossed it back to the coffee table next to his house key. Dropping his head back, he closed his eyes and planted his hands on his hips, cursing his actions. It was foolish to have talked to Alex in her house with the possibility that she would overhear. But it was even more wrong to have looked through her work papers without her permission.

Dropping his chin, he jerked his phone from his pocket and dialed her number, frustrated when it went to voicemail. Turning on his heel, he stalked to his truck and drove to her house.

He still had his key to her house but knocked on the door, hating that she did not answer. Looking up and down the street, he didn't see her car in its usual parking spot. Plopping down on the front step, he decided to wait. A few minutes later, Bob walked up and saw him sitting on the stoop. "Hey, Kyle, are you locked out?"

"No, she's not here right now. I just thought I'd wait for her outside."

"Yeah? How about some company?"

He wasn't sure how to politely say that he preferred being by himself and watched as Bob sat on his front stoop.

Bob surprised him when he said, "I'll be honest, Kyle. I saw Kimberly earlier and she said that you were investigating Kilton. That the robbery might be an inside job."

He looked toward Bob and held his gaze for a long time, impressed that the other man did not look away.

"My partner and I were going to come to see you today, but we got called away. I know that Tammy

Rutgers reports to you, so you're going to know all the shipping details."

"You want to make this official? Go ahead, ask me anything."

"Okay. I'm convinced that someone knew the route that the van was going to take. It was supposed to deliver to that particular pharmacy later in the afternoon but, even with the time getting moved up by several hours because of the change, the truck involved in the theft was already waiting there. Tammy knew the routes. You knew the routes. And the drivers knew the routes. I just found out today that Porter has that information as well. So that leaves me with a small pool of people that could have known what route they were taking."

Bob sighed heavily and looked out toward the street. "I know you've got to look into me, but I'll tell you, I had nothing to do with it. And I'd bet my life that neither did Tammy."

"Okay, if I take you at face value for right now, what does that leave me with?"

"That leaves you with Porter, Charlie, and Joe." Bob looked back at him and said, "But, of course, if I'm lying to you, I could just be setting them up."

"Yep, that's right. But I can already tell you that Charlie and Joe's stories don't match up."

Bob's gaze jerked back to Kyle and his brow lowered. "Damn."

"Tell me about those two."

Bob propped his forearms on his knees, clasped his

hands together, and stared down for a moment. "Did you know Joe had a stepbrother that was a user?"

"Fuck," Kyle bit out.

"Not raised together. Different dads and different last names. The only reason I know is that I stopped by the funeral home for family visitation when his mom died a few years back. He introduced me to his brother and then a couple of days later we were just shooting the shit and he mentioned that his stepbrother hadn't been out of jail very long. I think he mentioned using, maybe even dealing." With his head still facing down, he twisted around and caught Kyle's eye. "I've never had a reason to suspect Joe. And I sure as hell don't hold anything against him that someone in his family has ever done."

"Out of curiosity, when I said that their stories didn't match up and asked about the two, you told me something about Joe. Why is that?"

Bob's brow crinkled. "I don't know. I can't tell you who's lying when it comes to them giving different accounts, but I just don't know anything about Charlie that's suspicious at all. Hell, Joe's stepbrother doesn't make Joe suspicious either. I guess it's just something I thought of."

Kyle looked over as another car drove down the street and spied Kimberly. She parallel parked several doors down, bumping her back tire against the curb. If he wasn't so concerned about her state of mind, he would've smiled. Instead, he watched as she got out and threw a glare his way. The two men stood, and Bob turned to reach out his hand.

Grasping it in a shake, Kyle said, "Appreciate the information."

Bob waved toward Kimberly before going inside his house as she stomped up the front steps.

Opening her door, she marched inside, and Kyle followed. Rounding quickly, she said, "What were you talking to Bob about?"

"I'm not at liberty to tell you right now. It was official."

She reared back as her eyes bugged out of her head. "Official? You were questioning my neighbor officially?"

"He volunteered to be questioned officially, so yes. And not as your neighbor, but as an employee and a person of interest."

"A... a... a person of interest?"

He wondered if her eyes could widen anymore and sighed heavily. "Kimberly, I don't want to talk about this now."

"Well, guess what? We don't always get what we want, do we?" She held out her hand, wiggling her fingers. "Keys."

He was struck with déjà vu and wondered if she recognized the similarity from weeks before. Stepping closer, he said, "Sweetheart, I'm sorry."

She pinched her lips together in a tight line. "You betrayed my trust, but it's all supposed to be better because you say you're sorry?"

"No, not because I just say that I'm sorry, but because I truly am. What I did yesterday was wrong. I wasn't snooping, but the material was lying right there in plain sight, and I did start looking through it. All I could think about was finding out who's getting drugs on the street."

"All you care about is taking out somebody at Kilton."

"No, that's not true."

"How long have you been investigating Kilton Pharma? Since before meeting me the first time?"

"Yes, but—"

"Is that why you're with me?"

Hands on his hips, he shook his head. "You know that's not true. You know that who you work for has nothing to do with how I feel." He dropped his chin to his chest for a moment then lifted his gaze back to her. "Damnit, Kimberly, I'm not after Kilton. I'm trying to get the leak of prescription drugs off the street. The way I went about it wasn't right when I found your notes, but my motives were pure."

Indecision crossed her face, then she shook her head. "I don't have time for this right now. I'm going to a friend's house."

"Whose?"

"That's my business."

He wanted to argue that her business was his business but knew he should tread carefully. Sucking in a deep breath, he let it out slowly. "All right, but I'd like to know you accept my apology."

"Kyle, I'm still upset. And I need some time and space, and you're going to give me that."

He nodded slowly, hating to agree but understanding her need. "Okay, but will you let me know when you get in? Not because I'm trying to keep tabs on you but because I worry."

Her shoulders slumped as she held his gaze. "Yeah, I'll do that. I promise."

"Men suck."

Kimberly, sitting on the floor with her back to the sofa, rolled her head to the side and looked at Caitlyn. Not usually one for making such negative declarative statements, she was surprised. But then Caitlyn was on her third glass of wine, so her tongue was loosened.

"Hear, hear," Sandy agreed.

Sandy was sitting on the other side of the room, so Kimberly rolled her head toward her. "Come on, girls. They don't really suck. They're just... kind of sucky."

Bekki laughed and propped her feet on the coffee table. "Well, you're the one who started it by talking about Kyle."

She hadn't meant to go into all her problems when she'd shown up at Caitlyn's house earlier. After all, Caitlyn was Kyle's sister. But it seemed as though Caitlyn had had a bad day at school with a new principal, Bekki was frustrated with one of the men at the TV station, and Sandy... well, for all her flirting, she was always irritated with men.

"I know. He did apologize, though. It just seemed so underhanded."

Caitlyn set her wine glass down, pulled her feet off the coffee table, and leaned forward. "Okay, here's the thing that you've got to understand. Something that Bekki and I get in spades. So, listen and learn a few things that the nuns didn't teach you, darling."

Curious, she twisted around so that she could give them her full attention.

"My dad worked for the FBI. Bekki's dad is the Police Commissioner. She's got two brothers who are detectives, and another one who's a fireman. I've got two brothers who are detectives and another one who's a paramedic. My oldest sister is now married to a detective. Bekki's oldest brother is married to a detective, and another one is with a DEA agent. Are you getting what I'm telling you?"

"Yes. You're telling me that your family is mostly law enforcement. Uptight, always on duty, suspicious... am I on the right track?"

Caitlyn giggled, nodding. "Yes, but that's not all. You see, people aren't just in law enforcement as a job or a career. It's in their DNA."

"DNA?"

"It's who they are. They are always investigating. Always looking. Always searching," Caitlyn said.

"Always security conscious," Bekki threw out.

"And from what I've seen... always alpha," Sandy added with an eye-roll.

"Yeah, alpha for sure," Caitlyn agreed, "but not in a *me Tarzan, you Jane* kind of way. Just in a... a..."

"It's more of a *'I love you and want to protect you'* kind of way," Bekki finished. Leaning back in her seat, she sighed, a slight smile playing about her lips. "That's what I'm looking for and certainly didn't find it where I work."

"I *know* I don't find it where I work," Caitlyn said. "The most domineering man I work with is the principal and he's a prick."

Kimberly settled back against the sofa cushions, her legs spread out in front of her, and sipped the last of her wine. "You're right... Sister Honoria didn't teach me that at all." Grinning, she added, "Although Sister Francine did say that one day a man would sweep me off my feet."

"Was she right?" Sandy asked.

Looking at the curious faces of her friends, she grinned. "Yeah, she was."

"So, my brother's not such an ass after all?" Caitlyn asked.

"I never said he was an ass! He did apologize."

Sandy leaned over, her expression wistful. "Then what are you doing here? If I had such a man, I'd be with him."

"You could be, you know?" Caitlyn said. "Rory would—"

"Right! Like the biggest, flirtiest, playerist in town would settle down?"

"Playerist?" Bekki asked, her nose scrunched. "I don't think that's a word."

"Well, it fits Rory McBride!"

Pushing to her feet, Kimberly smiled and said, "Dearies, it's time for me to go."

Caitlyn moved over and wrapped her arms around

her. "Please, forgive my brother. I really want you two together."

Squeezing her in return, she leaned back and smiled. With hugs given all around, she called for a taxi and gave him the address.

Kyle sat in his living room, the TV on a game, but he paid no attention. Instead, his focus was on his phone, waiting for the text or call from Kimberly to say she'd gotten home safely. A car door slammed outside and a few seconds later he heard knocking on his door. Jumping to his feet, he looked outside and spied her standing on his stoop.

He threw open the door. "Babe? Are you okay?"

"I've been with Caitlyn, and Bekki, and Sandy."

It was then he realized her smile was a bit sloppy, and he looked behind her up and down the street. "Did you drive?"

"Of course, I didn't drive! I've had several glasses of wine, but I'm responsible enough to take a taxi."

"Why didn't you text me any information about the driver so if you disappeared off the face of the earth, I would've known who you were with?"

Still standing on his stoop, she narrowed her eyes and planted her fists on her hips. "Are you trying to be a jerk... again?"

He started counting to ten but only made it to four. Reaching out, he snagged his hand around her waist and gently pulled her inside. Staring down at her green eyes, all other thoughts fled his mind, and he simply wanted his lips on hers. Bending, he kissed her. A kiss to claim and possess, but he knew it was she who claimed his heart and possessed his soul. Finally, he lifted his head, sucking in a ragged breath.

She reached up, placing her palm over his wildly-beating heart. "Earlier, you asked for forgiveness. I give it."

The tight band around his heart eased, and he let out a long breath.

"Caitlyn and Bekki had a lot to say about the men in their families."

Brows lifted, he asked, "Was it good or damning?"

Her lips quirked and she said, "A little of both." She ran her tongue over her bottom lip and sighed. "They were raised in families with a lot of people in law enforcement. They told me it's in your DNA. I was raised with sweet nuns. I'm not sure my past experience makes it easy to always understand what you're thinking or going through."

The grip that had hold of his heart squeezed again, and he quickly said, "I don't want our pasts to keep us from the future, Kimberly."

She shook her head quickly. "That's not what I'm saying, Kyle. You and I look at people from two completely different perspectives. I'm just saying that I'm having to get used to being with someone who has such a suspicious mind."

He slid one hand over her shoulder and cupped her cheek, his fingertips gliding through her silky hair. He rubbed his thumb over her soft skin, drowning in her expressive eyes. "This is all new for both of us, sweet-heart. I can't change who I am, but I can promise I won't use you. And I'll share whatever I can about your work-place, especially to make sure you're safe."

"And Bob? What on earth does he have to do with anything?"

He hesitated, battling with what to say. Finally, still cupping her cheek, he admitted, "Kilton Pharmaceuti-cals is huge in the industry, one with ties to big money, lobbying, and politicians. Not all the strings that get pulled are the altruistic desire to find a cure. One of the biggest problems we have on the street is legal pharma-ceuticals getting into the wrong hands."

Her tongue darted out to moisten her bottom lip, but she remained quiet, simply nodding for him to continue.

"The street value is in the millions, something you know because you've been researching. Some of those drugs come from Kilton Pharmaceuticals." He watched as his words penetrated and her eyes widened. Expecting her to argue, he was surprised when she simply nodded again. Still choosing his words carefully, he added, "We have every reason to suspect the Kilton van theft was aided by someone at Kilton."

She gasped, sputtering "But... but Bob wouldn't—"

He slid his thumb to settle over her lips, stilling her protestation. "I didn't say he did it. But someone who knows the delivery van schedules would be a person of interest to talk to. I had some questions for him, and his knowledge is beneficial."

"Tammy? Or the drivers themselves—"

"I'm not going to speculate with you—"

"But I can get in there and ask questions. I can do some checking for you—"

"Oh, hell no, Kimberly. Absolutely not," he barked, wanting to throttle her but wondering if it was the alcohol making her reckless. "Okay?"

She sucked in her lips, thoughts working behind her eyes, then nodded.

"Hey," he said, pulling her attention back to him. "How drunk are you?'

A slow smile spread over her face. "Why?"

"Because I don't mind fucking you when you're tipsy, but not drunk."

"Oh, I'm definitely just tipsy—"

Breathing a sigh of relief, he scooped her into his arms and carried her up the stairs where he proceeded to show her just how much fun tipsy sex could be.

23

Kimberly made her way to Bob's office the next morning. Kyle's words about Kilton Pharmaceuticals ending
up on the streets of Hope City still rang in her ears.
Worrying her bottom lip as she walked, she wondered
how to keep interviewing employees for human-
interest stories while considering if they were involved
in something illegal. It also crossed her mind that if
Kyle's investigation proved true, Kilton Pharmaceuticals
would once again take a deserved hit in the media.

Along the way, she waved toward a few of the warehouse workers that she had met before. As she passed
by Tammy's door, the woman looked up, smiled widely,
and waved. She smiled in return but wondered if
Tammy could see the uncertainty on her face as she
thought back to Kyle's concerns that someone here had
tipped off the thieves.

"Good morning," she said. "I was... um... just
looking for Bob."

"Bob is probably still in a meeting," Tammy said,

then glanced at her watch. "Well, he might be getting out by now. Instead of going back out to the warehouse, go up to the third floor and I'll bet you'll catch him."

Thanking her, she jogged up the stairs to the third floor, remembering Niles' office was here. Just as Tammy predicted, a door opened and several people walked out. Bob caught her eye and smiled widely.

"Hey, neighbor. What brings you here? Still looking for some more stories?"

"Now that I decided to showcase many of the people who work here, it seems like I'm always finding a story." She smiled as a few other people walked past them and then lowered her voice. "I wanted to find you to see if you were okay after yesterday. I know you weren't expecting to be questioned by the police on your front stoop."

"Hey, it was no problem. He's got a job to do, and I respect that. He was there. I was there. It just turned out to be the right time to have a little chat."

Smiling, she placed her hand on his arm and gave a little squeeze. "You're the best, Bob. Thank you. Well, I'm gonna head back down to the warehouse. I've got an interview with a couple of drivers today." With a nervous smile, she headed back to the stairs.

Niles and Porter walked out of the conference room, both moving directly to Bob.

"I couldn't help but overhear, Bob," Niles said. "What did she mean by the police on your front stoop?"

"Kimberly is dating the detective that's in charge of the drugs stolen from the Kilton van," Bob said.

"You're kidding," Porter said, his mouth hanging open, looking between Niles and Bob.

"Is that a problem?" Bob asked.

Smiling widely, Niles shook his head. "No, I shouldn't think it's a problem. Not at all."

"What was she saying about one of our drivers?" Porter asked.

"She said she was going to interview him."

"Is she investigating now as well?" Porter continued pressing.

"I'm sure she's just looking for more employees to write about," Niles said. "Well, gentlemen, if you'll excuse me, I've got work to do." He turned and headed down the hall.

Porter and Bob walked to the elevator, neither speaking. Stepping out on the first floor, both men caught sight of Kimberly near the back doors, talking to Charlie. The two men looked at each other silently, then parted ways, each heading to their own office.

"I can't imagine how scary it must've been for you," Kimberly said to Charlie. "You've been driving for Kilton for a long time."

"Yes, Ma'am. Never had anything like that happened before."

"It's my understanding that while your job might not seem dangerous there are more and more thefts of pharmaceutical vans. The street value of the drugs that you transport between Kilton and pharmacies has a huge value."

Shaking his head, Charlie's brow scrunched. "I wouldn't know about that, Ma'am. I just know I've never been held up before."

"Do you think they were waiting for you?"

"They seemed to know what they were doing. Had guns and everything."

"Has it changed how you feel about your job? Do you still want to keep being a driver, or have you thought of something else you'd rather do for the company?"

"I used to work in the warehouse, Ma'am. I didn't mind that because I like to have a big area to work in... something that's not too closed in. But I really love being a driver. I don't mean that it's some kind of job I can slack off with. No, Ma'am. We have a schedule to stick to, deliveries to make, and we have to be careful with what we're carrying. But I like being outdoors. I never wanted to be a long-haul truck driver, but I surely love being on the roads in Hope City."

Smiling, she asked if she could take his picture for the Faces of Hope City, snapping it as soon as he agreed. "I don't know who all I'll be able to showcase in the material for Kilton, but I'm so glad I had a chance to talk to you today."

As they started to part, Charlie looked to the side and said, "Here's somebody you want to talk to. This is Joe, my partner."

She observed the other man with a small bandage on

his forehead, noting his gaze darted between her and Charlie, his expression proclaiming he would rather be anywhere than talking to her. With her bright smile, she walked over. "Joe, how nice to meet you. I hope you're feeling better."

"Uh… yeah… yes," he muttered.

"I was just talking to Charlie about the holdup. That must've been terrifying for you. Were you able to help the police in identifying the thieves?"

His eyes widened as he jerked his head back and forth. "No! They had masks."

"Oh, that's right. But they separated the two of you, didn't they? Charlie on one side of the van and you on the other. I wonder why they did that?"

"Couldn't say."

Charlie, still standing nearby, piped up, "You must've been brave, I'll give you that. I could hear y'all talking on the other side."

"Oh, really?" Turning her attention back to Joe, she cocked her head to the side and adopted a wide-eyed expression that she hoped looked more like awe than interest. "What were you talking about? Were you threatening them or telling them to leave you alone?" Giving her head a little shake, she added, "I can't imagine what I'd say to someone holding a gun on me!"

"I don't remember much," Joe mumbled.

"Well, I was just telling Charlie that I know how much street value those drugs were worth, and whoever robbed you must've known what they were doing and had a plan." Joe's gaze jumped to hers, his eyes widening ever so slightly. "I'm just so glad you weren't hurt more seriously."

Saying goodbye, she walked back through the warehouse, her insides quaking as she once again waved toward a few of the workers that she had met. *I would just bet Joe knows something.* Walking along the sidewalk between the buildings as she headed back to her office, she held her phone and dictated some of her impressions, never realizing how many eyes could be on her from the windows of the various buildings.

Kyle climbed the steps to the second floor of the rundown rowhouse. Just like his observations of the architecture of the old townhouses, this one was no different. Room in the front from the street, leading to the kitchen. Stairs in the middle, a couple of bedrooms on the second floor. Only this one hadn't been flipped. No renovations. No updates. In fact, he wasn't sure it had been cleaned this century.

Alex had his back, keeping an eye on the people on the first floor. Walking into the bedroom toward the back alley, he found the man he was looking for. A card table sat in the center, an old towel thrown on top.

Lifting an eyebrow, he grinned. "You gettin' ready for a card game, Marquee?"

"Yeah, Detective McBride. Just gonna be me and a few of my friends having a little game of poker."

"Poker, huh? And why the hell did your mama give you a name like Marquee?"

"Said she knew my name was gonna be all lit up one of these days." He laughed loudly, his open mouth exposing rotted teeth from years of using meth.

Kyle shook his head. "Jesus, man." Inclining his head toward the table, he said, "I take it you don't want me to lift that towel up to see your... *poker chips*."

Marquee's face fell, giving him a hound-dog appearance. "Aw, man. You got better stuff to do today than bust me. I got a few dime bags, that's all. That's not even enough to waste your time doing paperwork to haul me in."

"Word on the street is that you might know about some additives to put into your bags."

Shaking his head emphatically, Marquee replied, "I don't add nothin' to my shit."

"But you hear who does?"

Marquee scrunched his nose as though smelling something unpleasant, which Kyle found odd considering the entire house reeked of rotten garbage.

"I don't want no trouble."

Kyle said nothing, letting his silence speak for him.

"Shee-it," Marquee finally said on an exhale. "There's a place up on Baxter. From talk, there's someone there who gets the good stuff. Name is Raffie or somethin' like that. Sells huge to some major dealers. Hear he rakes in the money without getting his hands dirty."

"You ought to know, Marquee. Everyone in this business gets their hands dirty." Turning, he walked back down the stairs, the sound of Marquee's cackle turning into a cough ringing in his ears. Collecting Alex as they walked back outside, he sucked in a deep breath, needing to clear his lungs and nostrils of the stench.

"Get anything?" Alex asked.

"Yeah," he replied as he climbed into his truck. "We're heading to Baxter. Seems like Raphael might be who we're looking for." He called in for a pickup of Marquee, knowing the officers would get the bags Marquee was working on. Waiting until they showed, he gave them directions. A few minutes later, they walked out with Marquee in handcuffs and evidence bags filled with what Kyle was sure would be heroin, either pure or laced with something. Knowing Marquee, they'd be laced with something cheap just to make his heroin go a little further.

Pulling away from the curb, he and Alex traded one run-down area of town for another. Parking a block away from his destination, he glanced around, knowing Alex was doing the same. It didn't matter that they were both in jeans that had seen better days, faded T-shirts, jackets, and boots, or that their hair was long and their tats were showing. To many, they would fade into the background, but to the people that hustled this part of town, they'd still stand out as police.

As though the fates were smiling down on them today, it didn't take long to spy Raphael walking down the street.

"Looks like he doesn't have a fuckin' care in the world," Alex said.

Grinning, Kyle opened his door. "Let's give him something to fuckin' care about."

Raphael twisted around and saw them coming up

behind him, then took off running down the block, darting into an alley. With no words needed between them, Kyle and Alex separated while still in pursuit. Kyle took the more direct route, following Raphael into the alley.

Their prey was just turning the corner at the end of the alley when Kyle observed him tossing a bag to the side. Knowing Alex had everything under control, he jerked a glove out of his pocket and stopped long enough to snatch up the bag of pills. Racing around the corner, he heard a loud crash and 'umph'. Raphael was face down on the pavement, Alex securing his hands behind his back.

"You ain't got nothing—"

"Shut it," Alex barked, then looked up at Kyle and grinned when he saw the plastic bag of pills in his grip. Alex stood and hauled Raphael to his feet.

"Well, well, I figured we'd spend half the day looking for you and the other half trying to find where you had your stash. And here you were walking right down the fuckin' street with this shit in your pocket. Must be our lucky day."

"Fuck you," Raphael growled.

"It'd be luckier if we didn't have to be in the stinkin' alley with the garbage," Alex muttered.

"You talking about the garbage in the cans over here or the garbage you got standing right in front of you?" Kyle asked, dropping the plastic baggie of pills into an evidence bag. Looking up, he said, "We're hauling you in while we get these pills analyzed. You can save yourself a lot of hassle by going ahead and telling me what I got."

"Fuck you," Raphael repeated.

"I knew you were a dumb shit, but I figured you'd made it this far having some smarts. Looks like you don't even have that." He held the other man's gaze for a moment. Raphael was clear-eyed, his clothes clean and looking fairly new. Dangling the bag in his hand, he said, "You're clean. You're not using the shit you peddle, but if this turns out to be what I think it is, you'd be smart to start talking."

Raphael said nothing.

"If I call for a team to do a sweep of your apartment building and come up with the rest of the shit, you lose making a deal." He waited a few seconds and watched as the wheels began turning behind Raphael's eyes. "I'm telling you, man, I don't just want these pills off the streets, I want the ones higher up calling the shots. That ain't you, I know that much."

"Shit, man, I just get the stuff and move it on."

"You process it? You crush it and add it before *moving it on?*"

Raphael shook his head, his hair slinging back and forth. "No! The people that buy the shit can do what they want to with it."

"Like Marquee?"

Raphael's eyes jumped up to his. "Shit! That fucker gave me up?"

"Doesn't matter how we got you, we got you. And what you've gotta decide is what the fuck you're going to do."

They waited another minute, then Kyle growled. The stench of the alley following on the heels of the stench of Marquee's building had him lose his patience. Pulling out his phone, he called for backup.

"I didn't say I wasn't gonna let you know anything," Raphael bit out, his jaw hard.

"I don't think you get it. You're not calling the shots. And we're not standing in this fuckin' alley any longer. So, I got officers gonna do a sweep of your building, and you're coming down to the station where your ass is going to be in a chair while we have a little chat. And on the way, you can think real hard about how you want this to go down. 'Cause I got no problem nailing you for everything even though I want the higher-ups."

As soon as the officers arrived, they directed some to the apartment building and another car took Raphael down to the station. Scrubbing his hand over his face, Kyle said, "Let's go to the lab and see what we can get before we question him."

Glad that the lab was not overly crowded, they headed directly to one of the technicians. It didn't pass his notice that the antiseptic odor of the lab seemed daisy-fresh after having been in the stench of Raphael's and Marquee's residences.

The technician smiled as they approached. "What can I do for you?"

Alex handed him the bag as Kyle said, "Just need an identification off of these for now."

Nodding, the technician looked at the pills under a microscope, jotting down the individual notations. He grinned as he lifted his head and said, "I take it you're hoping these are from Kilton Pharmaceuticals since they had that van robbed? Well, it's your lucky day... these are definitely from Kilton Pharmaceuticals."

"I notice they're all the same kind. Can you tell us what the drug is?"

Rolling his eyes, he said, "Geez, come here sometime and ask me a hard question. What you've got here is their brand of fentanyl."

Alex had stepped to the side to take a phone call and Kyle felt his lungs deflate as the air rushed from them. He thanked the technician and turned to his partner.

Alex grinned as he disconnected his call. "Officers on the scene at Raphael's apartment building have discovered boxes labeled with Kilton Pharmaceuticals. We'll need to cross-check, but it looks like we may have found what came from the stolen van."

24

Kyle stalked into the interview room, slapping a folder onto the top of the table while sliding into the seat opposite of Raphael. Not in the mood to drag things out further, he flipped open the folder and began. "The drugs that were in your possession have been identified as being from Kilton Pharmaceuticals. The boxes of drugs that were in your apartment have been identified as being from the Kilton Pharmaceuticals van theft. Your fingerprints are on the bag that was in your possession. Your fingerprints are on the boxes, and we have identified from other fingerprints several of your comrades. They are currently being rounded up or are already in custody. The drugs that were in your possession in the bag have been identified as fentanyl. Right now, you're looking at multiple charges and a long stay as a welcome guest of the prison system."

Snorting, Raphael leaned back in his seat. "Then what the fuck am I doing here? Throw me in jail and be done with it. It's not like I can tell you anything that's gonna get me out of this."

"You're partially right. But just how long you're going to be a welcome guest could very much have everything to do with what you start telling me."

Raphael sat quiet, and Kyle took that as a positive sign.

"We know you're part of a larger scheme. What I want to know is who else can be connected above you. I'm not convinced you stole the truck or were driving it the day the Kilton Pharmaceuticals van was robbed. But that was armed robbery and a man was injured. I'll have no problem pinning that on you."

"It wasn't me!"

"Then give me something to go on."

"Hell, you think everybody sits around the table and plans this shit? It's not like I got some memo telling me who's doing what."

Kyle looked at Alex sitting next to him and grinned. "I like that. A memo." Turning back toward Raphael, his smile dropped. "When I get finished throwing everything at you that I think will stick—plus some that might not—you're going to wish you had a fuckin' memo."

Raphael slumped in his seat. "I wasn't in that truck. Wasn't part of the robbery. I was told that someone was gettin' shit to me. I start selling and keep a percentage."

"Honor among thieves? How the hell did someone know you were giving them the right amount?"

"Because the person talking to me knew exactly how much shit was given to me, what I can sell it for, and what their take was going to be after I had my cut. They had it figured out to a fuckin' penny. Plus, I got the feeling they were the kind of people that I shouldn't fuck with. Fine with me... I was gettin' plenty out of the deal."

"Who delivered the shit to you?"

"Just got a first name."

"And?"

"Dude named Jerry. Don't know his last name, but they call him Jerry D."

Shooting Alex a quick glance, he stood and walked out of the interview room, pissed that he hadn't brought everything in with him. Moving to the evidence board, he looked at the small notes they had tacked to the side. Joe Parson's brother's name was Jeremiah. Jeremiah Dempsy. Grabbing his phone, he called the lab. "The boxes brought in from Kilton Pharmaceuticals that we got from Raphael's place this morning. I know you're going to check fingerprints through more databases, but was there a match with Jeremiah Dempsy? He's had priors, so he's in the system."

Waiting for them to call back, he grinned when he gained an affirmative. Back in the interview room, he sat down and pierced Raphael with a hard gaze. "Okay, so we know who delivered the boxes to you. Now tell us how the payments go."

"I get a call. Shit's dropped off by Jerry D. I get another call and only deal with one person. They tell me where to meet, and I start making sales. As soon as money comes to me, I turn around and start paying."

"Seems like a lot of trust. He's actually trusting you to keep making payments?"

"Fuck, man. These people are connected. I want to keep breathing, I pay."

"Got a name?"

Scrubbing his hand over his face, Raphael grimaced. Sighing heavily, he said, "I don't know his whole name. He goes by Solten."

Kyle shot another glance toward Alex and nodded. *Finally, the fuckin' loose ends are coming together.*

Kyle and Alex had interviewed Roger Solten after Jon Ying mentioned his contact. They'd run a check on him that came back clean. At the time, they just wanted to verify that Hope City Linen and Uniform Service did own the truck that Mr. Ying had reported stolen. Confirming that, they'd had no other contact with him.

Now, pulling into the HC Linen building visitor parking, Kyle looked through the windshield at the warehouse-sized brick building. It was near the end of the business day, and employees were starting to leave through the main front doors. Not wanting to miss him, they hustled toward the front.

Moving to the reception desk, Alex smiled at the woman sitting on the stool, tapping on her cell phone. Her gaze lifted to Alex, then dropped to her phone before doing a quick double-take back up to him, her smile widening.

"We need to speak to Roger Solten."

"I don't think I've seen him today. Hang on," she replied, turning to a computer screen on the counter. With a few taps of her fingers on the keyboard, she shook her head slowly. "No, he's not in. In fact, he hasn't been in for two days."

Alex offered a chin lift and they turned to leave.

"Normally you could catch him after work at Hopkins Gym, down on Twenty-First Street." She shrugged and flashed a mega-watt smile. "I could show you if you want." She leaned her forearms on the counter, bending forward, creating the planned effect of pushing her breasts together, cleavage now showing at the neckline of her T-shirt. "I like to go and... work out, if you know what I mean."

Alex placed his hands on his hips, pulling his jacket open just enough to show the badge clipped to his belt. "Thanks, but I think we've got it."

Her gaze had dropped to his badge then back to his face as her mouth fell open.

Walking back out to the truck, Kyle chuckled. "You like doing that shit, don't you?"

"Not a lot of perks in this job, but sometimes it's nice to either get someone talking or get 'em to shut up by just looking at the badge."

They checked the gym and went by his apartment but didn't find him. By then, their shift was over and Kyle dropped Alex off at the precinct parking lot. "We'll pick this back up tomorrow morning. Have a good evening."

Alex waved as he climbed into his SUV and Kyle headed home. He had received a text earlier from

Kimberly letting him know that she was fixing dinner. Pushing aside thoughts of work, he grinned. He'd eat whatever she fixed, knowing it would be good, but he was especially hoping she had whipped cream for dessert.

Dressed all in dark clothing, a man slipped to the back door of the rowhouse and unscrewed the lightbulb by the door. Sliding back into the shadows, he waited for several minutes to make sure that a nosy neighbor had not seen and called the cops. The neighborhood remained quiet except for a few cars occasionally going down the street, a dog barking in the distance, and crunching near the garbage cans, indicating the possibility of mice, if not rats.

Using a crowbar, he popped open the back door and quickly moved into the house. The clock on the stove gave slight illumination to the kitchen and he walked silently into the living room and rounded the bottom of the staircase. Taking each step carefully, glad there was no squeak, he made it to what he thought was the top. Miscalculating, he stumbled on the last step, grabbing the banister to keep from falling. Heart pounding, he stayed rooted to the spot, barely breathing, listening for any movement. Not hearing a sound other than a slight snore, he continued toward the master bedroom.

He would've flipped on the light switch if necessary, knowing the brightness would temporarily blind his prey, but with curtains only partially closed over the window, moonlight and streetlight illuminated the lump in the bed. Pulling out his weapon, he stepped closer. Just then, the floor groaned slightly with his weight, and the sleeping owner roused.

Startled, he fired without taking proper aim. A cry from underneath the covers met his ears and he fired again while growling, "Shit, Kimberly. Shit." Whirling around, he raced down the steps, shoving his gun into his pocket. He continued through the first floor to the door of the kitchen. As soon as he was outside, he ran down several alleys until he came to his parked vehicle. Climbing inside, he wheezed, trying to catch his breath while his insides quaked. Swallowing deeply, he attempted to slow his racing heart, concentrating on breathing.

Knowing he needed to get out of the area, he fumbled with the ignition before placing his still-shaking hands on the steering wheel. Pulling out onto the road, he drove with caution, not wanting to bring undue attention to himself. *I shot her.* A nervous grunt erupted from deep in his chest at the thought. Scrubbing his hand over his face, he realized he had no idea if she was alive or dead. If she was still alive, at least she wouldn't be able to identify him.

Dragging in another shaky breath, he hated what he'd done, but was glad it was over. He was surprised they asked him to do it, but then they trusted him. Heartbeat settling as the adrenaline slowed, he continued driving, each mile allowing him to breathe easier.

Kyle jerked awake at the sound of his phone. Used to middle-of-the-night calls, he snagged his cell phone from the nightstand. Seeing Carter's name on the ID, his heart lurched, and he barked, "Talk to me. Is it Tara? Colleen?" He flipped on the lamp next to the bed and stood, immediately stalking toward the closet.

"No, it's neither of them. It's Kimberly."

His chest depressed as air rushed from his lungs, and he grabbed hold of the doorframe to steady his legs. Brow furrowed, he asked, "What? What the hell are you talking about?"

"Just tell me this first, Kyle. Do you know where she is?"

"Yeah, I'm fuckin' looking at her right now!" His gaze bore straight at her as she sat up in his bed staring at him, confusion marring her expression.

25

Kimberly glanced at the driver's side of the truck cab but chose to remain silent. The intense emotions pouring off Kyle filled the cab, and his white-knuckled grip on the steering wheel caused her to wonder how it did not snap under the pressure. Anger and fear combined into a rage that made her afraid. Not afraid for herself but for whoever he let loose on, depending on what they found once they arrived back at her rowhouse.

"You should've stayed at my place."

Ice dripped from each word. Keeping calm, she replied, "I need to be here. If Bob needs me—"

"He's already been taken to the hospital."

She sucked in a quick breath. The idea of her neighbor being shot while sleeping rocked through her once again. Kyle had not given her much information, but from what she discerned from Carter's call, the police had reason to believe that someone was after her. *But then why go into Bob's house? Why shoot him?* She wanted to ask but knew Kyle wasn't in the mood to talk. Turning her head, she looked out the passenger window as they hurried onto her street.

Another gasp left her lips as she viewed the number of police cars lining the area in front of the row houses. The early morning light was just beginning to cut through the night, casting the entire block with an eerie glow. Yellow caution tape had been strung up from the edge of her house to the road and around the corner, keeping the gathering onlookers at bay. Bob's front door was open, and several people were going in and out, blue paper booties on their feet and gloves on their hands.

Kyle turned the corner by Bob's house and parked in the middle of the blocked-off street. From here, she could see that the caution tape extended down the sidewalk by the side of Bob's house and around the back alley to where their back doors were located. Questions flew through her mind, but she said nothing, shock making it difficult to draw enough oxygen into her lungs.

Kyle jumped down from the driver's seat, barking a one-word order. "Stay."

Biting her tongue to keep from screaming, *I'm not a dog!'*, she jerked her head around and watched as he stalked toward Carter, Alex, and another man. Sighing heavily, she knew that he was right to tell her to stay in the vehicle. The stark reminder that Bob's home was a crime scene deflated her irritation. *He was shot... in bed.* Closing her eyes, she sent up a hasty prayer.

The four men continued to talk, but her gaze stayed

mostly pinned on to Kyle. His hands alternated between fists planted on his hips and lifting one to tear it through his hair. He finally dropped his chin to his chest and stared at his boots for a minute, and she continued to observe as the other three men shot glances toward her. Uncertain if she should disobey his order to stay, the choice was taken from her when he finally turned quickly and headed straight to her.

Opening her door, he said, "It doesn't look like anyone broke into your place. Let's get you off the street and into your home."

Nodding silently, she allowed him to assist her down and dropped her keys into his outstretched hand. Avoiding the front, he led her to the back and through her fenced patio. It did not escape her notice that Carter, Alex, and the other man surrounded her completely, providing a protective barrier between her and anyone else. *But why?*

Kyle opened her back door and she was hustled inside, the door closed behind them. Following him through her laundry room and into the kitchen, she waited until he stopped and turned around to face her. "Kyle, honey, what's going on?"

He stepped directly into her space and cupped her face with his hands. She held his eyes before he tilted her head down and placed his lips on her forehead, mumbling, "I've got you."

Uncertain of his meaning, she didn't have time to ask before he turned to the side, wrapped his arm around her shoulders, and pulled her close. He nodded toward Carter, and she turned her attention to him.

"Kimberly, you know Alex, and this is Evan, my partner," Carter began.

She offered a tremulous smile to the other detectives, clasping her hands together in front of her, glad for Kyle's presence.

"Here's what we know. A call was placed to 9-1-1 a little after two a.m. from a man who identified himself as Bob Trogdon, saying an intruder had shot him. He gave his address and police and rescue were dispatched. Evan and I were on call, and we got here right after the paramedics."

"Is he... will he be..."

"He was alive and conscious, able to talk when we got here, and he's been transported to Hope City General. He took one shot to his shoulder and another clipped his side."

A slight growl rumbled against her side, and she twisted her head around to look up at Kyle.

Carter continued, drawing her attention back to him. "Bob was able to give us a very quick statement before they took him away. The intruder did not turn on any lights, but Bob heard a noise and moved. I would guess that either the intruder was an incredibly bad shot, incredibly nervous, or incredibly stupid by not clearly seeing his victim."

"Or a combination of all three," Kyle mumbled under his breath, drawing nods from the other three detectives.

She sucked in her lips, rubbing them back and forth as she tried to make sense of what they were telling her. Finally, shaking her head slowly, she said, "I'm sorry, I just don't understand. I can't imagine why anyone would be after Bob, and you all are acting as though this had something to do with me."

The other men shared a look, and she twisted her head back up toward Kyle again. She spied fire in his eyes but was unable to interpret the expression. Carter called her name, and she gave her attention back to him.

"Please understand that we'll be questioning Bob more, but he was very lucid although in pain when we talked to him. He agrees that he cannot think of anyone who would want to harm him, but what he was very clear about was what the intruder said."

"And that was?" Her voice was barely above a whisper.

"Shit, Kimberly."

As she attempted to decipher the words, she shook her head slowly. "I… I don't understand…"

"Babe," Kyle said softly. He turned their bodies so that they were facing each other and bent closer. "Why would an intruder call Bob 'Kimberly' unless he thought he was talking to you?"

She jerked, but Kyle's hands about her waist tightened to hold her in place. Continuing to shake her head, she repeated, "I don't understand."

"We have to look at all possible scenarios, Kimberly," Carter said. "And one of those is that the intruder was not actually after Bob. It was dark in the room, and he simply fired at whoever was in the bed."

Eyes wide, she gasped. "So, they might have been after me? They just went to the wrong house?" Understanding slowly dawned on her, and her eyes bugged out even further. "Me?" She shook her head with vigor. "No, no! That makes no sense!"

"Sweetheart, listen to me," Kyle said, pulling her close to his chest, cupping the back of her head. "We don't know, but we have to look at all possibilities."

"But I'm nobody. Why would anybody want to shoot me?" Her legs felt like jelly, but she hated to show a sign of weakness.

"Let's sit down," Kyle said, and led her out of the kitchen into the living room. They sat on the sofa while Carter and Evan perched on the chairs.

"I saw you've got coffee pods in there," Alex said, jerking his head back toward the kitchen. "How about I make you some coffee?"

Too stunned to think clearly, she was aware that Kyle nodded, and Alex returned to the kitchen.

"Okay, babe, this is killing me to think of anyone after you, but let's break this down. Is there any reason you can think of why someone would want you to stay out of something?"

Shoulders slumping, she shook her head. "I don't do anything. I go to work. I come home or go to your place. Occasionally, I get with friends."

Carter asked, "I know you recently met with some women at the Cardboard Cottages. Did you talk to anyone else? Give your full name? Give anyone your contact information?"

Continuing to shake her head, she replied, "I only talk to those women, and we only use first names. They know me as Kimberly, but that's all. No phone number. No address. Nothing. They talked about their lives, and

I asked a few questions, but that's all that came from those conversations."

"Okay, then what about your work?" Kyle asked.

"You already know about that. I've talked to people in just about every department at Kilton. But all I'm asking about is their jobs, what they like about it, that kind of thing."

"Who at Kilton knows you're doing this?" Evan asked.

Lifting her hands to the side, she sighed. "Who doesn't know? All the vice presidents, most of the department supervisors, the people in my office and then, of course, anyone I've talked to. Again, there's nothing untoward about any of it. I've met some interesting people, and I've had a few interviews where I was bored out of my mind." Turning back to Kyle, she stared into his intense blue-eyed and squeezed his hand. "I just don't think this can be about me."

He looked over to where Carter and Evan were sitting. "Where are you next door?"

"Forensics is seeing what they can get. If the guy was smart, he was wearing gloves, but just in case, we'll get fingerprints around the back door where he broke in and the railing on the stairs. It doesn't appear that anything was taken or disturbed, so we assume that it was a hit and not a failed robbery."

"Robbery wouldn't make any sense anyway. Bob doesn't keep anything special in his house." She chewed on her lip as she ran possibilities through her mind.

"What about drugs? What about the possibility that

Bob is involved in drugs? Could he have something in his house?"

Before she had a chance to refute Kyle's question, Carter spoke up. "Forensic is doing a drug sweep as well."

"There's no way he was involved in drug theft! It's not like we hang out all the time, but I've been inside his house. I've known him for four years!" she defended.

Alex walked back into the room, and she looked up, surprised that he was not carrying coffee mugs. Instead, he had a piece of paper in his hand.

"Kimberly, you had mail lying next to the coffee maker, and I couldn't help but notice it. It's addressed to you, but it's not your address. It's Bob's address."

Waving her hand dismissively, she nodded. "Oh, yeah. HR at work initially put my address in as his. We get very little mail but, occasionally, a letter will come for me with his address on it. Bob always just brings the mail over to me when that happens."

No one spoke, but the room vibrated with electricity that she could not define. Looking between the four men, it was as though their thoughts snapped between each other. Suddenly, realization dawned, and she sucked in a quick breath. "What are you thinking? That the intruder got our addresses mixed up and went to the wrong home?"

Kyle jumped to his feet and began pacing the room, his hand squeezing the back of his neck. "This supports the idea that Bob was not the intended victim... Kimberly was. And that means the intruder was either someone from Kilton or was directed by someone from there." He whirled and stared at her. "Can you think of anyone you talk to that would've been spooked?"

"Other than questioning Tammy, Charlie, and Joe about the van robbery, there hasn't been anything out of the ordinary."

Jerking back as though hit in the gut, Kyle stared. "You questioned them about the robbery?"

"Yeah, honey. I thought it was interesting. I read an article that said that thefts of pharmaceutical vans were on the increase, and I wanted to know what they thought about it and if it made them want a different job."

She could have sworn he was counting to ten under his breath again, but Carter grabbed her hand and gently pulled her into the kitchen.

"Let's give him a minute to chill. Alex will know what to say to him."

She looked up at Carter, his kind eyes staring at her warmly. It dawned on her that as Kyle's brother-in-law, he could have that same title with her if she stayed with Kyle. She placed her hand on his arm and asked, "So much of this has been about me, but I really need to know about Bob. I can't believe he was shot, but I feel horrible if it was supposed to be me instead of him—"

"Get that outta your mind, Kimberly. The only person who did anything wrong is the one who shot him."

She nodded slowly, letting out a breath. Before she had a chance to say anything else, Kyle stalked into the kitchen. He moved directly to her, wrapping his arms around her, and placed a kiss on the corner of her eye before resting his lips against her forehead. "Pack what you need to get out of here, sweetheart. Clothes, toiletries, whatever. I don't want you staying here now."

Feeling a little lost, she sighed. "Okay. I need to call work and let them know I won't be in today." While Kyle stayed downstairs and talked to the other detectives, she went upstairs and packed. Not having any idea how long she would be gone, she filled one small suitcase with clothes, shoes, and toiletries, and she made sure to grab her e-reader and phone charger. Sitting on the side of her bed, she called her office.

"Marcus? Hey, it's Kimberly. Is John in? He wasn't answering his phone."

"No, he hasn't been in yet today. In fact, Helen was looking for him earlier."

"Oh, okay. I was just going to tell him that I'm not going to be in today either."

"Are you okay? You taking a sick day?"

"Let's just say I'm taking a mental health day."

Marcus chuckled. "I hear you, girl. Everybody needs those once in a while. If John comes in later, I'll let him know you're out today."

"Thanks. I'll see you tomorrow." Disconnecting, she looked up as Kyle walked into the room and glanced toward her suitcase.

"Is this all?"

"It'll do for now." She stood and moved straight to him, wrapping her arms around his waist. They stood embracing for a long moment, silently offering strength to each other.

Finally, whispering against her hair, he said, "Let's get you home, babe."

Technically, she was in her home but wisely kept her mouth shut. If he wanted her in his house, that was just where she wanted to be.

2 6

Kyle left Kimberly at his townhouse after helping her pack necessities and anything else she might want to have. She had not attempted to talk him into letting her stay at her place—not that she would have had a chance of doing so anyway. He hated to leave her, but since she was now designated as the intended victim of Bob's shooting, he was able to get an officer to sit outside his home.

Now, back at the precinct, he was forced to endure his captain's speech on letting the detectives in charge handle their investigation while he and Alex needed to continue theirs. While the captain agreed that most likely the two were linked, he warned Kyle to watch his step.

"You've worked too long and too hard to fuck it up now. If you give me the slightest provocation, I'll pull you from the case."

He nodded but gritted his teeth as he walked back into the workroom. Alex came over, clapping him on the shoulder. "I get it, Kyle, I do. You want nothing more than to tear Kilton apart piece by piece. But that's not going to help you find who's behind the stolen drugs or who called a hit on Kimberly."

Even though he knew what happened, hearing the words *'called a hit on Kimberly'* leave his partner's mouth sent shivers down Kyle's spine.

News traveled fast, and he fielded calls from Sean, Brody, Brock, and Kallie as well as his dad. Assuring everyone that Kimberly was fine, he had to assure them that he was also.

"Son, I get it, but you have to stay cool," his dad warned. "I can't tell you to not make it personal because it is, but you want to get them. That's more important than your personal vendetta. Chauncey won't call you now... he called me instead. But you've got his support."

Finally shoving his phone into his pocket, he planted his hands on his hips and stared at the evidence board. His eyes drifted over what they already had. Alex sidled up next to him and remained quiet while Kyle talked out loud.

"Someone knew the driver's route. That would come under Niles and Porter. Someone also knew how to get an employee address. HR is run by Sidney Kilton. The van theft and truck used can be traced back to a politician who is getting money to be supportive of pharmaceutical companies. Finance is run by Thomas Kilton. So, are we looking at more than one? Are we looking at people stealing drugs and a separate group of the Kiltons who want to protect the company's name?"

"We've got to get Roger Solten. I think if we can get

him, we can find out who in Kilton Pharmaceuticals is next in line."

Scrubbing his hand over his face, now wishing he had eaten breakfast before having three cups of coffee, he nodded. As much as he wanted to go home and just sit with Kimberly, staring at her to make sure she was fine, he knew Alex was right. "Okay, let's go. But I gotta hit a drive-thru breakfast on our way to Hope City Linen."

Three hours later, his stomach was no longer churning but they were no closer to finding Roger. He had not reported to work again. Was not at his apartment. Not at the gym. And not at the local watering hole that one of his co-workers said he liked to frequent. He swung through another drive-thru, this time for burgers and fries for them and the others in the precinct before heading back to the station.

Crossing over one of the highway bridges in town, he flipped on his blinker, changed lanes, and curved onto the exit ramp. Alex didn't bother to ask where he was going, but Kyle said, "We're close, so I figure I might as well go check in with Manny."

The Cardboard Cottages loomed ahead as the two climbed from his truck. The early morning cool had already burned off, and the temperature was supposed to be mild. Casting his gaze around, he thought of the residents who would be sweltering in another month. Sighing heavily, he scrubbed his hand over his face at the desolation facing those who called the Cottages their home.

"You okay?" Alex asked as their feet crunched over the hard-packed ground.

"Just bogged down by the weight of it all. I sometimes feel like we're fighting a losing battle, but then I get to go to a real home at night." Alex nodded but remained silent, which Kyle appreciated.

The burn barrel was lit, not for warmth but as a place for some of the residents to burn their trash. It was not lost on Kyle that even in desolation, there could be the desire to make their situation better. Unfortunately, the stench of unwashed bodies and refuse still hung in the air.

Approaching, they nodded toward Manny, who aimed his wide smile toward them.

"Afternoon, Dee-tectives McBride and Freeman. You come to check on your old friend?"

"Manny," he greeted, noting a few others moving around in the distance. "Yeah, checking on an old friend and seeing if there was anything you might want to let us know about."

Manny cast his gaze around before lowering his voice. "Sometimes I think it's real boring around here in the Cottages. Same old thing every day."

"So, nothing new?" Alex asked.

"Well, dee-tectives, that's what's interesting about this place. You just never know what's going to pop up."

"Manny, don't got all day."

Manny chuckled and, as usual, the sound turned into a deep-chested cough.

"We can get you to a clinic if you'll go," Kyle offered.

"Don't like doctors much, but it's real neighborly of

you to offer," Manny managed to say as he overcame his cough. Lifting his hand, he scrubbed his fingers over his rough stubble and said, "Lots of medicine around here. That's one thing about the Cottages, you can always find some medicine."

Kyle shared a glance with Alex, then looked back toward Manny. "Any recent *medicine* show up around here?"

"Well, now that you mention it, Dee-tective, had us a new *doctor* come visit us. Now me, I don't have the money or the inclination for his medicine. But got a man at the far end of the Cottages that don't mind paying." He leaned forward, whispering as though telling a secret. "I don't think he's a full-time resident, you understand. He just likes being the... *doctor's assistant*." Chuckling at his humor, he fell into another fit of coughing.

Kyle and Alex gave him a moment to gain control of himself before Kyle asked, "Got a name for this assistant?"

"Now, you know, Dee-tective, we're not much on names around here. Leastwise, not full names."

"Would a hamburger and some french fries help your memory?"

Alex didn't even wait to see the wide-eyed interest hit Manny's face. He jogged back to the truck and grabbed one of the paper sacks, pulling out a wrapped hamburger and small bag of fries.

Manny scrubbed his hand over his scruffy chin and scratched, his eyes never leaving the food in Alex's hand. Nodding slowly, he said, "Just heard him called

Jerry." Reaching out his hand, he took the burger and fries, lifting his gaze to Kyle's. "'Preciate it." With the dip of his chin, he turned and walked back to his cardboard home.

Climbing back into his truck, Kyle drove around to the other side of the Cottages, parking where he could observe the tents with children playing outside. "I know I bought lunch for us and some of the others. Do you mind if I—"

"You don't need to ask."

Nodding, he reached behind the seat and grabbed the rest of the burgers and fries and headed toward the tents. As soon as he neared, he recognized two of the women that had talked to Kimberly. The blonde's eyes were suspicious as she darted her gaze between him and the children. The dark-haired woman lifted her chin, her hands on her hips as she stared at his approach.

"Ma'am," he greeted. "I was here the other day with my girlfriend, Kimberly. Just happen to be in the area and thought you and the kids might like some lunch. I know it's not as healthy as what she brought, but it's yours if you'd like."

"You're a cop," the dark-haired woman said, her voice more accusing than commenting.

Nodding, he agreed. "My name is Kyle."

"And what are you looking for?"

"Nothing, Ma'am. I had to talk to some of the people in the Cottages." He inclined his head to the side, indicating under the bridge. "I had the food and thought about you and the children."

"Mama, it smells good!"

Kyle looked down at the little boy staring up at the dark-haired woman and smiled. He waited, watching as she reached out her hand, caressed her son's cheek, and her hard expression softened.

"Okay, but you know what to say," she said.

The little boy ran over to Kyle, soon joined by three other children. Reaching into the bag, Kyle handed out hamburgers and french fries. Looking up at the two women, he said, "There's some more in the bag, plenty for you."

"Thank you," the blonde said. "Tell Kimberly we said hello."

"I will. Be safe, and if you ever need anything, call the police and you can ask for Detective McBride."

He started to turn away, but the dark-haired woman called him back. She held his gaze a long time, and neither wavered. Finally, she stepped a little closer and said, "You said the food is a gift. We appreciate it. Charity isn't always easy to accept, but I'll do anything for my kids." She licked her lips, hesitating, then added, "My brother has a job at Sal's Market. He's clean, works hard, and is saving money trying to get me, the kids, and him into a place. Most of the time he keeps his head down and his nose outta other people's business. Safer that way."

Kyle nodded slightly, not wanting to break the sliver of trust this woman seemed to be ready to hand him.

"He's seen a man around here that he knows is dealing. Told me and Margo to make sure we stay away and keep the kids away. He's also seen him go in and out of the apartment across the street from Sal's. He does everything he can to stay away from that. I want my kids away from that."

Realizing the gift she just gave him, his lips curved slightly. "I'll be sure to tell Kimberly you said hello, and we'll come back with some better food soon."

With a quick nod, she turned and walked back over to the children and Margo, and he turned to hurry back to the truck. Giving Alex the info, he waited as his partner grabbed the address for Sal's Market. Pulling away from the Cottages, he could not help but stare into the rearview mirror, wondering more about the life of those who called it home.

Back on the roads of Hope City, he followed Alex's directions. Jerry as well as Roger had been elusive, and he hoped this tip would pan out. Parking just down from the market, they watched the building across the street. Typical, old-city block of buildings. Storefronts on the lower floor, two or three floors of apartments above.

"There he is," Kyle noted thirty minutes later, seeing Jerry crossing the street heading toward his building. Alighting from his truck, Kyle followed from behind as Alex moved into the alley that ran behind the block. With no security on the front door, Kyle had no problem following Jerry, watching as he climbed the stairs to the third floor and entered an apartment at the end of the hall.

Approaching, he knocked on the door and identified himself. Hearing a crash from the inside, he shouldered the door open, popping the chain off the wooden frame. Entering, he spied Jerry's foot dangling over the living room windowsill as he climbed onto the fire escape. Racing after him, he tripped over some of the debris scattered about in the room. Cursing, he scrambled to the window and climbed out onto the metal landing. Following in pursuit, he pounded down the metal-grate stairs, gaining on the fleeing man. Just as Jerry leaped at the bottom to the alley, he was slammed up against the building by Alex.

"*Augh*," Jerry managed to mumble with his face pressed against the bricks.

Kyle called for backup. Hearing a noise to the side, he watched as two large rats scuttled away from the garbage bins in the alley. Shaking his head, he looked at Alex. "I've spent as much time in the dump with rats the last couple of days as I ever want to."

Alex laughed and forced Jerry to a seated position to wait. As soon as the officers arrived and hauled him off to the station, Kyle, Alex, and more officers searched his apartment, finding boxes labeled Kilton Pharmaceuticals. Boxes were open and some of the drugs on the table were crushed. Once HazMat transportation had taken possession of the drugs to deliver them to the lab and Kyle signed off on all the forms, they walked out of the building.

Making their way toward his truck, he glanced toward Sal's Market and saw a dark-haired man wearing a Sal's apron standing at the front, arms crossed over his chest, watching them. The man gave a barely perceptible nod, then turned back to the store.

"I'm glad you got to meet Aleeta and Margo," Kimberly said, lying in bed with Kyle, her naked body half draped over his. He had come home from work and told her about the progress on the case and his trip to the Cardboard Cottages. Having been home all day, she'd fixed dinner, which he wolfed down, commenting that he had missed lunch.

Both exhausted, they climbed into bed early but soon discovered they were not *too* tired. Long kisses led to hands roving. Before they knew it, he had kissed down her body, his lips between her legs, and she lost herself in the sensations. Reciprocating, she flipped him to his back, sliding her lips over his erection.

Licking, sucking, using her mouth as well as her hands, she worked his cock, feeling it swell even harder under her ministrations. He warned her that he was close, but she was too far gone to heed what he was saying. Suddenly, she found his cock no longer in her mouth as he dragged her body upward.

"I come, I come inside," he growled.

With him still on his back, she nestled the tip of his cock at her entrance, sliding down until he was fully sheathed in her warmth. His hands found her breasts, molding the plump flesh as he tweaked her nipples. Head thrown back, her fingernails scraped along the tattoos on his chest before she dropped her chin and her hair created a curtain around them as she clung to his shoulders. This man, this connection, was what she craved.

Her orgasm caused her to shudder as her sex pulsed around his cock. Forcing her eyes to stay open, she wanted to see his face. Not disappointed, he soon followed her, his cock thrusting until there was nothing left.

Crashing onto his chest, the words, "I love you," were forced from her lungs. For a split second she cringed, wondering if it was too soon to let him know how she felt, but his arms tightened, and she relaxed. She had no illusions that he would repeat the sentiment or that he even felt those words at the moment, and that was fine. She knew what was in her heart and had no problem letting him know.

They lay, arms and legs tangled as heartbeats slowed, breathing each other in. He rolled to the side, keeping his arms banded around her. Bringing one hand to her face, he brushed her hair back, keeping his gaze pinned on hers. He kissed her lightly, the barest touch of lips. Mumbling against her mouth, he whispered, "I love you too, Kimberly."

She loved it when he called her 'babe', but at that moment, she loved that he used her name.

Sleep still proved elusive, so they lay wrapped in each other's arms. That was when she told him that she was glad he'd gone to the Cottages.

"It was the right thing to do, but remember, I still don't want you to go by yourself. We'll go together."

She smiled at the thought, then looked up as he shifted slightly, leaning back so that he could stare into her face.

"I want you to move into my place."

She blinked, her brow scrunching. "I am here."

"No, I mean permanently. Bob will have no problem finding a new renter."

"Kyle, I don't know that this is the right time to make this kind of decision. Things are really intense right now. I know you're trying to protect me, but we need to make sure we're solid."

"This doesn't feel solid to you?"

"Yes, it does. But giving up my house means that I have no backup in case something goes south with us." Seeing him about to protest, she huffed. "I'm not saying it's going to. I'm just saying that I want to make a smart decision."

He cupped her face, his thumb sweeping over her cheek. He nodded slowly and said, "I can't argue with your logic, but I do want you here with me. And our situation is intense, but that doesn't make you and me any less right."

"How about I move in with you, but I don't give up my house right away? After all, I've already paid rent through this month."

Grinning, he rolled her to her back and nestled his hips between her thighs. "Perfect, babe. As always, you're perfect."

27

Kimberly walked into her office, glad to arrive early so that few people were there. So much had happened in the last few days that it had been hard to focus on her job. While at Kyle's home yesterday, she'd spent time typing up her notes on the interviews from personnel in research, development, quality management, sales, and finance. She also finished the interviews with the vice presidents and department supervisors. After completing each interview, she dropped it into the shared folder with John to await his approval.

Having gained permission from several to include them in her Faces of Hope City e-magazine, she had forwarded those to her editor. Chuck loved them and could not wait to start the new series.

Facing her today was the last of the interviews from Niles' department, including Tammy's, Charlie's, and Joe's interviews. She wanted to wait until Kyle's investigation was over. When he confided that they were certain someone from the inside was in on the theft of the pharmaceutical van, it put a damper on her enthusiasm.

Flopping into her chair, she dropped her purse and satchel onto the floor and leaned back. She had called Bob early that morning to find that he'd left the hospital and was staying with a friend. Promising to visit soon and bring food over once he was home, she felt disheartened that he was injured because of her.

Sighing, she rubbed her forehead to ease the dull headache that had begun and stared at her desk. She reached forward to turn on her desktop computer when her fingers froze in place. The files on her desk were skewed. She was certainly haphazard about many things but remembered when she'd left the other day she had taken the time to straighten her desk.

Leaning forward, she flipped open the file and looked at the contents. Everything seemed in order, and yet, she could not shake the feeling that someone had been through her interview notes.

"Good morning."

She startled and looked up in surprise as Marcus walked past her, his hands full with two coffee cups.

He sat one on her desk and grinned. "Guess who's discovered a new coffee shop around the corner from my house?" he asked. "I got you a caramel macchiato, two sweeteners, and I told her to add an extra dollop of caramel." He glanced down at the drink confection and his brow crinkled. "Hmmm, the whipped cream has melted, and you'll probably need to zap it in the microwave. But it's the thought that counts, right? I figured if you needed a day off yesterday, you might need this today."

She laughed and nodded, popping off the top of the cup and seeing that he was right about the whipped cream. Taking a sip, it was lukewarm but deliciously sweet. "Oh, that's nice. Thanks!"

He settled at his desk and more people wandered in as well, ready to start the day. Leaning over so that she would not be heard by others, she asked, "Did you see anyone at my desk yesterday?"

"Like sitting at your desk or just near it? Why? Is something wrong?"

"I just thought it looked like someone may have gone through some of my files. Although I don't know why it would matter, I've sent everything to John. It just gave me the creeps this morning, that's all."

Marcus chuckled. "You know, you're the only person our age that still seems to print everything out."

"You know me! I'm always afraid something will get lost in cyberspace. So I save things to a bunch of different places and then print them out! That way I figure I'll always have something I need." Glancing up toward John's office, the lights still obviously off, she wondered if he was not coming in again today.

"Do you think the receptionist that was drooling over you will be there today and that she might know more about Roger than just what gym he goes to?" They had

Jerry, but now Kyle and Alex wanted to get their hands on Roger.

Scowling, Alex shrugged. "It's worth a shot."

"Well, she had her eye on you, so I'll let you do the talking again."

"Great," Alex grumbled.

It didn't take long to get back to their destination and, walking in, Kyle was glad to see the receptionist from yesterday. She looked up from her cell phone, her gaze bouncing between the two of them before settling on Alex with a wide smile on her face.

"Hi! I didn't think I'd get a chance to see you again."

Alex leaned his forearms on the counter, his smile cocky. "Hey, darlin'. We're still looking for Roger. We were here this morning, but he wasn't in. He wasn't at the gym either. I don't suppose you know of any other hangouts of his, do you?"

Kyle was almost certain her eyelashes fluttered but wasn't sure if that was even a thing. She mimicked Alex's stance, leaning on her forearms, once again causing her cleavage to deepen. Her voice oozed syrup and she giggled.

"I can't imagine what you want Roger for."

She began to twirl a strand of hair around her finger, and it was all Kyle could do to keep from rolling his eyes.

"He's got some information that I need, so I'm desperate to find him." Alex leaned forward slightly and added, "Are you sure you don't know where he might be?"

"Well, the only other place I've ever met him at is

Tingle's. It's a bar down on 46th." She whispered, adding, "He took me there once, but I thought it was a dive. I mean, if a guy's going to take me out, he should show me a good time, right?"

"Absolutely, darlin'. A guy taking you out should always show you a good time."

She giggled again, this time her breasts bouncing with the movement. "Is that an invite?" She asked, her smile threatening to split her face.

"Sorry, darlin'. I just don't think my wife would like that very much." He tapped his fingers on the counter, then offered her a wave and a smile. Turning, he walked toward Kyle and the two left the building.

Once outside, Kyle shook his head. "Harsh, man."

"Shit, I couldn't think of anything else."

"You're losing your touch."

"Just because you've got a girl waiting for you at home doesn't mean the rest of us do."

Kyle smiled at his partner as he climbed into the cab of his truck. "Well, I know a certain detective that looks like she wouldn't turn you down if you asked her."

"Birdie?" Alex sighed. "Yeah, she's special. But damn if I know how two detectives are ever supposed to get together for a date. I can't even imagine what that must be like."

"Brock and Kallie make it work."

"Yeah, because they started as partners. Me and Birdie... never happening, man."

Kyle let it drop as they approached Tingle's Bar. His eyes were on a parking space when Alex called out. "Isn't that him?"

Lifting his head around to look out the passenger window, he observed Roger walking down the sidewalk away from them. Turning at the corner, he drove past Roger and found an opening at the curb. A grin slipped across his face as he parallel parked perfectly. They sat for a moment until Roger walked past them, then bolted from the truck.

Roger spied Alex first and started to run, crashing into Kyle as he stepped in front of him. A flash of fear moved through his eyes just before Kyle pinned him against the wall.

"Don't try it," Kyle warned, pressing Roger's face against the brick of the nearest building. "I can see running in your eyes, and it won't go good for you."

Roger's head jerked in a nod as his feet remained rooted to the sidewalk. As though suddenly aware of their location, his eyes scanned the other people on the street as Kyle loosened his grip slightly. Looking back at Kyle and Alex, he said, "Do we have to do this here?"

Alex cocked his head for a second then turned to Kyle. "I like this. Nice and easy."

A chuckle erupted from Kyle's chest, and he nodded toward Roger. "I'd say it would be best if we took this to the station."

"Do I need a lawyer?"

"Your call."

Roger stayed still for a few seconds, then said, "Not now. But I reserve the right for representation later if I need it."

"Like I said, your call."

Thirty minutes later, Roger was settled in an interview room. Kyle and Alex were ready to walk in when an assistant, Jocelyn, rolled her wheelchair down the hall toward them, a sheaf of papers in her hand.

Handing them to Kyle, she winked and said, "Interesting reading."

As Alex looked over his shoulder, he flipped through the papers, skimming to the sections she had highlighted. After a moment, he lifted his head and grinned widely. Bending, he kissed her cheek. "You're the best."

Waving as she rolled away, she laughed. "That's what all the men say!"

Turning back to the interview room, he tucked her file folder underneath the other one in his hand and walked in. Alex leaned his back against the door while Kyle scraped the chair over the tiled floor and sat, slapping both files on top of the table.

"We know you get the money from the sale of the drugs stolen from Kilton Pharmaceuticals. We have one of your distributors in custody, and we're currently rounding up two more that we know of. The one in custody is playing this smart and has already given you up. We have you linked to the truck that was used in the latest theft of a pharmaceutical van, and we're working on gaining the physical evidence, including traffic cameras, to prove that you were the one driving. We know that you pass the drugs to Jeremiah Dempsy, who then gets them to your distributors."

He shook his head slowly and said, "I guess that's the part I really don't get. You trust Jerry to get the drugs to your distributors? A known addict?" He watched a specter of doubt move through Roger's eyes. "So,

Raphael distributes, takes the money, keeps his cut, and gets the payment to you. And before you're set to deny, we've got him, and he's ready to roll."

"I think I want my lawyer now."

"Wish you'd decided that earlier—it would've saved us some time." He closed the folder and said, "Once your lawyer gets here, let him know that you still have time to work with us. You take too long, that door's going to shut."

"I don't know anyone higher up other than the person I take orders from," Roger said suddenly.

"That's how we climb this ladder, man. One step at a time. Got no problem with that."

Roger rested his arms on the table, his fists clenched together. "Let me talk to my lawyer first."

Several hours later, Kyle and Alex were on their way to Kilton Pharmaceuticals.

28

Once again, Kyle walked through the door into Thomas' office. This time, instead of finding the affable Vice President of Finance, he and Alex were greeted with a scowl.

"Detectives, I understand your need to investigate and no one wants the criminals found more than me, but this is a most inconvenient time for an interruption."

"We understand, Mr. Kilton, but our investigations don't always follow *convenient* timelines." They had not been invited to sit, but Kyle moved toward the chairs in front of Thomas' large desk and sat, Alex following suit.

Heaving an exaggerated, audible sigh, Thomas lay his pen on his desk and leaned back in his seat. "Then, by all means, let's get this over with."

"We've—"

The door opened, interrupting Kyle, and the three men turned to see who was entering the room. An older, distinguished gentleman stepped in briskly, and Kyle recognized the president, Robert Kilton.

"I'd like to know what's going on. Thomas?"

"Dad, these two men are detectives with the Hope City Police who've been investigating our stolen drugs."

Dropping his gaze toward Alex and Kyle, the older man introduced himself. "Detectives. I'm Robert Kilton. Pardon me for the intrusion, but I've just been informed that this is now the second time you've been in to speak to Thomas. I can't imagine what information he would have for you, but I'd like to know what's going on with any investigation affecting my company."

"Dad, this is nothing for you to be concerned about. You've just gotten back from your trip and should be resting."

Robert waved his hand dismissively. "Nonsense. Everything about this company is my business. Everything. Don't forget that."

Kyle glanced toward Thomas, seeing his jaw working, but he did not stand and offer his father a seat. While Kyle felt no professional duty to do so, his upbringing stepped in. Standing, he waved his hand toward his chair. "Sir."

Acknowledging his offer, Robert replied, "Thank you, but I'll stand."

At that, Thomas jumped up from his seat and said, "No, Dad, please. Sit here."

Hiding his eye roll at the change of seating, he watched as Robert sat behind the desk, Alex moved to lean against the credenza, and Thomas sat in the chair closest to Kyle.

Glancing toward Robert, Kyle began. "Mr. Kilton, I don't know if you've been apprised of what's been going on since you've been out of the country for a few weeks."

"I was told about the van robbery which, of course, concerned me. But I was also told that the Hope City Police were working diligently to find out what happened to the drugs. I made sure the mayor stayed in contact with the police commissioner to keep me apprised of any developments."

Kyle said nothing, knowing Chauncey wouldn't know the particulars of the case, nor would he discuss them with the mayor.

"And I don't see what any of this has to do with me," Thomas reiterated.

Forgoing a conversation with Robert at the moment, Kyle returned to his original purpose. Looking at Thomas, he said, "Concerning your relationship with Congressman Dell, we know that this company and each of the vice presidents and department supervisors have made significant campaign contributions—"

"There's nothing illegal about a business or individuals making campaign contributions. If this line of questioning continues, I'm going to consider it to be police harassment."

"In talking with your vice presidents and department supervisors, all of them except one were surprised that their name was listed as a campaign donor. That would indicate that Kilton Pharmaceuticals has been making donations beyond the legal limit using employees as a cover."

"This is pure speculation and has nothing to do with what your investigation is supposed to be about! You obviously can't do your jobs and are now trying to besmirch this company," Thomas bit out, a bead of sweat forming on his brow.

Robert ignored his son and leaned forward, his gaze pinned on Kyle. "I'm concerned about what you've just brought up, but I'm curious how it ties into your investigation of the stolen drugs. Or is it a diversion as my son implies?"

"This case was somewhat of a labyrinth, Mr. Kilton. Not one that we couldn't move through, and certainly one that had a great deal of paths that led to nowhere but, eventually, we found our way to the end."

"This is ridiculous—"

"Thomas, quiet," Robert barked, keeping his attention on Kyle.

"We've known that some of Kilton's pharmaceuticals, particularly opioids such as your brand of fentanyl, have ended up on the black market, often used as an additive with heroin or cocaine, making it way more potent and way more addictive. Cash value on the streets is in the millions."

Thomas began to speak again, but a sharp glare from Robert caused him to snap his mouth closed, his fingers clutching the arms of the chair.

Continuing, Kyle said, "We were suspicious of the van robbery. While I wouldn't call it easy, there were too many variables that led to our concerns. The van had to get to the pharmacy earlier than normal, and yet the truck was already there waiting for them, indicating the thieves knew not only the regular schedule but the change in schedule. The driver who was struck, Joe Parson, had been taken out of sight and yet Charlie distinctly heard him talking, indicating Joe had a conversation with the driver in a tone that was not upset or concerned. The truck involved in the theft had been reported stolen from a local laundry business but was owned by a larger cleaning service. It was found, and while the thieves assumed the use of gloves on the plastic-wrapped cardboard boxes would suffice, trace evidence of the pharmaceuticals was discovered. The truck was owned by Hope City Linen and Uniform Service, which in turn is owned by Artog Shipping."

At this, he noted Robert's eyes widened. "I see you recognize that name. It has ties to both Kilton Pharmaceuticals as well as Congressman Dell."

Thomas scoffed. "This is ridiculous! This is nothing more than a convoluted fabrication that exposes the Hope City Police Department's inability to find stolen drugs. Hope City has a drug problem and the police are ineffectual in combating it, so they're coming after us with nothing but ridiculous political innuendo."

Kyle turned and looked toward Thomas, lifting his brow in skepticism. His lips curved ever so slightly and he continued without hesitation. "What was suspected from the beginning was that the robbery was either planned by or planned with someone from inside Kilton Pharmaceuticals. As it turns out, we now know how it was done and have arrested most of the players."

Alex's phone vibrated aloud, and after he checked the text, he looked toward Kyle and nodded.

"Detective Freeman has just been informed that Porter Myles has been taken into custody, and we already have Joseph Parson. At the moment, those are the only two employees of Kilton Pharmaceuticals that we have arrested. Joe knew that the robbery was going to occur. When the accident kept them from keeping to their original schedule, he had to inform someone, ensuring that thieves on the other end would know about the change. Officially, he called Tammy Rutgers, which would be the correct protocol. She, in turn, told Bob Trogdon, and that should have been the end of it. In checking Joseph's phone logs, we found that he also sent a separate message to Porter Myles, who responded that he'd take care of it. We know that Porter then contacted Roger Solten, who works at the Linen Service. He was the driver of the truck and made the change necessary to be at the pharmacy at the new time."

Thomas shifted slightly in his seat, and Kyle threw another glance toward him. "Roger took the drugs and delivered them to the next level, getting them close to the streets. He used Joseph's stepbrother, Jeremiah Dempsy, who would then deliver the drugs to various dealers. Roger kept a tight accounting on the dealers, and he had sufficient manpower to back up any threats he needed to make. The money started pouring in to him after the dealers took their cut. Then Roger began paying the person in charge of the entire operation after he took his percentage. Even with all that, the person at the top is making over a million dollars on this stolen shipment alone. And, of course, that doesn't include other stolen shipments around the world that occur when Kilton Pharmaceuticals uses Artog Shipping."

"Detective, please tell me that you've identified who was at the top so that we can plug this hole," Robert Kilton said, his blue eyes blazing and his voice hard.

"Yes, Sir, we have."

Alex stepped forward, flanking Thomas' chair. "Thomas Kilton, you need to accompany us down to the station, where you will be charged with the theft of the Kilton Pharmaceuticals drugs. I will also let you know that the FBI will be meeting us there as they are looking into the multi-national drug ring organization as well as racketeering considering money from your private account has been paying for the silence of Beth Washington and Douglas Tiller. Congressman Dell is already being questioned as to the discrepancies in the campaign finances. We're in the process of obtaining a search warrant for your computers, both here and at home, but the FBI is stepping in and taking over this case. It's our understanding that they will be freezing your accounts, including your offshore accounts and properties."

"Offshore accounts?" Robert asked, his palms slamming down on top of Thomas' desk as he pushed himself to stand, his gaze pinned on his son. "You've been stealing from the company? Our family?"

"This is preposterous! You've got nothing on me because I had nothing to do with any of this!" Thomas cried, jumping to his feet.

"We can do this easy where you walk out, or we escort you out in handcuffs in front of the other people in this building. You make the call," Kyle ordered, his voice low.

"Go with them, Thomas," Robert said. He walked around the desk, and Kyle noticed the older man's hands shook ever so slightly. "I'll call our attorney but, Son, I'll let you know right now... if you're guilty of what these detectives say you are, you'll get no help from me."

Alex placed his hand on Thomas' shoulder only to have the indignant Vice President shake himself loose. "I'll walk out on my own." Turning toward Kyle, he sneered, "You'll regret this."

Kyle stalked over, stopping only when the toes of his boots touched Thomas'. The men were almost equal in height, but Kyle shoved his face forward, forcing Thomas to lean back. "You're in enough shit, but if I find out you had anything to do with calling a hit on Kimberly Hogan and the subsequent shooting of Bob Trogdon... I'll bury you."

Robert gasped, but Kyle was done talking. Alex opened the door and motioned for two HC police officers to step into the office. After Alex placed Thomas under arrest and read him his rights, he had the officers escort him out.

A commotion was at the door and a woman rushed inside, her eyes wide. Kyle recognized Sidney Kilton from her pictures, but the harried expression on her face was not like the professional photographs.

"Dad! What's happening?" She hurried forward, placing her hands on her father's arms, pulling him close.

"It… it appears that your brother has made some… unwise decisions…" Robert's voice trailed off, his breath seeming to leave him.

Sidney, still holding on to her father, turned toward Kyle. "Can you tell me?"

"Ms. Kilton, at this time I can tell you that your brother is under investigation by not only the Hope City Police Department but the FBI for stealing pharmaceuticals from the company and arranging to have them sold on the black market. He is also being investigated for funneling money into the campaign finances of Congressman Dell, purportedly to ascertain favorable legislation for the pharmaceutical industry."

He had no idea what her response would be, but her face hardened like stone and she stiffened her spine, pulling herself to her full height. "That snake!" Jerking her head around, her face softened as she stared at her father. "I had suspicions about some of the financial decisions he was making, but I had no idea he'd sunk so low!"

Robert appeared as though he had aged just in the time that Kyle had been in the office. Turning to leave, Kyle was halted when Robert asked, "Detective, what did you mean by a hit on Kimberly and Bob Trogdon?"

Turning fully to the pair staring at him wide-eyed, he said, "Kimberly Hogan is an employee in your marketing department who had been seen talking to the driver that had been arrested. Bob Trogdon works in your warehouse and happens to be Kimberly's neighbor. Someone broke into Bob's house two nights ago and shot him as he slept, but evidence leads us to believe they thought they were in Kimberly's house—"

The gasps were audible coming from Robert and Sidney, but Kyle continued. "I'll add that Kimberly is my girlfriend. So, even though I have to be professional... this is personal."

29

Marcus leaned back in his seat and stretched his arms above his head, drawing Kimberly's attention from the editing she'd been working on for most of the morning. Glancing around, she saw the room was almost empty. John had finally come in but, with barely a nod to anyone, had gone into his office and his door remained closed.

"Oh, my goodness, I didn't realize everyone had gone to lunch."

"You hungry?" Marcus asked.

"Yeah, I am."

"Let's hit one of the food trucks downstairs." Marcus stood and turned, suddenly taking a step closer to the window, looking down. "Whoa!"

"What is it?" Her attention snagged, she hurried to the window and stood next to him, peering downward.

Suddenly, John's door opened, and he stepped out. He walked over to the window also, standing on the other side of her. "What's going on?"

As the three looked down toward the sidewalk, she saw two police officers and two of the Kilton Pharmaceuticals security guards escorting a man between them. "That looks like Porter Myles."

Marcus turned toward her, his brow furrowed. Answering his unasked question, she said, "He's over at the warehouse. I talked to him a couple of weeks ago."

"I wonder what he did."

She lifted her shoulders in a shrug but remained quiet. Suddenly, more movement on the sidewalk caught her attention and a gasp slipped out.

Marcus and John leaned forward also, all watching as Thomas Kilton was escorted by the police toward the parking lot. Both men turned toward her, and she glanced up between them, shrugging again.

Marcus continued to look at her, tilting his head to the side. "I get the feeling you know a lot more than you let on. You've been interviewing these people."

"With the drug thefts, it's an ongoing investigation. The police can't say much."

"Come on, let's get a bite. John, you want to join us? We're going to hit one of the food trucks."

A look of indecision passed over John's face before he nodded. The three left the office, taking the stairs and exiting the building on the side. Other employees were gathered in small groups, murmuring as everyone watched the police escort Porter and Thomas away.

Skirting around some of the others, the trio headed toward the closest food truck. "This is crazy," Marcus said. "Drugs being stolen, people in high positions being arrested, hell, even Bob getting shot."

Blinking in surprise, Kimberly jerked her head around and looked up at Marcus. *Bob getting shot? But how...?*

Hearing a growl on the other side, she jerked her head around and looked at John. His eyes were pinned on Marcus, his jaw hardened, and his mouth pinched into a tight line.

Marcus' gaze jumped between John and hers. "Shit!" His hand shot out, grabbing her upper arm, clamping tight. He pushed his way between a small group of people, dragging her along with him just as John shouted for them to stop, grabbing her as well.

Kyle and Alex stepped out of the headquarters building, having left Robert Kilton and his daughter to deal with the legal fallout for Kilton Pharmaceuticals. Pulling out his phone, he was shooting a text to Kimberly when a shout caught his attention.

A man was shouting for someone to *'stop'* while grabbing onto a woman who was being dragged by another man. Recognizing Kimberly as the woman now trapped between two angry men, all thoughts left his mind about the ongoing interviews and investigation, focusing entirely on getting to her.

People scattered as he and Alex pounded down the sidewalk toward Kimberly and the two men still fighting over her. Alex shouted their identification as police and one man dropped his hold of her as he turned toward them.

With his hands in the air, the man cried, "It's Marcus! He shot Bob!"

With no one pulling in the opposite direction, Kimberly was now pulled along by Marcus, and they were almost able to disappear around the corner of the building. Kimberly's toe caught on an uneven seam in the sidewalk, and she fell toward the ground, her arm jerking out of Marcus' grip. She landed face down, smacking the sidewalk with her palms. Kyle reached her as Alex yelled, "Police!" and made a flying leap, tackling Marcus.

Kyle dropped to his knees next to her and scooped her up into his arms. She kept repeating, "I'm okay, I'm okay, I'm okay." He shifted around and plopped his butt onto the sidewalk, pulling her into his lap.

The first man rushed up and squatted next to them. "Kimberly, are you hurt?"

"I'm okay, John." Looking toward Kyle, she said, "This is my boss, John Bennett."

Even as she was offering assurances, Kyle noted her palms, knees, and cheek were scraped and bloody.

"I had no idea! But as we were walking out, Marcus said something about Bob being shot. I knew nobody should know that!"

"I thought the same thing," John said.

Standing, Kyle helped her to her feet. Turning his attention toward John, he asked "How did you know something happened to Bob?"

Glancing around, John blushed slightly. "Because we're a couple. He's at my place to recuperate."

"Oh, I had no idea," she said, her heart still pounding.

"We felt it best to keep it quiet. Work romances can be hard under the best of circumstances."

By now, Alex had handcuffs on Marcus, and he was being loaded into another police cruiser. He glanced down at her knees. "First, let's get you checked out."

"It's just a few scra—"

He hushed her words with a light kiss, mumbling, "Do it for me, babe."

Grateful she acquiesced, he led her to the ambulance where they cleaned and treated her abrasions while he hovered, not wanting to let her out of his sight. Wrapping her in his arms, he whispered, "Hate like hell to do this, babe, but I need to get to the station, and you're coming with me."

Her eyes were warm as they stared at him. "Then let's go. The sooner we get this behind us, the sooner we can go home."

Looking toward John, she asked, "Will you stay with Bob?"

"Absolutely. Go do what you need to do, and I'll tell Bob you'll talk to him later."

Tucking her in close to his side, he bent and kissed her lightly. "Can't wait to get home, babe."

The station was busy. Thomas and his attorney were squirreled in one of the interview rooms, deciding how best to play the evidence stacked up against them as the FBI grilled him. Porter Myles gave up easily, choosing to admit to his part in the van theft and not minding who he took down with him.

Marcus was the surprise. Under questioning by Carter and Evan, he admitted that he'd been hired—or rather, coerced—by Thomas to keep an eye on Kimberly's interviews. Considering he was one of the dealers on a nearby campus, Thomas had him under his thumb. When it appeared that she was getting too close, he ordered the hit on her.

Kimberly sat in a hallway on a stiff plastic chair, staring at the comings and goings all around while clutching a cup of horrid coffee in her hands. Heavy footsteps were heard and she looked up just in time to see Chauncey King settle in the chair next to her.

"Kimberly," he greeted, his deep voice soft. He held her gaze and she was surprised as well as comforted by his presence.

"Mr. King… I mean, Commissioner King—"

"As soon as I heard you were here, I wanted to make sure you were okay." A deep-chested chuckle erupted as he added, "And Hannah and Sharon would never forgive me if I didn't get the intel back to them that I checked on you."

Her smile met his and she patted his arm. His smile dropped as his gaze moved over her abraded cheek, but she rushed to assure, "I'm fine. Really, I am. Just a few scratches."

He nodded and opened his mouth to say more when his phone vibrated. Pulling it from the clip on his belt, he looked at the caller ID and sighed. Connecting, he said, "I'm here, sitting right beside her. She's fine. Why don't you and Sharon fix something simple for dinner and make it portable in case Kyle wants to take her directly home." He listened and then added, "Because they may not want to come over... Kyle may just want her to himself this evening."

He hung up after endearments and she was unable to hold in her mirth at the huge police commissioner dealing with his wife and Kyle's mom. "Thank you for that. I'm not sure I'm up to company tonight, but knowing how much they care... well, it's nice."

As Kyle walked around the corner and approached, she and Chauncey stood. He wrapped his arms around her and kissed the top of her head. "Remember, we're all family, Kimberly. See you soon."

With that, he nodded toward Kyle and walked back toward the elevators. Kyle reached her and pulled her into his arms. "You ready to go home, babe?"

She leaned back and looked into his face, seeing the deep creases emanating from the corners of his eyes. She hated to see the toll his job took on him. Lifting her hand, she smoothed her fingertips over his face and smiled. "I'm always ready to go home with you."

He tossed a wave toward Alex and then turned with her tucked into his side. Once in the elevator, she said, "By the way, Chauncey said that Hannah and Sharon will bring dinner over to your house. He managed to talk them out of making us go there."

"Good man."

"I don't know what they'll bring, but I thought we could stop by the store on the way home. I'm in the mood for whipped cream."

It took a few seconds for her comment to sink in, but suddenly Kyle threw back his head and laughed. "Babe, anytime you want whipped cream, just say the word!"

With a much more light-hearted Kyle by her side, they walked out of the station, arm in arm.

30

ONE WEEK LATER

Kimberly looked to the side as Kyle turned off the street and headed his SUV toward the Cardboard Cottages. She had told him she would drive her car so that he did not need to bring his new SUV, but she was not surprised when he immediately nixed that idea. He glanced her way, meeting her gaze, and they both smiled. Parking not too far from the tents, she looked out, her heart twinging as usual when she saw the conditions.

"Oh, my, to think this is right here in our town," came the soft voice from the back seat.

Twisting around, Kimberly said, "I'm glad you came with me today, Sister Honoria."

"I'm blessed you asked me to come, dear Kimberly."

Kyle hopped out and rounded the front of his vehicle. First assisting Kimberly out, he then turned to the back seat and carefully made sure that Sister Honoria was steady on her feet. Kimberly moved to take the older woman's arm, and they began walking toward the tents, met by Margo, Aleeta, and their children.

Sister Honoria had brought some food and clothing which Kyle carried over and she distributed to the women as well as a few games given to the children. Several other people walked over from the ragtag structures, each greeting the smiling nun, thanking her for what she brought.

Kimberly moved to the side, standing next to Aleeta. "Will you be moving soon?"

Aleeta's smile was wide as she nodded. "My brother made the deposit yesterday. I've got a surprise, though. Originally, we were only going to get a one-bedroom apartment, but he said the manager had a two-bedroom for about the same cost. Margo and her two kids are going to move in with us."

Squealing with joy, Kimberly threw her arms around both women, hugging them. "What about furniture?"

"He found a deal on bunk beds for the kids. I don't mind sleeping on the floor, just knowing we have a real place will be worth it."

She glanced to the side and, receiving a nod from Kyle, turned back to the two women. "Well, as it turns out, I've got some furniture that I'm not going to need anymore. I have a bed, dresser, small table with chairs, and even a sofa to donate."

Her curls bouncing as she shook her head, Aleeta said, "Oh, no! We can't take that from you! That would be too much!"

Sister Honoria moved to them and overheard Aleeta's objection. "My dear, in allowing someone to be generous, you offer a gift as well."

Aleeta sucked in her lips, blinking back tears before grabbing on to Margo's hand. "I can't imagine. I can't imagine being in a home again."

Kyle stepped over and wrapped his arm around Kimberly. "Get the address to us, and I'll round up some men to help move the furniture."

A man walked over from the side and overheard Kyle's offer. "Well, well, Mr. Dee-tective. Look at you, being all good-deed and shit."

Turning quickly, Kimberly's eyes widened but Sister Honoria just smiled.

"Manny," Kyle growled, his eyes cutting toward the nun.

Manny had the good grace to blush and nodded toward Sister Honoria. "Sorry, Ma'am."

Kimberly hugged Margo and Aleeta goodbye, sharing her phone number so that they would be able to let her know when to help move furniture. "Remember, you two are going to be featured in the Faces of Hope City. I think I'll title it Perseverance and Resilience." She took Sister Honoria's arm and they began walking toward the SUV.

Knowing Kyle was close behind them, she overheard Manny say, "See you around, Mr. Dee-tective."

She glanced over her shoulder in time to see Kyle offer a chin lift. He caught up to her and they assisted Sister Honoria into the backseat, making sure she was buckled and comfortable. Walking around the back of his SUV toward her door, she caught Kyle's arm, bringing him to a halt. He cocked his head and waited for her to speak. Instead, she wound her arms around his neck and pulled him close. She whispered, "I love you, Mr. Dee-tective."

"I'd love to do nothing more than take you home, babe, and show you just how much I love you, too. But…"

"But we've got to get Sister Honoria back to Sacred Heart and then get to your mom's for the party."

"Yeah…"

"But after that? I'm all yours."

His arms spasmed around her and his blue eyes lit with the promise of good times to come… starting now.

For the next Hope City books, click here!
Ryker book 6

Don't miss other Maryann Jordan books!

Lots more Baytown stories to enjoy and more to come!

Baytown Boys (small town, military romantic suspense)

Coming Home

Just One More Chance

Clues of the Heart

Finding Peace

Picking Up the Pieces

Sunset Flames

Waiting for Sunrise

Hear My Heart

Guarding Your Heart

Sweet Rose

Our Time

Count On Me

For all of Miss Ethel's boys:

Heroes at Heart (Military Romance)

Zander

Rafe

Cael

Jaxon

Jayden

Asher

Zeke

Cas

Lighthouse Security Investigations

Mace

Rank

Walker

Drew

Blake

Tate

Hope City (romantic suspense series co-developed

with Kris Michaels

Brock book 1

Sean book 2

Carter book 3

Brody book 4

Kyle book 5

Ryker book 6

Rory book 7

Killian book 8

Saints Protection & Investigations

(an elite group, assigned to the cases no one else wants…or
can solve)

Serial Love

Healing Love

Revealing Love

Seeing Love

Honor Love

Sacrifice Love

Protecting Love

Remember Love

Discover Love

Surviving Love

Celebrating Love

Follow the exciting spin-off series:

Alvarez Security (military romantic suspense)

Gabe

Tony

Vinny

Jobe

SEALs

Thin Ice (Sleeper SEAL)

SEAL Together (Silver SEAL)

Letters From Home (military romance)

Class of Love

Freedom of Love

Bond of Love

The Love's Series (detectives)

Love's Taming

Love's Tempting

Love's Trusting

The Fairfield Series (small town detectives)

Emma's Home

Laurie's Time

Carol's Image

Fireworks Over Fairfield

Please take the time to leave a review of this book. Feel free to contact me, especially if you enjoyed my book. I love to hear from readers!

Facebook

Email

Website

Made in the USA
Coppell, TX
27 June 2024

34003404R00204